THE
SIX IRON SPIDERS

Books by Phoebe Atwood Taylor
available from Foul Play Press

Asey Mayo Cape Cod Mysteries

THE ANNULET OF GILT
THE ASEY MAYO TRIO
BANBURY BOG
THE CAPE COD MYSTERY
THE CRIMINAL C.O.D.
THE CRIMSON PATCH
THE DEADLY SUNSHADE
DEATH LIGHTS A CANDLE
DIPLOMATIC CORPSE
FIGURE AWAY
GOING, GOING, GONE
THE MYSTERY OF THE CAPE COD PLAYERS
THE MYSTERY OF THE CAPE COD TAVERN
OCTAGON HOUSE
OUT OF ORDER
THE PERENNIAL BOARDER
PROOF OF THE PUDDING
PUNCH WITH CARE
SANDBAR SINISTER
SPRING HARROWING
THE SIX IRON SPIDERS
THREE PLOTS FOR ASEY MAYO

Writing as Alice Tilton

BEGINNING WITH A BASH
FILE FOR RECORD
HOLLOW CHEST
THE LEFT LEG

PHOEBE ATWOOD TAYLOR

THE
SIX IRON
SPIDERS

An Asey Mayo Cape Cod Mystery

A Foul Play Press Book

THE COUNTRYMAN PRESS
Woodstock, Vermont

TO

MARIAN CHURCHILL WHITE

CHAPTER ONE

ASEY MAYO heard the thin ice coating of the puddles crack under his feet as he dashed along the lane in fruitless pursuit of his best gray felt hat, which capered like a chamois just beyond the reach of his outstretched hand.

During the course of the last few hours he had chased that elusive headgear over a wide cross section of Cape Cod, and he had no intention of letting it escape him now, practically within sight of his own home. So, ignoring the splattering slush and mud, he dove ahead in one final, desperate lunge—and managed to pick himself up from the gelatinous depths of a boglike rut just in time to see another gust of sour east wind send the hat soaring over the lane's locust boundary fence. It hovered for a moment above the bare quince trees of his orchard, then zoomed gaily away somewhere in the direction of the beach and the leaden waters of Cape Cod bay.

Asey shrugged, resignedly brushed the particles of ice and the morsels of mud off his best overcoat, and winced at the sodden spectacle of his best shoes. Then, turning up his coat collar, he tramped back to where he had left his kitbag, and proceeded to slosh his way up the curving lane.

This was definitely not turning out to be the homecoming that he had planned. Not that he expected any brass bands to blare at him, or any roses to be strewn at his feet, but after being absent for six months at the Porter Motors Tank Plant, he had taken for granted that either his housekeeper cousin Jennie Mayo or his good friend Dr. Cummings would at least drive over to the airport to welcome him and fetch him home. He hadn't figured on having to waste four precious hours of his two-day vacation in a laborious, sixty-mile hitchhike in the teeth of a February east wind.

He walked along more slowly after pausing to remove a fragment of gravel from his oozing right shoe, and wondered again at the odd sensation that had been haunting him since he left the main road for the lane, a sensation of strangeness and unfamiliarity with perfectly well-known and familiar objects. The lane was the same, the landmarks were the same. Nothing old was missing, nothing new had been added. Still, the lane seemed much longer and bleaker and more uphill than he remembered. Perhaps it was because he had been away since September—

"I'm on foot!" he suddenly said aloud. "By golly, that's what makes the difference! I'm on foot!"

The realization that he probably hadn't walked the lane in thirty years came to him as a distinct shock. That accounted for his lack of judgment in calculating the depth of the ruts and the velocity of the wind, and the distance, and the upgrade.

The low white house with the long kitchen ell loomed ahead in the gathering dusk as he rounded the last curve, and Asey lengthened his stride at the heartening sight of all the first-floor lights burning with festive lavishness. Jennie must have received his telegram, all right, but the news of his return had inspired her to dash to the kitchen to cook him a gala meal. Without doubt she'd jumped to the conclusion that if he were flying back, he would be flying with Bill Porter as he usually did, and that one of the Porters would drive him home. He would forgive all the slip-ups, from his hitchhike to his lost hat and wet feet, Asey thought, if Jennie had a clam chowder waiting for him. A real clam chowder, with clams, and without a lot of outlandish tomatoes.

"For Pete's sakes!"

Setting down his bag, Asey planted his hands on his hips and surveyed with bewilderment the strange assortment of vehicles lined up by the picket fence at the foot of the oystershell walk.

Except for its four spanking new, nonballoon tires,

the object nearest to him could hardly be dignified by the title of automobile. It lacked a top, hood, fenders, running boards, doors, or upholstery, and still it had too much of the rigid dignity of antiquity to be thought of as a jalopy. Beyond it was a small, dilapidated truck against whose homemade tailboard three bicycles were propped. A blanketed horse attached to a moth-eaten buggy, and a long, sleek Porter town car—one of the Porter factory's last custom jobs, Asey decided critically—completed the bizarre little collection.

"For Pete's sakes!" he said irritably, "didn't Jennie *get* that wire I sent? What in time's she got my house filled with mobs of people for?"

There certainly was a flock of people inside, for he could see figures flitting past the small-paned windows of the living room. Jennie must be throwing a party— but not for him. She knew that when he had a vacation, he wanted peace and quiet. Besides, he had never in his life seen any of those vehicles before. They didn't belong to any of his friends.

Striding up the walk, he cut across the lawn and peeked through the side window.

Then he blinked, and looked again.

It *was* his living room, unquestionably. He could see the five-masted schooner "John B. Mayo" in full sail over the mantel; there in the corner was his grandfather's mahogany desk, and jammed against the wall was his own favorite easy chair.

But who in the name of all that was holy were all these strange people, and what were they up to?

They couldn't be the Ku Klux Klan back in action, he told himself, and yet there was more than a touch of Klannishness about the figure stretched out on the hooked rug in the center of the room, covered with a sheet, and wearing on its head a clumsy, baglike hood with slits cut for eyes and nose! The fact that the bag said "Domino Sugar" on it didn't in the least lessen the generally macabre effect.

Suddenly an elderly woman, a pleasant-looking person with white hair and small, fine features, detached herself from the little group near the hall door, crossed the room, and, after kicking the recumbent Klanner in a most unladylike fashion, rudely wrenched off the slitted hood.

His discovery that the recumbent one was only a store window lay figure relieved Asey, but still failed to clarify the situation to any extent. Why, he asked himself wonderingly, should a bevy of utter strangers de-hood dummies in his living room? Why, in fact, had they troubled to adorn the dummy with the sugar bag in the first place? Where was his cousin Jennie during all these goings-on?

He was about to march in and request an explanation when a young girl with shoulder-length blond hair entered from the hall, lay down beside the dummy, and then almost at once jumped up and started arguing violently with a fellow in dungarees and a flannel shirt —and the most flourishing beard Asey had seen since the last time he bought a package of cough drops. An elderly man in tweeds and a younger, sandy-haired man in a blue serge suit joined the dispute, and although Asey could hear only the sound of their voices and not their words, it was evident that no two members of the quartet agreed on anything, nor did they particularly appear to want to, very much.

None of them paid a whit of attention to the white-haired woman who was now kneeling beside the dummy, pulling the sugar bag over its head again, and she, in turn, ignored the dark-haired mastifflike woman who stood behind her, kibitzing.

It must be a game, Asey decided, when still another woman came in, petulantly trailing a white streamer behind her. None of these people were Cape natives, obviously. They must be winter visitors, and he had had some previous experience with games devised by apparently normal outlanders to while away the long winter evenings. He specifically remembered "Hoople," a madcap time-whiler that had culminated in a murder and several of the most exciting days he'd ever spent. But "Hoople" and all the other games devised by bored winter visitors were gay, light-hearted affairs usually accompanied by spasms of violent laughter. These people here were grimly, even pugnaciously serious. It was a tossup in his mind as to whether the blonde girl would take a good yank at Dungarees' black beard before Elderly Tweed picked up Blue Serge and spanked him. And the petulant woman with the white streamer was just on the verge of taking a crack at the hefty black-haired Kibitzer when a whistle blew shrilly.

Everyone stopped dead, as if a curtain were going up on a tableau.

"What in time," Asey muttered, "*are* they playin', Still-pond-no-more-movin'?"

Or had Jennie, in his absence, decided to turn an honest penny by renting his property to some upper-class madhouse?

He gasped as a woman strode into the living room and blew another strident blast on her whistle.

His Amazonian cousin Jennie was a pretty awe-inspiring sight in a house dress, but Jennie Mayo in gray flannel slacks!

"Wow!" Asey said. "Golly! Oh, my! Oh—oh, wow!"

His tall frame shook so with silent laughter that he had to grab out and take hold of the window ledge for support.

"Looks," a familiar voice behind him commented critically, "like the 'Queen Mary' in battle gray, doesn't she?"

Asey swung around to find the stocky figure of Dr. Cummings at his elbow.

"Hi, doc! I was so busy watchin', I never heard you —doc, for Pete's sakes, what *is* all this?"

"First Aid," Cummings told him.

"First *what?*"

"First Aid. Jennie's an instructor. Didn't you see her arm band?"

"Arm band? I never looked that far," Asey said in a choked voice. "*I* can't get beyond them slacks. Jennie in slacks! Whyn't someone *tell* her she shouldn't ought —huh, I s'pose Syl tried, an' got nowheres. I guess it's a good thing I come home! Who's the rest of that crazy crowd?"

The doctor peered in. "That's the East Aspinnet outfit—oh, God, traction splints! Duck!"

Asey obediently ducked, and then, in a whisper, asked why.

"Because Jennie looked this way," Cummings said, "and I don't want her to find me here. I refuse to be dragged in and pumped about traction splints. The whole damn county's just getting to traction splints, and they hound me about 'em night and day. I tell you, Asey, they're so mad about traction splints, they'd slap one on you if you got a splinter in your big toe. I'm going to print a little tag."

Asey still felt confused. "Uh—a tag, doc?"

"Yes." Cummings peered in the window again. "A little tag to tie around my neck. It's going to say, 'You leave me right here in the ruins until an accredited

M.D. can be located. No traction splints. This means *you!*' These First-Aiders—there, now, you hear that fellow on the floor yelping? He'll be limping for a week! Tch, tch, tch! Tch—"

Asey interrupted the doctor's horrified tongue-cluckings.

"Doc, I still don't seem to catch on to all of this."

"You mean," Cummings turned around and stared at him, "you never took a First Aid course? Honestly? Man alive, how'd you miss it? What've you been doing in your spare time, anyway?"

"Makin' tanks," Asey told him a little wearily. "That's all. Just makin' tanks an' overseein' the makin' of 'em, an' testin' 'em, an' ironin' out bugs. An' then makin' more tanks. Didn't I ever write you?"

Cummings snorted. "Write me! You sent me a picture post card of a concrete highway near West Abernathy, and on the back you wrote, 'Near here we make tanks.'"

"Well, we do," Asey said. "We make 'em till we drop, an' then Bill Porter an' I retire to his office an' a couple of camp beds, an' sleep till we hear a whistle, an' then we go make more tanks—you sure I didn't ever write you? I meant to."

"One measly post card," Cummings said, "is the only indication I've had of your continued existence—except for the week that picture of you and Bill Porter bobbed up on the cover of *Newsorgan.* You looked like a couple of old coal miners—Asey, did I hear you mutter something then? Man, didn't you *know* you were man-of-the-month, or something?"

"To tell you the truth," Asey said, "all I get time to read is the headlines, an' Joe Palooka, an' once in a while maybe Skeezix. Does *Newsorgan* still call me a Hayseed Sleuth an' Cape Cod's Codfish Sherlock?"

Cummings nodded. "They've coined a new name for you, too. 'Tankexpert.' All one word. 'Lean, salty Asey Mayo, ex-Porter yacht cap'n, Jack-of-all-trades, now Porter director and Tankexpert—' "

"Say, doc," Asey interrupted, "*all* the women in there are wearin' slacks! I just noticed!"

"Haven't you," Cummings asked with irony, "seen women lately?"

"Wa-el, there's waitresses in the place where Bill an' I eat," Asey said, "but I only see the half of 'em that's above the counter. I never noticed the rest of 'em."

"Lucky man!" Cummings said feelingly. "My wife says it's treason for me to wisecrack about good patriotic women going to war in sensible, economic slacks, and I keep telling her I'd never open my peep if they all looked like Katharine Hepburn. But they don't. They're either superdreadnoughts like Jennie, or string beans like my wife—she threw a potted begonia at me," he added with a chuckle, "when I said I was going to stand her out in the garden to scare off the crows. My, she's a ghastly sight! Asey, I figured you wanted to be met at the airport, and I fully intended to be there waving a flag, but I got delayed with Minnie Silva. Triplets, this time."

"So?"

"Now go on," Cummings said eagerly, "and ask me what she named 'em. Go on, ask me!"

"What?"

"Winston, Franklin, and Douglas!" Cummings told him with pride. "And they've already been photographed for the 'Standard-Times,' caption to read, 'Triple threat to Axis.' "

"An' what," Asey inquired slyly, "was Minnie's own nominations, doc?"

"Oh, well, maybe I did influence her a wee bit," Cummings returned, "but it was the opportunity of a lifetime, and I simply couldn't bear to let it slip out of my fingers. Particularly since her oldest boy's named Joe. Man, it's good to have you back! But it's going to take years to catch you up with all the changes and things. We've had invasion scares and parachutist scares and sabotage scares and spy scares, and one honest-to-goodness tire theft. Someone swiped the Hazards' spare the very day they finally got delivery on that new Porter—by George!" the doctor lowered his voice. "Asey, look down toward the picket fence, quick! Am I seeing things, or is that someone prowling around behind that Porter, right now?"

Asey peered through the darkness. "I don't see—

yes, by golly, there *is* someone sneakin' back towards the truck! But, doc, nobody'd try to swipe a tire with us standin' right here!"

"Don't kid yourself!" Cummings retorted. "They stole that spare when the Porter was parked on Main Street in front of the Congregational Church! Something funny's going on, Asey! Anyone coming late to Jennie's class would march right in, they wouldn't dally around down there! We ought to investigate—but don't you do any quarter-deck bellowing at 'em, mind! You'll only rouse Jennie and her mob, and let me in for a long interlude of traction-splint trouble. Can't you grab whoever it is, and scare the daylights out of 'em?"

"That's sort of what I was considerin'," Asey said. "Tell you what, you march down the walk toward him boldlike, an' I'll circle around the garage an' be ready to cut him off if he beats it away from you. Ready? Start along, then."

Ten minutes later, Asey came panting back to where the doctor was impatiently waiting by the assortment of parked vehicles.

"Makin' tanks," he said in reply to Cummings' eager question, "isn't good for a body's wind. I don't know who 'twas."

"You mean you didn't catch 'em? Didn't you," Cummings demanded, "even see their *face?*"

Asey shook his head. "There's one big rut puddle

yonder in the lane that's my nemesis," he said as he brushed off the shoulders of his overcoat. "Last time I dove into it, I lost a hat, an' this time I lost a shoe. Anyhow, they got scared off, an' I don't think they'll be in any hurry to come back—what you holdin' out in your hand?"

"Two fifty-cent pieces," Cummings told him "Maybe it's a tip, but I think they just bounced out of her pocket when she started to run—it was a woman, wasn't it?"

"I wouldn't know," Asey said. "I never got near enough. It might've been a woman in slacks, but I just took it for granted it was a fellow in pants. I haven't caught on yet to bein' slack-minded—doc, why aren't the lane lights on, like they should be? I noticed Melrose's are out, too."

"All independently controlled side-lane lighting is out for the duration," Cummings said. "We had a lot of trouble with people blacking out their houses, all right, and then bumping around for hours trying to find the outside control switch. Or else they sailed off for the evening and left their lane and driveway lights on—I'm *sure* that was a woman, Asey! What d'you suppose she was after?"

"If it was a woman, I don't think she had any more sinister aim than to call on the Melroses, or maybe the Snows at the Point. With all the lane lights out, she probably got mixed up."

"Look, Asey, you didn't bring home any secret plans or blueprints, did you?" Cummings asked suddenly.

Asey looked sharply at him, but the doctor seemed perfectly serious.

"All I got in my bag, doc, is a lot of soiled shirts. I'm just home on a vacation, an' no E. Phillips Oppenheim about it. Honest, if I was you, I wouldn't give that woman another thought."

"But she ran away! If she was hunting someone, she'd have asked us the way! She just turned and fled!"

"I nearly turned an' fled, myself, at the sight of these things," Asey indicated the parked vehicles. "They're enough to scare anyone—what's the big idea?"

"In the quiet, secluded ivory tower of your tank plant," Cummings asked sarcastically, "have you happened to hear any faint rumors about civilian rubber problems? Tires, and all? And by the way, where's your roadster? You had one when you left here. A long black thing. Remember?"

"Bill an' I gave our cars to the Red Cross to turn into ambulances," Asey said. "Doc, I'm cold an' wet an' hungry, an' I want to change my clothes an' eat—"

"I wonder if she's the new woman spy my wife was talking about this evening," Cummings interrupted pensively.

"If *who's* the new woman spy? And what'n time d'you mean, *new* spy?"

"The woman you chased. She worries me. And I call her the *new* spy, because Jonah Ives, that fellow with the black beard in there," Cummings nodded toward the house, "is generally referred to about town as 'Our Spy.' Frankly, Asey, I don't think it would do a bit of harm if you took a few minutes off to look into him. He spends all his time snooping around the old wood lanes on his bike, and he's always asking questions, and looking at maps."

"So? An' what," Asey said, "d'you think he's spyin' on, exactly? Woodlots, or Cousin Barney's chicken farm, or the bayberry candle factory? An' speakin' of chicken farms, I want some food!"

Cummings put a restraining hand on Asey's arm.

"You don't want to go barging in there! Come home with me and get a snack. That mob'll probably knock you down and slap a traction splint on you before you could grab a stale crumb out of the pantry. Besides, I want to talk to you—"

He broke off at the sound of Jennie's whistle, emitting shrill, urgent blasts.

Asey, looking curiously up at his house, could see figures darting excitedly past the living-room windows, and then suddenly the front door burst open, and people started streaming down the path.

"Get back! Get out of their way!" Cummings yanked at Asey's arm and pulled him around into the shadow of the garage.

"But what—"

"Ssh! There go the Hazards!"

Asey watched while the elderly man in tweeds and the white-haired woman got into the Porter town car and rolled off, closely followed by the battered truck, which was driven by the young fellow in blue serge.

"Bob Corner," Cummings said. "Corner Hardware. You know, used to be Lem Snow's store."

After a brisk tussle with the crank, the dark, mastiff-like woman roared off in the nineteen-seventeen touring car, whose lusty backfires drowned out Cummings's identifying comment.

"And here's Jonah Ives, Asey," the doctor added. "See him, with the beard, on the bicycle? Foreign bike, too, you'll notice. And that's Phil Mundy's daughter, that blonde girl on the other bike."

"Who's the woman wavin' the white streamer from the buggy?" Asey inquired as the horse leisurely ambled off.

"That's no streamer, that's her practice bandage," Cummings said. "She's John Tuesome's widow— never let her get near you, I warn you! She'll either practice bandaging you, or make you shell out for some fund—ah! here comes Jennie, now!"

But before Asey could step forward and speak

to his cousin, she had swung onto the third bicycle and was scorching off down the lane with her whistle blasting shrilly.

"Well?" Cummings said as the sound of the whistle faded away. "Can't you say anything, after that?"

"I never need to see any elephants fly," Asey said. "I seen everything. I seen Jennie Mayo, in slacks, take a racin' start on a bicycle! Say, where'd she ever learn to ride?"

"You ought to ask when, not where," Cummings returned. "It was the week after Pearl Harbor. I know. I treated her bruises. Sometimes I think the greatest mistake the Axis ever made was in underestimating the Jennies of our civilization. She damn near broke her neck, but she learned!"

"Jennie," Asey said, "has a cast-iron will. Doc, what was all that? It looked like the start of a dash for free land."

Cummings glanced at his watch. "It was time for the class to end, so probably Jennie decided to give 'em a problem."

"From here," Asey said, "it seemed more like she'd given 'em a mass hotfoot. What d'you mean, a problem?"

"Problems," Cummings explained, "are encouraged by some of our powers that be. Idea is to train people to get to any given spot where they may be needed, using whatever vehicles they may have at hand. Probably Jennie announced a code number, blew her whistle, and said 'Go!' The problem is for everybody to reach the proper spot within a certain allotted time." The doctor paused, and chuckled.

"An' do they?"

"Well, my wife got her code signals balled up, the night of the big blizzard last month, and spent three hours over in the pine woods by Harding's Swamp, waiting for the rest of her group. They kept phoning me and asking me where I thought she might be, and how they could find her, and I told 'em if the woman didn't know enough to come home out of a blizzard, all I could suggest was for 'em to find a St. Bernard and send it out to her with some hot cocoa—what're you going to do, come to my place and eat, or go in and scratch up a meal for yourself?"

"Scratch," Asey said. "Golly, when I think how the dream of a clam chowder sustained me all durin' that hitchhike from the airport—uh-huh, that's how I got home. Come along. While I scramble me some eggs, you can catch me up with the rest of the news, an' changes, an' alterations."

Cummings nodded his approval, a few minutes later, when Asey, dressed in familiar corduroys and flannel shirt and yachting cap, came into the kitchen.

"Now," he said, "you look like yourself. I never can get used to seeing you in city clothes. There's no sense," he added, "to your bothering to look into that refrigerator. I did, and it's full of blue yarn."

"Blue yarn?" Asey opened the refrigerator door and stared in bewilderment at its blue wool contents. "Now *why*, for heavens' sakes?"

"Jennie's probably conserving electricity and keeping food in the pantry, like my wife does," Cummings said. "I don't know why she should choose to put yarn there. Handy for her, I suppose. Try the pantry."

The pantry, Asey discovered, was filled with packing cases stenciled with the legend, "Bundles for Bluejackets."

"Where's she *keep* things!" Asey demanded. "She must eat! She has to feed Syl—say, I started to ask you about Syl, an' then I got side-tracked. Where's Syl, off first-aidin', too?"

"Didn't Jennie write you about her better half?" Cummings inquired.

"Jennie sent me a box of food at Christmas," Asey said, "an' a card last month, remindin' me to pay my state taxes an' the insurance. She said things was fine— Syl isn't sick?"

"He's back in the Navy."

Asey blinked. "But he's too old!"

"It wasn't Syl's age they objected to as much as his false teeth," Cummings said. "But when they rejected him, Syl fumed his way into Admiral Buck's office—

remember Buck? He had the Kents' place in Weesit one summer. Syl said he couldn't see why the best ex-chief machinist's mate in the country should be turned down because of a few damn molars. Said he had no intention of biting either the Japs or the Nazis. So they took him back—isn't there any food in that closet, either? You'd best come home with me."

"It stands to reason there's somethin' to eat some place in the house!" Asey said. "Huh! Maybe Jennie's usin' the old shed buttery."

He swung open the back door to the woodshed, and, without bothering to turn on the light, stepped down to the lower level of the ell.

Cummings jumped to his feet and bustled to the doorway at the ensuing thud and miscellaneous clatter.

"What's the matter?" he snapped on the electric switch. "Trip, did you? Hurt yourself?"

"Why," Asey ruefully rubbed his shin, "should Jennie leave pails of sand standin' out here? An' snow shovels! An'—what'n time is that fool contraption on the end of my best eel spear?"

"Guess you must have stumbled into Jennie's incendiary-bomb department," Cummings said. "Your eel spear is now a bomb scoop—Asey, don't you know *any*thing about Civilian Defense?"

"Wa-el," Asey said, "I do remember Bill Porter yelpin' with rage about Civilian Defense an' fandancers—or was it badminton players? You see, doc, the factory where I live an' work is a modern black-out plant, fireproofed an' camouflaged. Only thing you're liable to trip over is guards with Tommy guns. S'pose, before I break a leg, you warn me what else in the line of home defense I might be likely to stumble into?"

"Oh, stirrup pumps, garden hose, bomb-snuffers—there's no end to the stuff people may have around. Just watch your step."

"Here I was thinkin'," Asey said, "that I had my finger plumb on the pulse of defense, but somehow, I keep feelin' like Rip Van Winkle. Aha!" he added as he opened the buttery door and jerked at the string leading to the overhead light. "Here's the larder—an' there's that dummy, too, over in the corner. I wondered where they left it when they went rushin' off. It wasn't in the livin' room, or in the front closet when I hung up my coat."

"When I peeked in and saw 'em doing traction splints on that fellow, I noticed that dummy and wondered why in blazes they didn't practice on that—Asey!"

"Uh-huh?" Asey, bearing a butter crock and a wire egg basket, stepped gingerly past the sand pails and the converted eel spear.

"Come back here, quick! Asey! Asey, this isn't any dummy!"

" 'Tis, too," Asey spoke from the kitchen. "I saw

it lyin' on the livin' room floor when I first came, sugar-bag hood, an' all. Looked like the Ku Klux—"

"Asey, come here!" there was a note of frantic urgency in Cummings's voice. "It's no dummy, I tell you, it's a *body!*"

CHAPTER TWO

"*BODY?*" Asey stood in the buttery's doorway and stared unbelievingly at the figure beside which Cummings was kneeling. "*Body?* Golly, doc, you're right! It *is* a body!"

"I told you so. Come here and help me ease off this sugar bag."

"If only I'd troubled to take more'n half a look— got the end, now? But like a chump, I just assumed it was the dummy when I spotted the hood. Doc, who in time is he? D'you recognize him?"

Cummings nodded slowly. "His name's Mundy. Philemon Mundy. He's been living over in East Aspinnet this winter. By George, take a look at the back of his head, Asey! By George, what a blow that must have been! That's no self-inflicted wound, or any casual accident, either! He's been murdered, Asey!"

"D'you suppose—" Asey began, and then abruptly stopped.

"I was just going to ask you," Cummings got to his feet and held the sugar bag up to the light, "if *you* supposed the same thing, but the words stuck in my throat, too. But it can't be, Asey, it's altogether too fantastic! I can't believe that Jennie's First-Aiders would bash Phil Mundy and then thrust him into your buttery as if he were—well, a broken egg, or something! I can't believe that!"

"Neither," Asey returned, "can I. But golly, doc!"

"Those First-Aiders aren't so dumb they couldn't manage to distinguish a body from a dummy!" Cummings said. "And even if they were that dumb, Jennie could never be fooled! But, Asey, someone put him in here! Someone bashed him, and then put him in here afterwards. There's no question about that—see here, take a look at this sugar bag. See this little bloodstain? Now, look at his head. For all that he was struck a terrific blow—I'm sure he never knew what hit him, which is small consolation to him now—for all the force of that blow, there's just this tiny cut here on the back of his head, see?"

"Meanin' he was bashed with a reasonably blunt instrument?"

Cummings shrugged. "You know the futility of guessing about this sort of thing. Maybe someone hit him with the flat side of a broadsword. Or a golf club. Or a rolled-up copy of 'The Saturday Evening Post.' Or a frying pan—Jennie's medium-sized iron spider hanging up there would make an elegant weapon. On the other hand, maybe it was just a whale of a rabbit punch. After half an hour in the laboratory, I can probably be more specific, but right now any guess is good. Point is, after he was struck, that cut bled just a little. But he didn't bleed any after he was put here, because that hood was twisted around and the part of the bag with the stain was about here," the doctor indicated the side of Mundy's neck, "when I took the hood off. Of course, Asey—"

"Of course what?"

"Well," Cummings said slowly, "of course there was that fellow up the Cape who volunteered to play ambulance patient to some one of these defense outfits, and what with the girls being new at the rescue business, the stretcher got dropped once or twice. And no one was more surprised than the women to find, when they reached the hospital, that their poor devil of a patient had a fractured skull and a couple of cracked ribs. There have been some other pretty crazy episodes. But I can't believe that Jennie Mayo would let an accident like this happen, and if it did happen, and she found out, I'm sure she'd have done something! Damn it, Asey, I keep wishing they hadn't rushed off that way, though, as if they were running away from something! I wish—where are you going?"

"To call Hanson an' the state cops," Asey said, "an' then see if I can't locate that dummy that I seen."

"Wait," Cummings said. "Now, you told me you came around seven o'clock. Right? Asey, are you sure you saw a dummy, and not Mundy?"

"I'm positive it was a dummy." Of course it was a dummy, he added mentally. Aloud, he said, "Yes!"

"I know," Cummings said. "That's just the way I feel. I saw a dummy lying beside whoever the fellow was they were putting a traction splint on—I couldn't see his face. I'm positive it was a dummy. But then I keep having this sneaking suspicion that maybe it wasn't a dummy at all—d'you remember seeing Mundy in the rest of the group? I don't."

"They were all strangers to me," Asey said, "an' when I peeked in, I was a lot more interested in what they were doin' than what they looked like. But I don't think Mundy was there."

He crossed over to the buttery door and looked down at the still figure. Mundy was short and stocky, with powerful shoulders, and black hair that was beginning to grow gray around his temples.

"Sure?" Cummings asked.

"I'm sure I never seen him, doc. 'Course, he might have been in the dinin' room, I s'pose, or in the hall— I'm goin' to phone the cops."

Half an hour later, Cummings looked inquiringly at Asey as the latter entered the woodshed.

"No soap this time, either?"

Asey shook his head. "The cops are all still busy

with special detail work about the canal bridges durin'
a special practice blackout. An' the new phone girl
at central's just given me a piece of her mind for askin'
her if she had any idea where Jennie might be. Says
she's busy with Army calls in connection with some
practice maneuvers hereabouts, an' I mustn't clog the
lines with silly questions unless I'm on fire."

"Oh, that girl!" Cummings said. "She's a substitute.
Very earnest and literal, and wears blue denim—did
you suggest to her that this was a little matter of a
murder?"

"Uh-huh, an' she give me the state cops again, an'
there's no one there but a rookie phone operator, an'
whereas he's very kindly an' sympathetic, he says he
can't call anyone in from special detail unless it's a
problem of sabotage. He says nobody gave him any
instructions about murders."

Cummings snorted. "I suppose," he said with irony,
"we might get results if we lighted a few small fires,
and then rushed out and broke a few of your front
windows! Oh, God, I suppose they'll ultimately iron
out some of this fool red tape—did I tell you that if
my wife becomes a casualty, I'm not permitted to at-
tend to her?"

"An' why not?"

"Because some fool drew a line in red ink, and cut
our house in two," Cummings explained. "My wife
sleeps in the west wing, and consequently she's

Greeley's patient, and must wait until Greeley drives forty-one and three-tenths miles to care for her. I clocked the distance on my speedometer and then wrote Washington a perfectly corking letter about it —what's that notebook you've got with the Red Cross decorations? Where'd you get that?"

"I noticed it on the phone-table shelf," Asey said. "It's Jennie's First Aid records—golly, doc!"

"What?"

"Look, here's the attendance record of the East Aspinnet groups—for Pete's sakes, doc, Mundy must have been here, whether we saw him or not! See, Jennie's checked him off as present tonight! J. Mundy —that's the blonde girl? J. Mundy, check. P. Mundy, check!"

"Oh, let's just stop kidding ourselves, Asey!" the doctor said wearily. "We both say we saw the dummy on the floor, and we both keep hoping it wasn't Mundy we saw all the time—and yet we can only find Mundy's body, and we can't find a trace of the dummy! It certainly isn't in the house, and we certainly didn't see anyone take it out of the house, and—oh, it's fantastic to think that Jennie's class could produce such a catastrophe, but don't let's try to kid ourselves any longer that it didn't! Mundy was here, according to Jennie's book. Mundy was killed—when did that rookie at the barracks think the cops would get here? I want to get busy at the lab!"

"He said he'd tell 'em when they got back from their special detail. Doc, how long has Mundy been dead, do you think?"

"All the years I've known you," Cummings said, "and you still persist in asking such idiotic questions! Listen, X can die two hours ago and look as if he'd been dead a million years—"

"Uh-huh, an' Y can be dead a million years, an' it seems like only yesterday, or words to that effect," Asey said. "I know. One person reacts one way, an' another don't. But give a guess!"

"From two to four hours, more or less. I wish you'd look around and dig up some clews!"

"Not for me. I'm home on vacation," Asey returned. "This business belongs to the cops."

"I suppose," Cummings studied the tip of his unlighted cigar, "you've considered the fact that Jennie was the last person to leave the house, and that she didn't emerge until after the rest of the bunch had left the lane?"

"But no one would ever suspect Jennie of killin' this man Mundy! Why, she doesn't even know him! That is, no more than she knows the rest of the people in her class! Jennie isn't the sort of person to go around killin' anyone—an' least of all strangers!"

Cummings grinned. "Since you've been away, my fine Codfish, there isn't the same fine distinction between natives and visitors that there used to be. All those women in slacks have turned out to be more sisterly under the skin than you'd ever have suspected. Jennie knows Phil Mundy as well as she knows any native she's seen around town for the last twenty years. You get to know people quickly, in these various classes."

"Then say that Jennie knows him," Asey conceded. "I still say, what of it? What earthly motive could she have for killin' him?"

"Mundy," Cummings said, "has been a thorn in Jennie's flesh for some time. You see, she's fallen into the habit of calling me up and getting the dope on questions people have stumped her with, and she's specifically mentioned Mundy as being a pain in the neck. He was inclined to be a bit peremptory and officious—came to me to be treated for a cold, and then told me exactly how he wished to be treated— and there's no doubt in my mind but what all the First Aid class knows there's been a lot of friction between him and Jennie. Probably the whole town knows it."

"Are you," Asey asked gently, "tryin' to get my goat? You know, an' I know, that Jennie never killed this fellow Mundy, no matter how much he may have provoked her."

Cummings shrugged as he got up from his chair, walked across the kitchen floor, and rather elaborately scratched a match on the stove lid.

"You can't tell," he said as he lighted his cigar,

"what people may say or think, these days. I've done rather a large business in the jangled-nerve department. There'll be whisperings. 'Jennie was sore with Mundy.' 'Mundy goaded her.' 'Jennie's strong as an ox. She bashed him.' 'They say it was half an hour before she left the house to go after the rest of the group.' Of course," he added, "maybe they won't say a blessed word. But you can't ignore the fact that there's a perfectly good possibility of her being personally involved."

Cummings sat back in his chair and puffed at his cigar until he figured that the smoke screen was adequate to conceal from Asey's keen eyes any telltale expression that might betray his real purpose in egging him on to find the murderer of Philemon Mundy. Not for a moment did the doctor suspect Jennie Mayo, but he knew that Asey would do things for her sake that he would never do for himself.

He had very nearly given himself away when he brought up the jangled-nerve department, Cummings thought as he flicked his cigar ash onto Jennie's spotless linoleum floor. What Asey Mayo needed wasn't any rest, but a good, violent change. Something to erase the tanks from his mind. And chasing down a murderer filled Cummings's mental prescription to a T. While Mundy's death was a grisly and unfortunate occurrence, it also, he decided with a grim smile, was just exactly what the doctor would have ordered.

"Well?" he said aloud.

Asey sighed.

"All right, doc. You win. I can't let Jennie run the risk of gettin' into any trouble. I'll start to work. But I must say, this isn't the sort of vacation I had in mind when I left the plant this mornin'! Nice, quiet rest! Huh, in a pig's eye!"

He sounded genuinely annoyed, but Cummings noticed that he didn't begin to look as tired as he had only a few minutes before.

"What," Asey continued, "was the big idea of that sugar-bag hood?"

"Face bandage, or a variant of one," Cummings said. "Have you thought of that woman you chased?"

"I thought of her the minute I seen Mundy's body, but we can't do much about her, even in the line of figurin', till we solve a few other problems. Now, let's see Jennie's list an' do some countin' an' checkin'. Mundy's checked as bein' present, but we never seen him. We seen the Hazards, the older couple in the Porter—who are they, anyway?"

"He was the head of a Boston brokerage office," Cummings said, "until he retired a year or two ago. Gave his Boston house for a service canteen, and they're now living in Standing's place at East Aspinnet for the duration. Okay on them. Okay on their daughter Tiny, too."

"But didn't you say the little blonde was Mundy's daughter?"

Cummings chuckled. "Tiny Hazard is the black-haired woman, the one built like a brick house, who roared off in the old Buick."

"*Tiny*, they call her?"

"They do. They say she was terribly small as a baby. Just too tiny. Check on her. Check Bob Corner —he bought Snow's old hardware store last fall, after you left. Doing rather well with it until the war."

"Check Corner, alias Blue Serge," Asey said, "an' check on your spy with the beard, Ives. Check Mrs. Tuesome, the bandage-waver. An'—say, doc, this doesn't come out right! Here's another Mundy! *K.* Mundy, listed as present!"

"Kay Mundy? She's Phil's sister," Cummings said. "I never saw her, did you? Asey, we've got to find Jennie and straighten this mess out—what did you say?"

"I said," Asey tossed Jennie's notebook down on the kitchen table, "what puzzles me more'n all these Mundys is why, when you stop an' think of all the available places in this world, did anyone choose my buttery as the ideal spot to leave a corpse?"

"Like the blue wool in the refrigerator, I suppose it seemed a handy place," Cummings said. "Asey, pick up that book and see if Jennie's got a list of problem spots there anywhere. It's theoretically time she was back home, but sometimes when people get lost, it takes half the night to round 'em up. If we can find out where they might have gone, we can track her down. Here, give me the book. She probably keeps the list at the end, where my wife does. Aha."

Asey peered over his shoulders. "Hell Hollow, Harding's Swamp, Silver Marsh, Great Meadow—what damp spots!"

"I've had a fine runny-nose and sore-throat business from 'em," Cummings said absently. "Damn, Jennie hasn't checked any one place! We'll just have to drive through the list, that's all. We ought to bump into some of the crowd somewhere."

"You think we ought to leave?"

"I'm a medical examiner," Cummings said, "and I've made a preliminary examination. Death caused by blow on cervical plexus, by person or persons unknown, strong possibility of blunt instrument being employed, and so on and so forth. Seems to me safe enough to leave him here if we lock the place up. No one knows about this but the murderer and us, and if the murderer's gone to all the trouble of thrusting his victim into your buttery, that's obviously his conception of the *ne plus ultra* in corpse disposal. Hm. I wonder—"

"Yes?" Asey said encouragingly as the doctor paused.

"I wonder, do you suppose some thwarted ex-student wanted to embarrass the First Aid class? Quite a few have been dropped, you know, with resulting hard feelings. Maybe someone's working out an old grudge against you. Well, let's find Jennie, or one of her group, and get the facts on who was here, and when Mundy came, and when he left. Asey, d'you suppose the woman you chased could have been Kay Mundy?"

"Could be, except that she didn't come from the house there, where Jennie's records say she was. What about the cops, doc?"

"If they snarl things up in this practice blackout as thoroughly as they did in the last one they sprang up-Cape," Cummings said, "those cops won't be here until daybreak. I'll phone them, and then I'll try to locate my wife and see if she's any suggestions as to where Jennie and her mob might have gone."

The sound of his heated altercation with the literal-minded telephone girl carried out to the far end of the woodshed, where Asey finally located his favorite canvas duck coat hanging from a rusty hook.

He put it on, noticed that the back shed door was locked, and paused for a moment in the doorway of the buttery.

He couldn't quite fathom out the reason for Cummings's goading him to work on this. It didn't seem possible that anyone could consider attempting to involve his cousin Jennie. Still and all, things had changed since he'd been away, and probably Cummings spoke the truth when he said you couldn't tell, these days, what mad notions people might jump on and cling to.

"I wonder," Asey murmured, "if maybe p'raps the doc hasn't sort of been yearnin' for a little excitement, himself. Must sort of thwart him, sittin' here namin' triplets, after the work he done last war at old Base Hospital B. I wonder if that's why he egged me on, just in the hope of seein' some action! Wa-el, now let's consider this."

The dummy on the living-room floor had been partially covered by a sheet, but he remembered the fixedly wooden smile when the white-haired woman yanked off the sugar bag, and he remembered dark trouser cuffs, and brown feet. The dummy either had on brown shoes, or else the feet had been painted to give the illusion of brown shoes. That was all he could recall, except his fleeting impression that the figure must have been snatched from a local store window.

And Mundy wore dark-blue trousers, a short windproof jacket of blue gabardine, and brown sneakers.

Asey rubbed his chin reflectively. It was like being asked the time. You looked at your watch and confidently gave the required information. But if someone asked you again, a second later, you always nervously looked again at your watch before answering, as if you hadn't really been quite sure the first time.

For his part, he was sure that he had seen a dummy on the floor. But what he remembered of the dummy bore more than a passing resemblance to Mundy.

He bent over and scrutinized the brown sneakers on Mundy's feet. They were brand new, bone dry, and completely free from caked mud or water stains.

"Huh!" Asey thought of his own soaked, oozing Oxfords, and frowned. Mundy never could have walked to the house. He must have come with someone in one of the assorted vehicles parked outside. "Huh!" he said again. "How in time could anyone have bashed you durin' that class, an' lugged you out here with apparently no one bein' any the wiser? They couldn't have!"

"Who couldn't have?" Cummings appeared in the kitchen doorway. "What're you muttering about?"

"All this," Asey said. "Any luck with the cops?"

"That rookie says they've got to investigate two reported cases of attempted sabotage before they can bother with us. He has no idea when they may get here. So we might as well improve the shining hours and find Jennie. I've just thought of something, Asey. Look out of the way."

Brushing past Asey, the doctor knelt down and put the sugar-bag hood back on Mundy's head.

"There!" he said with pride. "Notice anything, Sherlock?"

Asey shook his head.

"Why, man alive, the slits fit his eyes, and nose, and mouth, see? That bag was custom-cut for him! And if you'll look closely, you'll see it's been pretty neatly cut, too. No ragged notches, no saw-tooth edges. Just neat, curved scallops!"

"Nail scissors," Asey said.

"Or embroidery scissors. It's the work of a woman. Not a man. Women always have scissors with 'em. At least, my wife always keeps a pair of little ones in her pocketbook. But if a man wants to cut something, he saws away with his pocketknife. Well," the doctor arose, "there's my diagnosis for you. The murderer was a neat woman with nail or embroidery scissors on her person, and the full use of both hands—takes two hands to get that bag on. Now I'll go see if Sourpuss's managed to phone around and track down my wife."

"How'd you get her to do it for you?" Asey inquired. "Tell her you was in flames?"

"I remembered, in a heaven-sent flash, that her sister's going to have a baby shortly," Cummings told him. "Gives me a certain hold over her."

He marched back to the telephone, and Asey stepped forward and knelt down beside Mundy and lifted up the sugar bag.

For several minutes he studied the small cut and the thin gray line, almost like a pencil mark, underneath it. Then he looked thoughtfully up at the iron frying pan hanging on the buttery's side wall.

That pan, properly wielded, would have delivered a terrific blow; it might well also have caused a cut and have left a mark.

But then, so might any one of a hundred other things. As Cummings had sensibly said, there was no use in speculating which blunt instrument out of all the blunt instruments available in the world might have been used to kill Mundy. Cummings would settle that in his laboratory. It was better for him now to try and find some extraneous object that might serve as a clew. Or something misplaced, or out of order.

He glanced around the floor. There was a molasses jug, a brown crock of water-glass eggs, a collection of empty milk and cream and tonic bottles that wasn't yet large enough to get into Jennie's way and provoke her into returning them to the store. He scanned the shelves, with their jars of pickles and relish and pre-serves and beach plum jelly and "put-up" vegetables. Then he looked over the miscellaneous pots and pans, all too good to be thrown away, that had been rele-gated to comparative limbo out here. Some day, proba-bly in the feverish bustle of Jennie's spring houseclean-ing, some of the accumulated has-beens would be sent to the dump. In the meantime, they cluttered up the buttery.

But Asey could see no trace of anything that a movie detective would pounce on and pronounce a clew. There were no cigarette butts, lipstick-stained or otherwise, no provocative hairpins of pure gold, no thin platinum lockets engraved with impressive crests, no gossamer handkerchiefs delicately scented with strange perfume. The buttery looked much as it always had looked since he was a child, and it had the same smell of scrubbed pine floor—and catnip. Every winter a bunch of dried catnip was always hung up on the inside of the door to be doled out at intervals to the current house cat.

The only extraneous object in the place was one of the fifty-cent pieces Cummings had picked up after the woman had fled down the lane. Probably it had dropped out of the doctor's pocket.

"Asey!" Cummings called. "Hey, Asey, hurry up! Sourpuss got hold of my wife, and *she* says she thinks they've probably gone to Great Meadow, because Jennie asked her this morning about the quickest way to get there—come on, hurry! My wife thinks the whole bunch may be planning to go on to some rally afterwards!"

"Okay." Asey put out the buttery light, snapped out the rest of the house lights, and followed Cummings down the oystershell walk.

"You lock the front door?" Cummings asked.

"I snapped it," Asey said. "I can't lock the tumbler,

because I haven't a key. Come to think of it, I don't know who does have a key. I'm sure Jennie hasn't, because she left the latch up. Tell me about this fellow Mundy," he added as he got into the doctor's coupe. "Whee, ain't those whitewalls new?"

"The rationing board," Cummings said, "practically choked those four new tires down my throat. People look at 'em wistfully and then say that if anyone gets tires, they're glad it's me. I always felt it would take a global war for me to be properly appreciated by my fellow men. Why, d'you know that some of my older deadbeat patients have actually started paying me in little dribblets—"

"Is that a *lunch* basket up on the shelf back of your neck?" Asey interrupted hungrily.

"By George, yes, and it's full," Cummings started the car. "Take it down and feed yourself. You see, having been given tires, I thought I should conserve 'em as much as possible, so I lunch wherever I happen to be instead of bothering to drive home. I forgot all about it today, what with Minnie and her triplets. I know quite a lot about Mundy," he added as he headed the coupe up the lane. "Met a fellow at a medical dinner who lives in Dalton and tended him. He's a war casualty."

"Army or Navy?"

"Neither, he's a civilian casualty. Came from a good old Dalton family, parents died when he was about fifteen, leaving him with a baby sister and practically no assets to speak of. Relations took the sister and the assets, and he went to work. The rest is practically Horatio Alger, in a small way."

"Successful, was he?"

"As of last year," Cummings said, "he owned Dalton's biggest garage and car agency, a string of garages and car agencies in all the neighboring towns, a small factory that made junk jewelry, a string of shops that sold the stuff, a chain of tire and radio stores, and a lot of real estate. As of today, he owns a garage or two, with some real estate. This Dalton doctor put it rather well. Said Mundy wasn't even back where he started out twenty-five years ago. He was behind back of where he started, considering his taxes and rentals and leases and notes and all that sort of thing."

"How'd he happen to land in East Aspinnet?" Asey wanted to know.

"This Dalton chap sent him down here in mid-December after a nervous crack-up and a bad bout of grippe. Hoped the rest and quiet would build him up and pull him together. Within a week," Cummings said, "Mundy had a finger in every pie in town, from organizing fire fighters and plane spotters to selling baby bonds. He's just one of those men with tre-mendous drive and energy. Couldn't keep still unless you tied him down."

"Would you say he had any enemies?"

"Well," Cummings said, "I told you he was inclined to be officious. That type often is. Of course, he rubbed a lot of people, including Jennie, the wrong way, but I think on the whole that people respected his knowledge of how to organize and tackle things, and his ability to get things done. He's made some irritated acquaintances, but I wouldn't say he'd made any mortal enemies. How's my lunch?" he added as he turned the coupe from the lane onto the main road. "On the stale side?"

"Best sandwiches I ever ate. Mundy had a sister and a daughter—what about his wife?"

"Died last summer. Been divorced for years. I don't think he ever saw his blonde daughter until she joined him here last month. I've an idea that his financial problems cut short her expensive schooling. Spoiled looking child, terribly convinced of her own importance. The sister's rather a pleasant sort, my wife said. Twenty-five or -six. Another war casualty. She was secretary to the president of an importing firm that folded. The three of 'em live in Collins's house out at the Bluffs, and take their meals at the Inn."

"Aren't you," Asey peered out the car window, "kind of takin' the long way around to Great Meadow?"

"I avoid wood roads," Cummings said. "Can't risk having a stump gouge my whitewalls. And in case you do any driving while you're home, I want to warn you very pointedly that forty is the speed limit, and you're no longer given any benefit of doubt."

"But the little short cut—"

"No!" Cummings said firmly. "No short cuts, and no, I'm not going to let you take the wheel! This car is virtually a national resource, and I refuse to expose it to your maniacal driving!"

Asey grinned. "Okay, doc, but if you're goin' in for patriotic conservin', stop ridin' your clutch! Tell me, why are all these group-problem meetin' spots in such swampy places?"

"Idea is that a plane making a forced landing would try to land on a flat place, and the only available flat spots in this vicinity are all marshes and swamps. My wife said we ought to find 'em just south of the meadow at the crossroads. That's where her group met."

He stopped the coupe under a street light at the crossroads and peered expectantly around, but there was no sign of Jennie and her group, or any of their vehicles.

"Damn!" Cummings said. "My wife sounded so positive, I felt sure we'd find 'em milling around here! Well, we'll just have to run through all the places on Jennie's list, I suppose."

"Wait a sec," Asey said as the doctor started up the car. "Look ahead at the dirt ruts, doc. There's some fresh tire marks that look to me like the arrow tread of that Porter town car. Lean over while I look at the other fork—yup." He focused the coupe's spotlight. "See? Bicycle tracks. An' they're fresh, too."

"Are they going that way, towards the Meadow, or coming back this way?"

"That way—see the mark of the bike's rear wheel?" Asey focused the light again. "See? Drive on along, an' maybe we'll catch up with 'em."

"I am not," Cummings said firmly, "going to drive this car down either prong of this fork! I know where these lanes lead to! Dead-end mudholes, that's what! And the ruts are full of sharp stones and tree stumps. I will not do it!"

"Okay," Asey said, "we'll walk. We can't miss 'em, because they got to come back this way. As I remember, both lanes come out on the Meadow's edge about a hundred yards apart, don't they? By the old dyke? Well, you take the left lane. That's shorter. I'll take the right. Here," he removed a flashlight from its clamp on the steering post and held it out to the doctor, "use this, an' mind your step, an' yell when you reach the Meadow. Signal me if you should sight any of 'em. Say, doc."

"Yes?" Cummings said as he got out of the coupe.

"What *do* you think about that iron fryin' pan of Jennie's out there in the buttery? I can't seem to get that iron spider out of my mind. It could've made that cut, an' left that mark. An' it was awful handy. Mundy could've been killed there, left in one position, an' then been moved to that corner, thus accountin' for that stain on the sugar bag. Honest, that spider worries me!"

"It's haunting me too, if you want to know," Cummings returned. "I never heard of anyone using an iron spider as a lethal weapon, but the more you think of it, the more—Asey, I saw a light flash over yonder in the woods! Let's get going!"

"Okay, doc!" Asey started off down the right lane at a loping run.

Half an hour later, Cummings angrily pitched his now worn-out flashlight far out into the soggy stretch of meadow before him.

"Damn!" he said hoarsely. "Damn, damn, damn! Damn it, where *is* he? Where'd he *go?* Why doesn't he *an*swer? What's the *mat*ter with him?"

Muttering under his breath, he stumbled his way along the ruts back to the crossroads.

The coupe was there, all right.

But Asey wasn't.

"Asey! A-sey May-o! Asey!"

Cummings called until his tired voice cracked, and trailed off into a thick whisper.

Then he put his thumb on the car horn, and shoved the button down.

Then he called again, and when his throat gave out, he whistled.

But nothing happened.

No one answered.

"Damn it!" Cummings muttered. "He can't have vanished into thin air!"

If Asey had seen Jennie or any of the First-Aiders, he certainly would have yelled at them. If anything untoward had happened, Asey would certainly have made the welkin ring!

"Damn!" Cummings said. "The man's had an accident. That's the only solution. He's tripped or slipped or fallen, and knocked himself out!"

Fishing around in the cluttered contents of his ubiquitous black bag, the doctor finally unearthed a small flashlight, and marched off down the right fork that Asey had taken.

At the Meadow's edge, he stopped and delivered himself of a vehement summary of the state of affairs as he saw it, and then he tramped back to the coupe and sat down wearily behind the wheel.

He had for so many years been exposed to the problems of life and death that neither Minnie's bouncing triplets nor Mundy's violent death had upset his equilibrium to any great degree. After all, he had once ushered quadruplets into the world, and he had once spent a breathless afternoon dodging a berserk patient whose brandished ax had already accounted for five victims. Those things were all a part of his day's work.

But to have a bicycle, its rider, a Porter town car,

its occupants, and Asey Mayo himself all evaporate soundlessly and apparently permanently into the curling mists of Great Meadow!

"That's not foul play!" Cummings muttered. "That's —that's sabotage! Hm. Sabotage—"

He turned the car and headed back to town. He'd bring the cops running!

CHAPTER THREE

ASEY emerged from the right-hand lane just in time to see the taillights of the doctor's car disappear around a curve of the tarred road.

"Not over forty! Huh!" Asey murmured. "Nearer sixty-five, I'd say, an' I'll bet he's ridin' that clutch, too!"

He rubbed his wrists, twisted his head and stretched his neck muscles experimentally, and then sat down on the ground and leaned wearily back against the street light post.

The doctor, he decided, had put it mildly when he said that the Cape had changed during his absence. After the sixty fantastic minutes he'd just spent in the vicinity of Great Meadow, Asey was beginning to wonder if he'd returned to the right Cape. He was fast reaching a point where he wouldn't turn a hair if Superman came swooping out of the starlit sky, or if a couple of gnomes jumped out of the lamppost behind him.

And the difficulty in trying to piece things together to make some sense was that there was so little to piece!

He'd started off down the lane, gone perhaps thirty yards, and then—wham!

Without a sound, and in a second and a half, flat, he'd been grabbed, gagged, blindfolded, and trussed up like a fowl. He never saw the pair who jumped him, and they'd never said a word. All he knew was that the trussing job was not the work of an amateur, or of any overzealous First-Aiders. No city gangsters could have been brisker or more efficient.

He'd been left there in the bushes for a while, and then he'd been picked up like a baby, carried some considerable distance into the woods, where he was finally dumped down on pine needles. Dimly, as they started to lug him away, he'd heard Cummings's voice calling out his name.

The couple carrying him must have heard the doctor, too, but they ignored the sound. And Cummings must have been aware of footsteps scrunching and twig-snapping that accompanied his involuntary tour to the pine grove. To Asey, as he was being jounced along like a bag of meal, the trip had all the sound effects of the Porter Tank Plant out for an evening stroll.

But probably Cummings had been too far away to hear, or else he had been making too much noise himself to hear anything else. Perhaps the couple who'd jumped him hadn't realized from what direction Cummings had been calling. Perhaps they'd assumed that he was yelling to someone back on the main road.

"Huh!" Asey said. "Quaint Cape Cod, as we used to laughin'ly call it!"

He got to his feet, and stretched. His ankles and arms were still stiff from being bound up, and his muscles still ached from all the wriggling about into crazy positions that had been necessary to free himself. If that pair had been just a wee mite cannier in their choice of knots, Asey thought, he'd probably still be squirming around those pine needles like a caterpillar stuck on a pin.

He wondered, as he turned and looked across to the pitch blackness of the Meadow, whether he might not have displayed more wit by sitting there placidly where he had been dumped. He certainly couldn't have been any more in the dark than he was now, and perhaps, if he'd stayed there long enough, he might have gleaned some faint inkling of what was going on.

A brief study of the bicycle tracks and the tire marks in the ruts of the road forks left him feeling even more baffled. After seeing Cummings's car speed out of sight, he'd jumped to the conclusion that the doctor and the cyclist and the occupants of the Porter, after vainly hunting for him, had all hurried back to town to round up additional help. Maybe a posse. Certainly some lights.

But the rut tracks remained just as they had been when he first set off down the lane over an hour ago. Unless the cyclist had pumped back through the woods, or unless the Porter had been flown back, they must still be there where he expected to find them in the first place.

Asey rubbed his chin reflectively.

If Jennie or any of her blessed group had heard the doctor calling, they surely would have done something about it!

Or would they?

Cummings seemed to feel that you couldn't predict what havoc an enthusiastic First Aider might wreak. But would they go so far as to lurk in a bush two miles from nowhere, leap on an innocent passerby, truss him up, gag him, blindfold him, and dump him half a mile away in a pine grove?

None of it, Asey thought, bore any remote connection with his own private conception of first aid.

Could it be some other group practicing something?

Asey shook his head. It didn't seem likely.

After all, this was still Cape Cod, and whatever changes the war might have caused, certain facts remained unchanged. What, in peace, amounted to assault and near-battery and kidnaping in a small way, amounted to the same thing in war. And murder, he reminded himself, was still murder.

Could someone in the First Aid class have gone mad?

"Golly, whatever they're doin', they're still at it!"

Asey's voice echoed some of the frustrated bewilderment he felt as a light flashed on suddenly in the woods beyond the meadow, and then as suddenly disappeared.

He turned and looked back up the tarred road. Cummings knew something was wrong and, without doubt, Cummings would return. But he couldn't wait for help, or for the flashlight he really wanted. The time to make sense out of this mess was now.

He started cautiously down the left lane that Cummings had taken, stepping softly and stopping every now and then to listen.

He reached the end of the road without seeing any trace of a bicycle on it or beside it, and he knew that it wouldn't be worth the effort or the danger of lighting a match to peer at the ruts for tire tracks, because the ruts were as full of sharp stones and mud puddles as Cummings had prophesied.

Ducking, he sneaked past the Meadow's edge to where the right lane ended, and tiptoed along it to the place where he had been grabbed.

There was no sign of the town car!

Asey stepped off the lane, leaned against a pine tree, and considered the situation.

The bike could have been wheeled off into the

woods, or tossed down anywhere in the bushes. Not locating that didn't mean much.

But no one could pick up a car with the Porter's wheel base, and march off with it tucked in his hip pocket! And beyond any shadow of a doubt, the Porter had gone down that lane, and it hadn't come back!

It took him twenty minutes and two round trips up and down the lane before he finally located the town car, driven off the lane, and practically hidden from sight by a thicket.

Only a madman, Asey thought, would choose to park a car like that in among bushes and brambles and saplings—and enough tree stumps to make Cummings burst into tears!

He listened for a moment, then tiptoed over to the car and watched it intently for several minutes before reaching out and opening the rear door.

The inside light flashed on, showed that the car was empty, and Asey quickly and quietly closed the door.

He found himself swallowing.

The light had been on only for a second, but that had given him ample opportunity to see, sitting smack in the middle of the back seat, an iron frying pan! A twin of Jennie's spider hanging at home on the wall of his buttery!

"Golly!"

He stepped back from the car and ducked down at

the sound of low voices coming from the meadow end of the lane.

There were two people, one of them wheeling a bicycle.

A cigarette glowed, and Asey recognized the bearded face of Jonah Ives.

"Know what *I* say, June? June, where are you now! Did anyone," there was a note of irritation in Ives's voice, "ever tell you that you're an awful dawdler, Miss Mundy?"

"My moccasin came off again." The girl stopped a few feet away from Asey, put a hand against a tree trunk to steady herself, and replaced her footgear.

"Why the hell didn't you wear proper shoes?" Ives demanded. "You know Jennie warned us about outings like this!"

"Oh, she's so deathly *grim* about things!" the girl said querulously. "She reminds me of our Latin teacher. All these *warn*ings all the time—wait, Jonah! It's come off again! It simply won't stay on. The stitching's broken or something fatal like that."

"Haven't you anything you could tie it on with? Well, take my tie, then, and see what you can do with —oh, God, June, give it to me! Now, hang on to that tree trunk and hold up your foot—and damn it, stand still!"

"You're so *mean* to me!"

"You ask for it," Ives said matter-of-factly, "by being so damned irritating."

"If I'd known everybody would be so horrid to me, I wouldn't ever have signed up for that old class in the first place!"

"If everyone had known what a horrid little—er—thing you could be, I'm quite sure," Ives returned, "that they wouldn't have allowed you to sign up with them in the first place."

"Well," June said indignantly, "I say the hell with the old class! I'm not going again! I've gone to my last First Aid class, so there!"

"That," Ives said, "will suit the rest of us fine. For my part, I say the hell with hunting Mrs. Tuesome. I've hunted her for the last time. If she gets lost again, she can stay lost, so there! Now, will you make that moccasin stay on, please?"

"You've tied it too tight, Jonah! Now I can't walk at all!"

"My best hand-woven tie," Ives said. "I gallantly ruin it, and you complain. Of course, you'd complain if I stoically let you stumble on, too—hold your foot up again, and if this doesn't suit your ladyship, you can damn well stomp home barefoot—what became of your father tonight? Where'd he go?"

Asey got the impression that Ives really didn't care a whoop where Mundy had gone, and that he asked more to change the subject and relieve the somewhat charged atmosphere than to get information on Mundy's actual whereabouts.

"The hell with him," June said. "I don't know. Or care."

"Don't care much for your father, do you?"

"I loathe him," June said. "He's perfectly horrid to me. Mother said he always was horrid, always thinking of himself all the time, and always wanting his own way."

"And so, of course, your mother brought you up differently." Ives's smooth irony sailed over the girl's head. "To be sure, to be sure—there, is that damned shoe all right now?"

June took several experimental steps.

"That won't ever stay on! That's perfectly *ter*rible! It drags, and then it slips right off—Jonah, how'll I get home?"

"As a concession to your family, who have been very kind to me, and for other purely humanitarian reasons," Ives said, "I will break down to the extent of trundling you home on my handlebars—after we get back on the tarred road."

"*Han*dlebars?" June sounded as if Ives had announced his intention of wrapping her in a mantle of venomous snakes and dragging her off by her hair. "*Han*dlebars?"

"See here!" Asey could hear Ives draw in his breath sharply. "See here, young woman, someone ought to have told you that there's a limit to human patience! You can go home on my handlebars, or you can rot here! I don't care which—God, this is all your own fault! Don't you know better than to dump your bike down in the woods at night without at least *try*ing to mark the spot? How'd you expect to locate it again, with a divining rod?"

"I never meant to lose it! I just simply put it down— Jonah, listen! There's that funny noise again, hear it?"

"You mean that rustling we heard?"

"Yes! Listen now—hear it? And look—I just saw a light down at the end of the lane!"

Asey's eyes narrowed. He was in an excellent position to see any light at the end of the lane, but he hadn't. Neither had he been aware of any funny noises or rustlings.

"Here," Ives said, "hold the bike while I run back and take a look—maybe it's that idiot Tuesome wandering around, though personally I think there's something screwball going on here, and God knows I'd really try to look into it in a big way if I didn't have you dangling like a millstone around my neck! Now don't you lose *this* bike, my young blonde beauty, or I'll repair an omission of your youth and spank you so hard you'll be taking your meals off a mantel for at least a month. Hear me?"

He ran off down the lane.

The girl turned and watched him, and then, with a triumphant little giggle, she swung herself up on the bicycle and sped away before Asey had a chance to extricate himself from the bushes.

"The little brat!" he murmured. "She did that on purpose!"

He could have called after her and ordered her to stop, but he was under no illusion that she would have stopped at his command, or anyone else's. Probably, since Ives also seemed to feel that something odd was going on, it was better for the girl to be out of the way.

Now he would locate Ives, Asey decided, and the two of them could look into things together. And Ives could tell him where Jennie was, and who had been present at the class.

At any rate, he thought as he set off down the lane, he could feel sure that neither Ives nor June Mundy had been the pair who jumped him!

He was nearing the edge of the meadow when the soft pad of footsteps behind him caused him to duck quickly into a clump of scrub oak.

At the sight of the martial silhouettes of the two tin-hatted figures approaching, Asey's eyes opened wide. He began to understand the situation, and the soft-voiced conversation that took place directly in front of him cleared up the trussing episode in one fell swoop.

"Why're there so *many*, huh?" The shorter soldier removed his tin hat and wiped his forehead. "You *sure* we done right jumpin' 'em?"

"Listen, chum, you wasn't with us last week!"

"Yeah, but—"

"Listen, chum, I keep tellin' you, *I* learned my lesson last week, see? *I* let the old lady with the basket of eggs go by, see? And she turns out to be a Blue Captain, and he captures us, see? We ain't lettin' anybody by!"

"But you let that fellow and his girl go by!" the short soldier objected.

"Oh, that! That's different! We should bust in on them! They was all right. They got some *reason* bein' here. But what else reason would anyone else have for bein' in this godforsaken place? Answer me that one, chum!"

The short soldier admitted that maybe there was some truth in that.

"But," he added plaintively, "I keep thinking maybe we should've put 'em all together. How we going to find 'em?"

"Oh, there's only four!"

"Yeah, but how we going to find 'em?" The short soldier persisted.

"Well, maybe we should've put 'em together," the other conceded after a short pause. "We would of, if we hadn't of got sort of mixed up ourselves. What matters is, we got 'em. That's what matters. Nobody made up like somebody else has got by *us!*"

"Yeah. You think we ought to keep *on* grabbing everybody?"

"Listen, chum, we got our orders, didn't we? Nobody gets by! Okay. So *no*body gets by! Come on. I still think I heard someone down this way."

Asey grinned as the pair padded along the Meadow's edge.

He should have caught on quicker. The telephone girl had told him that some Army unit was maneuvering in the vicinity. He ought to have guessed.

So the pair had disposed of four people. He accounted for one. And the other three, in all likelihood, were the Hazards, who had apparently been hunting the lost Mrs. Tuesome, and probably the lost Mrs. Tuesome herself. And unless Jonah Ives was extraordinarily alert, Asey guessed that he would shortly turn out to be Number Five on the list.

If he attempted to trail the soldiers and explain the situation to them—Asey dismissed the idea. The incident of the lady with the basket of eggs was too firmly fixed in the tall soldier's mind. He would only be jumped on again, and he didn't feel up to a scuffle with that pair. Nor could he possibly locate the trussed-up trio by himself. The quickest way to solve the whole problem would be to get to a phone, bully the telephone operator into connecting him with the officer in charge, and tell him all that had happened.

He tiptoed out of the bushes and once again started up the lane toward the main road.

When he was almost abreast of the hidden Porter, a flashlight beam picked him out and focused on his face.

"Halt!"

Asey obediently halted, and a figure strode out of a thicket and marched up to him.

"What are you doing here?" There was a grimly authoritative note in the youthful voice that barked at him.

"I—er—"

Asey hesitated. He couldn't quite bring himself to tell anyone with that kind of bark that he was primarily hunting his cousin Jennie, a largish lady in outsized slacks.

"I said, what are you doing here?"

"D'you mind tellin' me, mister, why it's any business of yours?" That, Asey figured, would have been the probable response of the average independent native of his acquaintance.

The flashlight beam swung away from Asey's face and onto the newcomer just long enough to allow Asey to see the latter's cap and collar insignia.

"Oh!" Asey said. "I'm sorry, lieutenant. Have I run into somethin' I hadn't ought to have?"

"What are you doing in this area? How did you get here?"

"Why, I drove here," Asey told him. "I didn't know you Army fellows was—"

"What kind of car do you own?" the lieutenant interrupted crisply.

"Wa-el," Asey said, "I don't exactly own a Porter, right now, but I've always driven one."

"Chauffeur, eh? Didn't you see any of our signs?"

"Signs?" Asey said.

"This place is posted as a military area for the time being, and why you people can't—when'd you drive that car here?"

"I didn't exactly drive it here." Asey felt that he should skirt the truth as far as possible. "Mr. Hazard drove it—"

"I see, I see! He got stuck, and sent you to get it out. Well, *get* it out!"

"But—"

"Get it out, get on your way, and don't come back here tonight!" the lieutenant said. "Hurry up!"

"Okay."

Asey got into the Porter, felt a surge of relief at finding the keys in place, and, under the suspiciously critical gaze of the lieutenant, expertly backed the car out onto the lane. It was his impression that if he had been a whit less expert, this young shavetail would have grabbed him and marched him off as a suspicious character.

"What're you waiting for?"

"Well," Asey felt that he should at least make some effort to rescue the Hazards and Mrs. Tuesome, "I was wonderin'. You see, *I* never noticed your signs, an' I was wonderin' what'd happen if any of your men happened to meet up with anybody who hadn't noticed your signs either, an'—"

"You hang around here just thirty seconds longer, and you'll find out! Now, get along!"

"But—"

"Beat it!"

"Okay, okay!" With a shrug, Asey abandoned his direct-rescue attempt, and headed the Porter up the lane.

The Hazards and Mrs. Tuesome—and probably Ives had by now joined them—would all just have to wait until he could carry out his original plan of phoning the outfit's commanding officer.

Even if that shavetail had been inclined to listen, he thought, explanations would have been pretty complicated.

"An' how," he murmured, "did you know people had been trussed up in the first place, Mr. Mayo? An' why did you choose to let our Lieutenant Fuzzface think you was a chauffeur when you're not a chauffeur? Just what *was* you millin' around these woods for?

Who? Indeed! *In*deed! What a peculiar place to hunt one's cousin Jennie! An' just why were you seekin' her? Oh. A *mur*der! A murder in *your* house? Indeed!"

Ultimately, somewhere around daybreak, everything would probably have been ironed out to everyone's complete satisfaction. But a phone call to the top would be a lot simpler.

He had a lot of phoning to do, Asey thought as he sped along the tarred road to town. First to the Army, then to relocate Cummings, then to get down to brass tacks and find Jennie, without any more beating about the bush. Or, he amended, being beaten about the bush, either. The new little phone office was just up the road. Quicker to make his calls from there.

Two minutes later he was rattling the doorknob, and three minutes later, with the aid of a kitchen match, he was deciphering the notice tacked on the door which announced that the office closed at ten.

"Hey!" Asey tapped on the windowpane and vainly tried to get the attention of the earnest-looking girl who sat at the switchboard. "Hey, couldn't you let me in? It's only six seconds after ten! Hey, this is important!"

The girl heard him, all right, but she never even turned her head.

Muttering under his breath, Asey got into the Porter and drove on half a mile to the town's drugstore.

As he entered, he made his usual gesture of reaching

out and pocketing a tin of his favorite pipe tobacco.

"Hi, Marvin, I—oh." Instead of Marvin, a strange girl stood behind the rear counter, and the look with which she favored him could only be summed up as skeptical. "Oh. Good evenin'," Asey said. "I expected to see Marvin standin' here—where is he?"

"Mr. Holmes has been in the Navy since December. That tobacco," the girl added coldly, "will be thirty-five cents, *if* you please!"

Asey, feeling vaguely guilty, hurriedly gave her a half dollar.

She surveyed it mistrustfully, bounced it on the counter, and then with reluctance gave him his change.

"I want to use your phone," Asey said. "P'raps you could give me two nickels for this dime?"

She gave him the nickels, sat back on a high stool behind the counter, and fixed on him an unblinking stare that somehow seemed to penetrate the glass and golden oak door of the phone booth like an X-ray.

It never wavered during the next ten minutes, and it remained unchanged when Asey stepped out into the store and asked her, in the deadly calm voice of a man tried beyond endurance, if she happened to know the phone operator.

"An' if so," he continued, "d'you happen to have any influence with her?"

"She's my sister." The girl took a pair of shell-rimmed glasses off the counter and started to polish them carefully. "Why?"

"Huh," Asey said. "I'd ought to have guessed! Look, will you talk to her, for the love of heaven, an' ask her to put my call through? She won't connect me with an Army outfit over in the woods without I give her a password!"

"This is war," the girl returned.

"I know it's war! I—oh, no matter! Give me some more change. I'll do this the hard way!"

He opened his wallet and laid a bill down on the counter.

"What's *that?*" the girl demanded suspiciously. "I never saw a bill like that one!"

"It's a hundred-dollar note. I'm sorry, I haven't anything else—say, is Mrs. Holmes here?"

"She's on duty tonight."

"Where?" Asey asked.

"Just on duty." The girl pressed her lips tightly together, and Asey had a feeling that neither a firing squad nor a drove of hungry lions could compel her to reveal Mrs. Holmes's whereabouts.

"Well, keep the bill, then," he said, "an' give me about five dollars in change—" He broke off and sighed at the look that came over her face. "No matter. Forget it. I'll reverse the charges. They know me in Abernathy, anyway."

"Say, what're you talking about? What are you trying to do?"

"I'm tryin'," Asey said, "to effect a simple rescue of some innocent citizens. What I'm goin' to do is to call the Porter Plant collect, get Colonel Leigh, our Army expert, to call camp headquarters, an' ask them to call this maneuverin' outfit an' explain to them gentle that some errors has been made."

The girl sniffed her disbelief.

"An' furthermore," Asey told her five minutes later, "I done it. Any chance of your refundin' the money I paid you for this tobacco, so's I can squeeze out a few more local calls?"

"We're always glad to refund money," the girl said, "if there's anything the *matter* with merchandise. What's *wrong* with that tin of tobacco? You haven't even opened it!"

Asey leaned over the counter and patted her lightly on the shoulder.

"Some fine day, sister, someone's going to give you a wooden nickel," he said cheerfully, "an' the snickers you'll hear in the distance will be comin' from me. So long!"

Out in the Porter, he sat back against the seat for a moment, and considered things.

Before his stock of nickels had given out, he'd managed to call Cummings's house, but the maid had no knowledge of the doctor's present whereabouts. And no one had answered the phone at his own house. That meant Cummings wasn't there, nor had the cops arrived as yet. And neither of the two friends of Jennie's whom he'd called had been in, nor would anyone in either household venture a guess as to where Jennie might be located.

Asey's fingers beat a little tattoo against the Porter's steering wheel. He would go over to East Aspinnet, he decided, and track down the members of Jennie's class in person. The hardware man, Corner, and the Hazard daughter, and Mundy's sister should all be available. And by this time the Mundy daughter ought to have reached home on Ives's bike.

In his preoccupation he forgot the forty-mile speed limit the doctor had warned him about, and so he had whizzed well past the cyclist on the East Aspinnet cut-off before he realized that it had been June Mundy.

He braked, started to turn the car, and then abruptly pulled over to the side of the road, shut off the motor, snapped off the headlights, and waited.

Perhaps young Miss Mundy, if she were thrown into a good fright, would crash through with all the information he was seeking, and more besides. A good, unexpected grilling before the girl knew what had taken place might prove to be of considerable value. She was just enough of a brat to blurt out things that an adult would hesitate to mention.

That infernal iron spider home on the buttery wall

popped back into his thoughts as he waited for her to catch up with him.

A spider seemed to fit in so well with everything. It seemed such an ideal weapon. Of course, he thought, it was always simple to visualize someone swinging a blunt instrument, and then when you swung it yourself, you found complications arising. Swinging a golf club always appeared easy to a nongolfer, but it wasn't, and it took a deceptively large amount of space, too.

"Huh! I wonder!" Asey said.

Could anyone have swung the spider in the narrow confines of the buttery without smashing a lot of preserves, or at least bringing a pan or two crashing to the floor?

"I wonder," he said again, "if I ain't been takin' too much for granted—huh, what an old fool I am! I can always find out how much room you'd be needin' for a swing!"

He had forgotten that frying pan he'd seen on the Porter's back seat, and he reached over and groped for it in the darkness.

While it seemed strange that the Hazards should be carting an iron spider around with them, they doubtless had good and sufficient reason for doing so. Probably they were lending it to someone for some outdoor cooking. Jennie's spider was always being borrowed during the summer for beach picnics. Of course it was a coincidence that he should see the Hazards' spider after being so forcibly impressed with Jennie's, as it hung there on the wall over Mundy's body. It reminded Asey of Cummings's classic murder story where, directly following the discovery of a pitchfork killing, twelve men showed up, each and every one of them carrying a pitchfork over his shoulder.

"Ouch!" After twisting his shoulder in an extended grope, Asey got out, opened the rear door, and blinked as the interior light flashed out.

The iron spider wasn't there!

Asey lifted up the crumpled lap robe, ran his hand around the car's carpeted floor, and peered into the door's side pocket.

No spider.

"Huh!" Asey said. "Now you see it, now you don't! For Pete's sakes, what goes on!"

When he knew the spider was there, its presence had seemed merely a coincidence. Now that the spider had disappeared, it began to achieve an aura of suspicion in his mind.

Who, Asey asked himself, had taken the thing? And when?

Had there been someone else creeping around the woods besides the Army? Or had some Main Street humorist swiped it while he was in the drugstore laboring with his telephone calls?

Or what?

Asey shrugged. He had certainly seen a spider there

in the back seat. That had been no optical illusion. And iron spiders didn't crawl off by themselves.

"Maybe," he said, "you better stick to tanks, Mayo! You can understand them!"

He slammed the car door, turned, and strode impatiently back up the road. It was high time for Miss Mundy to arrive on the scene.

A car coming from the direction of East Aspinnet overtook him, passed him, and then stopped with a great squealing of brakes.

Asey started to run, and then realized that it was not Cummings's coupe stopping for him. It was a larger car, and the driver got out quickly and called to someone just out of the headlights' glare.

"June!"

Something in the person's quick movements struck a responsive chord in Asey. The woman he had chased down his lane earlier in the evening moved with that same lithe quickness.

"June Mundy, what in the world are you doing with —what *is* that, a frying pan?"

CHAPTER FOUR

ASEY stopped stock still, and then cautiously moved around to the right and rear of the coupe until he reached a spot where he could hear but not be seen.

"Where," the woman from the car inquired, "did you ever get that, and what *are* you doing with it, June?"

"It's absolutely none of your business!" June retorted. "And I think you're poisonous, Kay, the way you keep hounding me and following me around!"

So, Asey thought to himself, it had been Mundy's sister, Kay, who had been sneaking around his house!

"I'm not hounding you." Kay Mundy's voice contained the same note of irritation coupled with a determination not to lose her temper that had characterized Jonah Ives's voice when the latter was talking with June. "I never followed you around, and you know it! I don't care if you see fit to bury a hundred frying pans! It does seem odd of you to choose this spot and this time, but it's your business, and I'm not interested. What I do want to know about is your father. Where is he, June?"

"I don't know. I'm not my father's keeper. And I don't care where he is! If I never see him again, that's perfectly okay with me."

"June," Kay took a step forward, "is that Jonah's bike you've got?"

"So what? I've been out with your boy friend, and he lent it to me to ride home." June lied so smoothly that if Asey hadn't known differently, he would have taken her statement as gospel truth. "And what you see in that *poi*sonous brute! How can you go for him!"

"Look, June, where is your father? Did he go to First Aid?"

"That loathsome thing! I've given it up," June announced. "I'm never going again!"

"Frankly, I'm delighted," Kay said. "I think the whole class will sigh with relief. June, was your father there?"

"Why do you care whether he was or not?"

"June, I'm in no mood for nonsense! Was your father there?"

"Why do you care?"

"Because," Kay said, "he was in such a temper when he left the house that I've worried about him ever since! I do wish you'd stop fighting with him, June!

He isn't well, he's working much harder than he should, and you ought not to provoke him so!"

"You can't say much!" June returned. "You've been fighting him yourself all week! I hate you!" she added with a sudden fierceness. "And I hate him! And I hate this godforsaken sandspit! I'm going to run away and go on the stage!"

"I almost think," Kay said, "that it would serve you right. Look, June, your father's lost practically everything he's worked for since he was a boy. Success meant a lot to him, and he's taken all this in his stride. Eventually everything will be solved, and straightened out, but in the meantime you torture him by wanting things, and teasing for things! Can't you try and help, for a change? Can't you just sit and take it, and wear the clothes you've got, and stop talking about dude ranches and dramatic schools and mink coats and diamond bracelets?"

"He's just so selfish! Mother always told me he was a selfish pig who never wanted anyone to have anything!" June said. "Or any fun! Mother always told me *she* had to squeeze every cent out of him! She always told me—"

"Sometimes," Kay interrupted, "I wish I could have met your mother! I should have enjoyed telling her a few things! Look, June, try to be decent, just for the hell of it! Phil doesn't know how things are going to work out. He simply doesn't have ready cash, and until he finds out where he stands, he can't indulge your little whims! He'd like to give you things, but he can't! It's up to you to get along and make the best of it. And particularly, you've got to stop begging for money!"

June walked slowly from the side of the road into the glare of the headlights, and stood in front of Kay with her head held high and her chin thrust out stubbornly.

"Oh, you hypocrite!" she said. "You rant at me, and toss out all these noble sentiments! I should think they'd choke in your throat!"

"June, what are you talking about?"

"What am I talking about, she asks me in a voice dripping with hurt surprise! I'm talking about *you!* Why, you've been scrounging money out of father ever since you came! I've heard you a hundred times, with my own ears! You just *or*der him to give it to you—you don't even go through the motions of *ask*ing him for it!"

"I've asked him for my own money that he's been keeping for me," Kay said. "Now, June, you've had a lovely time being dramatic. You've managed to change the subject, and you've tried to put me in a hole. But you can't sidetrack me and provoke me into losing my temper the way you do your father. The point is that you've got to snap out of this streak and stop badgering Phil!"

"All I want is the money that father's keeping for me!" June said angrily. "He's taken all my money since I came here! I haven't had my allowance from mother's bank, I haven't had a single cent of my rightful money! Nothing! He's a thief! A common thief, a—"

"Stop it, June!" Kay said sharply. "If Phil's been holding your money back, he probably has a perfectly good reason for doing so! He's your legal guardian—have you ever stopped to think how really tough he could make things for you, if you provoke him enough? It's worth your consideration. Now, tell me, was he at First Aid?"

"Where were *you?*" June retorted. "Jennie was simply frothing when you didn't show up!"

"I've been trying to find your father," Kay said. "After that hideous scene with you this afternoon, when you flounced off in a huff, I went upstairs to change my clothes. And when I came down, Phil was gone. He didn't take the car, or his bike, so I thought he'd gone on to the Inn for early dinner. But he wasn't there, and he never came near the place, and nobody'd seen him except that old Nickerson fellow, and he said Phil went storming off toward the woods when he left the house. June, I'm worried about him! Do you realize that you—"

"Have you got a cigarette?" June interrupted. "Oh. Those things. I don't want one of those. I'll get my

spare pack out of the glove compartment, unless father's swiped 'em again—"

Once in the car, she slammed the door, and before
either Asey or Kay guessed what she was up to, the
coupe was speeding up the road.

Asey bit his lip. There was probably a better word
than brat to apply to that blonde chit, but until he
could think of it, thorough-going brat summed her up
very well.

He walked over to Kay, standing forlornly by the
side of the road.

"I wouldn't cry if I was you, Miss Mundy," he said.
"Honest, I don't think she's worth one of your tears!"

Kay swung around. "Who—who are you? Where
did you come from?"

"I'm Asey Mayo. I been sort of rudely eavesdroppin'
on you here."

"*The* Asey Mayo? Jennie's cousin? Oh, I'm so
glad! And so relieved! I've seen dozens of pictures of
you, and Jennie's talked about you so often, I feel I've
known you forever. I've been wishing for hours that
you were back in town—look, Mr. Mayo, did you
overhear all our conversation?"

"Uh-huh."

"Well, that's a sample of what her father—my
brother Phil—and I have been exposed to ever since
she came. First I thought it was just adolescence and
the wrong schools, and then it seemed to me the child

couldn't be normal—but she is," Kay added. "I mean, Phil showed me her school records, and if anything, she's got a superior mind—did you say something?"

"I said," Asey observed, "there's nothin' slow about the way her mind runs! She's caught me flat-footed twice so far tonight. What *is* the matter with her, just pure cussedness?"

"Some of it is," Kay said, "but mostly I think it's the fault of her mother. Ethlyn was divorced from Phil when June was only a baby, but apparently she never stopped fussing and complaining about him till the day she died. I think that sort of warped June's point of view. She just won't *try* to like her father."

"Offhand, I'd say she didn't try very hard to like anyone," Asey said. "Or to make 'em like her, either."

"As a matter of fact, I've a sneaking suspicion she wants desperately to have people like her, and doesn't know how to go about it," Kay told him. "I'll admit she's goaded me, but it's nothing to what she's done to Phil. She's almost driven him to distraction. She's really got under his skin—Mr. Mayo, that's what's worrying me so, now. Phil left the house this afternoon after a quarrel with June, and I can't find him!"

"So?" Asey said. "Where've you hunted for him?"

"All over East Aspinnet! I was upstairs and didn't hear him leave the house, but the handyman at the Inn remembers seeing him stalking off towards the woods

—and no one's seen him since! He never came back to the Inn for his dinner, or anything!"

The girl sounded genuinely upset, but Asey found himself wondering if Jennie, for example, would break her heart with worry if he himself, or her husband Syl, walked out of the house and failed to appear for a meal. To the best of his recollection, Jennie's only complaint in such circumstances was about the food she wouldn't have bothered cooking, and Asey couldn't picture her distractedly searching short cuts.

"P'raps," he said casually, "your brother just wanted to get away from everythin' an' be by himself. If I had that blonde chit around the house for very long, I can see where I'd get to yearnin' for solitude."

"But Phil isn't the sort who wants to be alone, ever! Not if he can help it! That's why *I'm* here," Kay said. "He sacked his nurse the week after he came, and he got so lonesome, he begged me to join him. Probably it sounds silly to you that this business should upset me so, but you see—look, d'you mind my telling you all this? It's a crazy time and a crazy place to be pouring out intimate family details to an utter stranger, but I feel as if I knew you—when I stopped for June, I was on my way to your house to ask Jennie's advice. Maybe you'd rather I didn't bother you with my problems. Maybe I'd better pour it out on Jennie's shoulder."

Asey chuckled. "If you can locate Jennie's shoulder,

you'll be two jumps ahead of me. I can't find anyone who'll even take a crack at guessin' where she is."

"Isn't she home? Oh," Kay said. "Probably she went on duty after class."

"Now what would you mean, on duty?" Asey inquired. "Where would that put her?"

"Well, if she's spotting, she might be in any one of a hundred places—no, come to think of it, her turn doesn't come till next week. She might be busy with some special test or other, or she might be at the report center."

"An' where's that?"

"Oh, dear!" Kay said. "I was afraid you'd ask me that! I honestly don't know! It was changed so many times the first month, I completely lost track of it. But Phil could tell you. It's one of his pets. Truly, it's hard to say where Jennie might be, if you see what I mean!"

"I think I get the gist of it," Asey said. "Maybe Jennie's hither, an' maybe she's thither. Huh! Why are people so secretive about bein' on duty?"

Kay laughed. "I'm not being secretive. If I had the vaguest idea where Jennie was, I'd willingly tell you, even though this is a mum week—you see, one week we boast to the skies about the work we do, and the next week we decide that we've been giving too much aid and comfort to the enemy, talking so much, so we're very mum."

"I've run into considerable mum," Asey said. "Sisters, in fact. Well, I s'pose I'll locate Jennie before I leave, an' in the meantime, tell me about your brother."

"You really don't mind my unburdening myself? Because I *am* worried!"

"I'm interested in your brother," Asey said with perfect truth. "Dr. Cummings has told me about him, an' how hard he's worked organizin' an' plannin' things."

"Oh, then Phil isn't a complete stranger to you, is he? Well, Mr. Mayo, this is what bothers me. That scene between Phil and June this afternoon was really horrible. June threw things, and struck him, and then rushed out of the house screaming that she loathed us, and Phil just sat there—I'd left the room during the thick of it, because there's a limit to my endurance, and I found myself wanting to spank both of them. I came back after June went, and there was Phil, sitting there, crying. It—well, it's hard to see a grown man weep. Perhaps the doctor told you about Phil's business? Well, this afternoon June was the—the—"

"Last straw?" Asey suggested.

"Yes, only it was something sharper than a straw. Phil was really broken up. He didn't seem to notice me at all. He just kept muttering one thing, over and over. I got him a drink, and after a while he snapped out of it and seemed all right again, so I went upstairs to change my clothes. And when I came down, he'd gone!"

The girl, Asey thought privately, was still too upset over this. Her worry was out of all proportion to what had happened. At least, to what had happened as far as she knew.

"Don't you think," he asked, "that your brother probably took a walk to get the whole quarrel out of his system? Syl, Jennie's husband, chops wood after he's had a good fight. Durin' election times we have the biggest kindlin' pile in the county, out behind our barn."

"But what Phil kept muttering, when I found him crying there in front of the fire, was that he was going to kill himself!" Kay said. "Don't you see, that's what's been on my mind! He said it over and over and over."

"So?"

"You don't seem moved! But I tell you, Mr. Mayo, he meant it! He said it as if he meant it! He wasn't acting!"

"My friend Cummings will tell you," Asey said, "that people who say they're going to kill themselves very rarely do so."

"Your friend Cummings doesn't know my brother Phil!" Kay returned. "If he says something, he means it! He doesn't make idle threats! When he didn't turn up at the Inn, I began to worry—you see, he doesn't like to walk. He hates taking walks. And he hadn't touched the car, or his bike, and no one had seen him except old Nickerson, who said he was heading for the woods. All I could think of was all those ponds! I've walked around more pools, hunting him! Then when it was time for First Aid class, I walked over to your house to see if he was there. And—"

"You know," Asey interrupted casually, "you'd have saved a lot of trouble if you hadn't run away then. Why did you?"

"How do you know I ran away?" Kay demanded.

"Because," Asey said, "I chased you."

"You? *You* chased me? That was *you?*"

"Uh-huh. Why'd you dash away like that?" Asey asked. "Why didn't you just up an' say what you come for?"

"Because," Kay's voice sounded different, Asey thought, rather as if her throat hurt her, "because I'd gone up the lane next to yours, by mistake. They all look alike at night. And I had rather a disagreeable time with young Pete Melrose, whom I accidentally bumped into. I think he was drunk."

Asey nodded. Drunk or sober, the Melrose son was the sort of fellow who could be very disagreeable on a darkened lane.

"I got away from him," Kay continued, "and then when someone leapt at me in your yard, I thought that Pete had somehow managed to track me down again. So I ran. Frankly, if you had been in my place and if you had been feeling the way I felt then, I think you'd have done exactly the same thing, and run just as hard."

"I'm sure I would have," Asey agreed. "But why was you dallyin' down there by the cars? Why didn't you march straight in an' ask Jennie if your brother was there?"

"It occurred to me that if Phil wasn't in there," Kay said, "Jennie would never let me leave until the class was over. She's pretty adamant, you know. And I couldn't see any sign of Phil—Mr. Mayo, what are you doing here? How does it happen that you're here?"

"Wa-el," Asey said slowly, "my bein' here isn't anythin' you can exactly sort of sum up in a few well-chosen words, Miss Mundy. Fate decided to put me here, an' here I am."

"Something *has* happened to Phil!" Kay said. "Something *must* have happened to him, if you're busying yourself with—look, you *were* hunting June, weren't you? And she was riding Jonah's bike—tell me, Mr. Mayo, what's happened?"

"Wa-el," Asey didn't want to tell her the truth about Mundy just then if he could avoid it. "Wa-el, beginnin' back this afternoon, I got out of Jimmy's plane at the airport, after a very bumpy trip because we had to stick to the course we was ordered to take, an' found no one waitin' for me, so I hitchhiked home, an' then—"

"Oh, don't fence, Mr. Mayo! After my life with June, you've got to be pretty expert to sidetrack me!

I know something's happened to Phil! I feel it! I've felt it all afternoon! Why were you here? *Were* you hunting June? What's she been up to? She—she hasn't done anything silly and got into any trouble, has she? *Tell* me!"

"I wish," Asey said, "that you'd tell me why she should be interrin' an iron spider out here at this time of night—what in the world would she be doin' with an iron spider any time, anyway? Can you guess?"

"I can't imagine," Kay said helplessly. "And *why* should she be riding Jonah's bike?"

"Whereabouts was she buryin' the spider?" Asey poked his foot around in the soft sand shoulder of the road.

"Just beyond you, in front of that lopsided scrub pine. What an ab*surd* thing for June to do! I can't understand it. I can't understand her having Jonah's bike, either. He never lets anyone ride it. It's the pride of his life."

"June swiped it from him."

"Swiped it?" Kay repeated blankly. "June *swiped* it?"

"Uh-huh." Asey knelt down and groped around in the sand until he found the spider's handle, and then he deliberately passed over it and busily continued to grope. He was glad to find that Kay Mundy could be sidetracked a little, if you piqued her curiosity sufficiently. Perhaps, if he could manage to fumble around long enough, he might be able to extract a little more information before she found out about her brother, and before her attitude underwent the inevitable change which he knew from experience always accompanied such tidings. "June swiped the bike from him just the same way she swiped the coupe from you."

"How d'you know?"

"I was there at the time, over by Great Meadow woods."

"Great Meadow woods? June and Jonah were there?" Kay asked sharply. "Together? Why?"

Asey smiled to himself at that breathless "together." It confirmed his guess about Miss Mundy and the bearded Ives.

"From what I gathered," he said, "Mrs. Tuesome was bein' hunted."

"Oh. Oh," Kay said. "I see. That poor woman, she's been lost more times!"

"How come?"

"She learned the first code beautifully," Kay said. "Then they changed it, and she's been confused ever since. She simply can't get it straight, and she refuses to cheat and carry the list with her, the way I do. Mr. Mayo, you might as well stop playing around in the sand, and pick up that spider, and tell me what's happened."

Asey picked up the spider and got to his feet.

"Okay, Miss Mundy, okay." Asey's Cape drawl was drawlier than usual, and Cummings, or anyone who knew Asey well, would have recognized it as a danger signal. "I'd sort of hoped I could keep you talkin' about other things for just a spell longer, but I see you're too smart to be fooled. P'raps it's just as well, because time is fleetin'. It ain't good news, an' I'm sorry I have to be the one to tell you, but—"

"Please, Mr. Mayo," Kay interrupted, "do let's skip the preamble! If there's one thing I cannot bear, it's having things broken to me gently!"

"I s'pose," Asey said thoughtfully, "that nothin' can really be as bad as all the awful things you've probably been imaginin' about your brother ever since he left the house, can it? I s'pose—"

"Please get to the point!"

Asey wished he could see the girl's face better, but the dim starlight wasn't much help. She sounded worried and tense, as if knowing the fate of her brother was the only thing that mattered to her in all the world. But was that, Asey wondered, the way she really felt? She had a flexible, expressive voice, and she knew how to use it to her best advantage. She'd held her own with June very largely by a trick of inflection.

"Mr. Mayo, I don't think you're being fair to me!"

"Your brother," Asey said, "has been killed. Doc Cummings an' I found him in the buttery over at my house."

Except for the sharp intake of her breath, the girl didn't utter a sound. For a full minute she was as silent and motionless as a statue. When she finally spoke, her voice was both composed and under control, but there was something strange about it which Asey couldn't at once diagnose.

"I—I can't say anything." She made a vague, helpless little gesture. "I was prepared for almost anything but that."

"The car I'm drivin' is down the road a piece," Asey picked up Ives's bike and put the iron spider in the handlebar basket. "Come along, Miss Mundy, an' I'll drive you home. Or anywhere you'd like to go."

As he wheeled the bicycle over the hard-packed dirt road, she walked quietly beside him, her hands thrust deep into the pockets of her jacket.

She didn't speak again until they had almost reached the Porter.

"I suppose you've seen any number of people react to this—this tragic sort of thing." She paused, and Asey suddenly realized what was wrong with her voice. It was higher, almost as if she'd changed the key. "I wonder, does everyone think the same way? Are they first so stunned and horrified that they can't sort out their thoughts at all?"

"Sometimes," Asey said.

"And then, when their throat stops being dry, and they can talk, do they scream out and ask you who did

it? And then in the same breath start sort of uncon-
sciously to justify themselves to you, to prove to you
that *they* didn't do it? Because," Kay said, "that's
just what I find myself wanting to do now. *Do* you
know who shot him?"

"He wasn't shot," Asey corrected her. "He was
struck a heavy blow on the back of the head. The doc
an' I don't know with what, yet."

Kay stopped short.

"A heavy blow?" she reached out a hand and pointed
to the bicycle basket. "The spider! So that's what you
were doing when I drove up! You were watching
June dispose of that iron spider! You think—oh, no,
no! What am I saying! What an insane thing for me to
say!"

"As a matter of fact, a spider did enter our minds,"
Asey told her.

"But not June! I know the child is exasperating, but
she never in the world—" Kay left the rest of her sentence dangling in the air. "Oh, and all the things I
told you about her! What you must have been thinking of her! And of me, for telling you! Your cousin
Jennie was certainly right about you!"

"So? What'd she have to say about me, in her ma-
lignin' way?"

"She said that you had an odd knack of inveigling
people into blurting things out to you—and you do! I
never regaled anyone with my family problems be-

fore in my life—but I poured them all out to you! And to think I did it gladly!"

"I wouldn't worry about it much." Asey opened the Porter's rear door. "If you hadn't told me, I'd have found things out from somebody else. Only it would've taken longer, an' just that much more time would have been lost in gettin' to the root of things."

"But I played into your hands—is this your car, Asey? It looks like the Hazards' little gem."

Asey chuckled. "It is. But the Army ordered me to get into it an' drive away, so I did. Get in front, Miss Mundy, an' try not to think of this for a while. Owin' to the First-Aiders rompin' off on a problem, an' Jennie disappearin' into the blue, an' the cops bein' balled up with a practice blackout up-Cape, an' me gettin' tied up with the Army—huh. Maybe I'd ought to say *by* the Army. Anyway, the interests of National Defense have kind of thwarted us tonight, Miss Mundy. Kind of presented us with what you might call a delayed start. There's no proof that a spider was what someone used to kill your brother. We're not sure of that, or of anythin' else. So don't start worryin' till we find out what should be worried about. Now, I wonder!"

"What's the matter?"

"It's this bike. Wa-el, if the Hazards can carry their own iron spider on their back seat without any protectin' coverin', or any consideration for Bill Porter's super de luxe upholstery, I guess they won't mind if I stick the bike in back. I'll drape the robe over the seat an' be as careful as I can. Look out for your head."

"Did you," Kay asked as he arranged the bicycle, "say something just then about the Hazards carrying a *spider?*"

"Uh-huh. It was on the back seat here, but somehow, durin' the course of events—duck, will you?—it disappeared."

"The *Hazards* had a *spider?*"

"Just like the one June was buryin'."

"The *Hazards?* The Hazards did? They had a *spider?* I know," Kay said, "that I sound like a parrot, but I'm still not thinking any too clearly, and for the Hazards to be carrying an iron spider on their back seat is asking a lot of my mind, right now. You don't actually mean *they* had a spider!"

"What's so amazin' about it?" Asey inquired. "People fry things every day. Why should the Hazards be an exception? Why shouldn't they have an iron fryin' pan?"

Privately, he wished that Kay Mundy would present him with three good reasons why. Or even one. For his part, he hadn't been able to figure out any at all in the last twenty minutes. After all, when you came right down to it, iron frying pans and Porter town cars didn't exactly go together.

For the first time since they had met, Kay laughed aloud.

"There's no reason why the Hazards shouldn't have a spider. Or a dozen. If they felt the urge, they could buy up all the spiders in New England with ease. Only I can't think why they'd want to. Frankly, I don't think the Hazards know a spider from a skillet. They'd be charmingly grateful if you gave 'em either, but I'm sure they couldn't guess what you did with 'em."

"So? Don't they eat," Asey inquired, "or don't they cook?"

"They're cooked for."

"So 'm I," Asey returned, "but I know a spider when I see one."

Kay laughed again.

"Nobody's told you much about the Hazards, have they? I thought not. They have a chef, and a couple of squads of servants, and their idea of really roughing it is—well, driving this car in a tweed coat, say. Or going to the post office to get their mail—what did you say?"

"I said," Asey told her with a chuckle, "after tonight they're goin' to have a brand new conception of the life rough. Courtesy of the Army. So the Hazards are hothouse plants, huh?"

"I shouldn't crack at them," Kay said. "They're such dears, and so charming and kind, and they mean so well. And they've been awfully nice to me. It's just that they were brought up in such a different world from mine, and they live in such a different world from the rest of us, they sometimes leave you gasping a little. You feel as if you'd been plummeted into a tea party in a Beacon Street drawing room of fifty years ago. And they're trying *so* hard to be democratic, and do the right things, and not hurt anybody's feelings."

"Hazard," Asey said thoughtfully. "The doc said he owned a brokerage office—hey, he isn't Hazard of Markham Hazard, is he? Honest? Why, he's the head of more things than you could shake a stick at, half a dozen banks, an' Coastal Mills, an' United Tap'n Die!"

"You sound just as awed as Phil did when he found out," Kay said. "They gave up their Boston house to some serviceman's organization and moved here for the duration. I'm sure this is the first time they were ever away from Boston for more than six weeks." She giggled. "And I'm sure that to them, settling down in East Aspinnet was probably the equivalent of establishing themselves among the aborigines of darkest Africa."

"How do they get on with our natives?" Asey asked as he finally got the bicycle placed to his liking, and shut the rear door. What he really wanted to know was how the Hazards got on with her brother, but he guessed that would probably slip out.

"You'd have enjoyed seeing Mr. H's face the night Jennie told him he was the stupidest man she'd ever met—he *is* clumsy with his hands, heaven knows. And Phil said he looked punch drunk when the local men began calling him 'Sterlin'.' Then he seemed to like it. I suppose after you've been accustomed to deferential low bows from the waist, a slap on the back can be very disconcerting. Phil finally broke down and admitted he was a genius with paper work, and he's the only man I've ever seen who can run through a government bulletin and tell you what it means. But I still don't think the Hazards would know a spider if they saw one—where are you going?" she added as Asey started the car.

"I was just goin' to ask you, will you come to my house—Jennie ought to be back by now—or do you want to go to yours?"

"Yours, please," Kay said after a moment's hesitation, "if you don't mind. I don't feel like seeing June just now. And maybe Jennie'll be willing to come back and spend the night. Jennie can handle June—you know, the only other people who can quell that child completely are the Hazards. They have such lovely manners, she's frightened to death of them. Oh, what *was* that phrase Phil used to describe that pair? Something about carriages."

"Carriage trade?" Asey suggested.

"That's it. They've always been so—so awfully safe, so cushioned from everything. Truly, I can't think of two people less likely to have an iron spider about them! Of course," she added, "I suppose they *might* be considering a beach picnic."

"I thought of that," Asey said.

"Except that their preparations for outdoor living include an elaborate charcoal broiler thing that looks like an operating room on rubber tires, and they have a man wheel it to the beach if they think there's the slightest possibility of anyone wanting to munch on a sandwich. No, I must say I can't see why they'd have an iron spider!"

Certainly, Asey thought, as the car sped on towards town, certainly if it should turn out that an iron spider was what had been used to kill her brother, she had managed to make the Hazards' possession of one a fine and mystifying thing!

"Asey," Kay said tentatively, eyeing the speedometer.

"Uh-huh?"

"They're fussy about the speed limit. Look, Asey, I don't know whether I should blurt this out now, or keep quiet about it and then have you pounce on it as a suspicious fact, but I bought an iron spider today, myself."

Asey slowed down to a pace which in other days he would have looked on as a mere walk.

"So?" he said.

"I bought it as a present for Phil's birthday tomorrow. He fancied himself as a cook, and he's kept saying that if only he had the kind of pan mother used to use, he could make the kind of pancakes she used to make. Asey, you don't suppose that the pan June had could have been mine!"

That's right, Asey thought to himself. Admit to having a spider, and then bounce it off onto June!

"It don't seem likely," he said aloud. "She was empty-handed there in the woods when she swiped Ives's bike. Where was this pan of yours?"

"I've been racking my brains trying to remember where I left it when I came home this noon. Somewhere in our house," Kay said. "The hallway, or the kitchen, or the back entry. I intended to hide it, but something distracted me, and then Phil and June quarreling drove it out of my mind entirely."

"Huh!" Asey said. "You had a spider, the Hazards had one, June had one, an' we started in with one hangin' on the buttery wall. Wa-el, I know what the doc will say when I tell him. Pitchforks."

"Pitchforks?" Kay demanded.

But Asey didn't seem to hear her question, nor did he pay any attention to her finger when she pointed it accusingly at the slanting speedometer needle. And although he took the proper turns, Kay had an uncomfortable feeling that he made them from memory more than anything else.

The house was alight when he stopped the Porter by the picket fence.

"Ah!" Asey said. "That'll be Hanson an' his state cops—mind stayin' here for a few minutes, Miss Mundy? I'll send Jennie out."

He ran lightly up the walk, and Hanson opened the door just as he reached the top step.

"Hi!" Asey said. "I'm glad to see you—what's the matter?"

Hanson's face was glowering, and he ignored Asey's outstretched hand.

"That's what *I'd* like to know, what *is* the matter, anyway? All of you gone stark crazy mad down here?"

"What d'you mean?" Asey demanded.

"To think," Hanson said, "how I nearly broke my neck rushing down here—where'd Cummings find you? He *did* find you, didn't he?"

Asey shook his head. "No. Is he huntin' me?"

"*Is* he hunting you? Listen, I get to the traffic lights at the four corners," Hanson said hotly, "and there's the doc, all of a lather. Says something's happened to you. You've evaporated into a meadow. You're a tank expert, he says, so it must have something to do with spies. It's sabotage. So—"

"*What?*"

"That's what he says. Sabotage. To hear him talk, you'd think you was a government arsenal being set on fire. So he grabs Daly and Mike and rushes off to rescue you, and tells me over his shoulder to come here and break in and see this body—and to think they're howling for me over in Axton, right this very minute! Honest, Asey, what's the *matter* with Cummings? What was the big idea?"

"Come down to earth, Hanson," Asey said. "What's the matter?"

"You got the nerve to stand there and ask me what's the matter! Listen here, did you happen to *see* that body?"

"Sure I did! The doc an' I—"

"You come here!" Hanson grabbed Asey's arm, pulled him out to the kitchen, opened the cellar door, and, ignoring Asey's protests, led him forcibly down the cellar steps.

"Now!" he pointed to the floor. "You got the nerve to call that a body?"

Over in the corner lay the dummy which Asey and the doctor had seen earlier, lying on the living-room floor.

"There, there!" Asey said soothingly. "Calm down, Hanson! I'm glad you found that—Jennie must have dumped it down here, and I'll admit it's the one place I didn't bother to look. Now you come upstairs, an' I'll show you the real body. This ain't no hoax. We got one."

Hanson, not much mollified, followed him back up the stairs.

"Out here," Asey continued as he snapped on the woodshed light. "An' be careful of Jennie's incendiary department—"

"What's she got those pails of sand out *here* for? They ought to be in your attic!"

"You'll have to take that up with Jennie. Now," Asey opened the buttery door, "here you are, Hanson. Here—uh!"

The buttery floor was bare.

Mundy's body had gone.

CHAPTER FIVE

"I DON'T care if you saw it!" Hanson was still hotly striding up and down the kitchen fifteen minutes later. "I don't care who saw it, I don't care if the whole damn Supreme Court saw it! It isn't there now, is it?"

"No," Asey said gently, "it ain't. Now, s'pose instead of rampin' around, you pull yourself together an' we figger out what happened, an' start in an' do somethin' about it!"

"*I'm* pulled together," Hanson said irritably. "I know what I don't see! I know when something isn't there! What is there to figure? Look, when I came, the doors were all locked. I know. I tried 'em. I tried the windows. They were locked. The only way I could get in was to bust out a pane in your dining room, and reach in and unlock the catch. Now, no corpse ever walked out of a house and then locked up after himself all neat and careful!"

"You're not honestly tryin' to kid yourself into thinkin' there wasn't any body here, are you?" Asey inquired.

"Well," Hanson said, "well—oh, hell, if you and Cummings both think you saw a body, I suppose you must have! But where the hell is it now? What did you go off and leave it for, anyway? Haven't you two any *brains?*"

"Hanson, in your vast an' varied experience, has it been the rule for bodies to disappear from the place where you found 'em? No, it ain't! It ain't been my experience, either," Asey said. "The doc an' I figgered that if someone'd gone to all the trouble of leavin Mundy in my buttery, then that was the place where they meant to leave him, an' the place where they meant him to be found. It never for a minute entered our heads that someone'd fly in through a keyhole an' whisk him away. Now, there was a body, an' it was Philemon Mundy, an' he was lyin' on my buttery floor. There still is a body, somewheres. It's just got removed to two other places, that's all."

"Yeah. That's all. *That's* all! Just taken somewheres else! You sound," Hanson said bitterly, "as if all we had to do was to reach out a hand and pull him out of the air—Asey, don't you realize we may never find that fellow's body again? There's the whole damn bay practically outside your house, and the whole damn Atlantic Ocean only a mile away! Why, all anyone had to do was sling him into either, and that's the end of that!"

"Not unless he was an awful landlubber," Asey said. "The tide's comin' in, Hanson. Even if someone took Mundy away right after the doc an' I left, they'd have had a tide problem, an' they'd still be havin' it now."

"Well," Hanson said, "think of all the damn little ponds around! They're handy, and you can't have any tide problems with them. See here," he swung around suddenly, "who's got keys to this house?"

Asey shrugged.

"I don't know. I wondered about that when the doc an' I left. I'm sure there must be keys somewheres. I never use 'em myself, though, an' Jennie doesn't either except durin' the summer."

"You mean, you only lock your doors in summer?" Hanson demanded. "Why?"

"Jennie says you can't trust the summer folks," Asey told him. "She claims they pry. But in the winter, there's only people around that she knows, an' she says why would they come bargin' in if she wasn't here."

Hanson sniffed. "Well, she must have keys, Asey!"

"She probably does, but I don't think she's got 'em with her," Asey said. "She left the front door unlocked when she went. Now, listen. Let me catch you up with things."

Beginning with the First-Aiders and what had been going on when he arrived, Asey progressed to the

finding of Mundy's body, and then briefly summed up
what had happened to him since then.

"Things like this don't happen when you're away
from the Cape!" Hanson said plaintively. "Why don't
you just stay put there at the Porter plant, and make
tanks?"

"I been wonderin' that, myself," Asey said. "I come
home for a nice rest. Anyway, Hanson, I snapped the
front-door catch. Jennie'd left the catch up. So I doubt
if she has keys with her. I'd look around to see if there
was any here, only I don't even know where she keeps
'em. She usually has to hunt around for 'em, herself."

"First woman I ever heard of who didn't lock things
up all the time and have a pocketbook stuffed full of
keys," Hanson commented. "Say, did you tell me she
came out long after the rest of the First-Aiders left?"

"Not 'long' after." Asey recalled Cummings's
prophecy that there might be those who wouldn't
consider Jennie herself entirely free from suspicion.
"Only a few minutes. Look, Hanson, suppose we consider where that body might—"

"She know this fellow Mundy?"

"He was in her class," Asey said. "Look, why would
anybody move a body? Seems to me—"

"So Jennie knows him. Aha!" Hanson said. "Aha!"

"You sound like a dog that's just found a big juicy
bone," Asey said. "Be sensible, Hanson! I run through
this angle with the doctor. Jennie don't like Mundy.

He got her goat. Some people do—matter of fact, you never inspire her with much brotherhood of man, yourself! Jennie stayed in the house a few minutes after the others left. All right. That's true enough. But what of it?"

"Where," Hanson demanded, "is she now?"

Asey shrugged. "If she isn't here, she's just still somewheres else."

"Where?"

"If you can find out, you'll do a lot better than me," Asey said.

"The phone operator'll know," Hanson started for the hall. "She always knows where everyone is in this hamlet."

"Don't waste your time," Asey advised. "It isn't Daisy. It's a new girl, an' she won't tell anyone anythin' without they got a password or written permission from the War Department. I've had words with her, an' it's like beatin' your head against a stone wall."

"Oh, she'll tell me!" Hanson said as he marched off to the phone.

His face was redder than usual when he returned.

"Well?" Asey said.

"This war certainly does things to people!" Hanson sat down at the kitchen table. "She says even if she knew where Jennie was, she wouldn't tell me—Asey, I don't like this business of Jennie disappearing along with the body! It looks pretty funny to me!"

"You've been going to the movies too much," Asey said. "I thought as much when you started sayin' 'Aha!' like that. You know Jennie as well as I do. You know she's no killer!"

"Only last month, one of my best friends shot his wife," Hanson returned. "That taught me not to trust anybody. Oh, I wish Cummings would get back with Daly and Mike! We've got to find Jennie and locate that body—Asey, can you think why anyone should have moved it?"

"If you'd stop jumpin' to silly conclusions about Jennie, an' give me half a chance to think," Asey said, "maybe I might be able to figure things out some. That buttery seems an odd place for anyone to put a body in for temporary storage. I wonder, now. S'pose someone had some reason why they had to leave the body there for a certain length of time. S'pose they wasn't in any position to dispose of the body after they killed Mundy. Huh! I'm willin' to wager that no one guessed the doc an' I found him."

Hanson wanted to know why.

"Be sort of foolish for anyone to bother movin' it then," Asey said, "with us knowin' all about it."

"Yeah," Hanson agreed caustically. "Yeah. Knowing about it sure has done us the hell of a lot of good, hasn't it?"

"We know it was there, we know it's been moved," Asey went on thoughtfully. "I wonder, now, if we ain't maybe one up on the fellow that moved it. He don't know that we know."

"What makes you think that?" Hanson demanded.

"If he had any suspicions that we'd found out," Asey said, "I wonder if he'd have dared to come back here an' take the body away, Hanson. If he'd been peekin' in a window, say, an' seen Cummings an' me findin' Mundy, or even if he was just lurkin' around an' just guessed we'd found the body, I think he'd been inclined to beat it away from here in a hurry, an' start fixin' himself up a nice watertight alibi. Knowin' we'd found out, it don't seem to me he could afford to take the chance of gettin' into the house after we left, either. He wouldn't have been able to reckon how soon we might come bargin' back. Nope, I think no-body knows we found him. I—"

"Hey, I've got it!" Hanson interrupted excitedly. "Someone was right here in the house all the time! That's the answer!"

Asey shook his head.

"Why not?" Hanson wanted to know. "Sure that's the answer!"

"Nope, I don't think so," Asey said. "I pretty much covered the house huntin' for that dummy, like I told you."

"But you didn't hunt in the cellar!" Hanson said with triumph. "That's where he was, hiding down there! See, Asey, if someone was here all the time, then they wouldn't have needed any key to get in! After you two left, they could have taken the body and gone out, and left the latch the way it was! Yes, sir, that's the answer! Because if someone'd come in after you and the doc went, they'd have to have had a key. And from what you say, nobody knows where the key is except Jennie—say, does she know you're home?"

"She rushed off before I had a chance to speak—see here, Hanson, don't get that 'aha' look on your face again! Jennie had nothin' to do with this business!"

"If she didn't know you were home," Hanson looked at Asey and then decided it might be wiser to say it another way. "What I mean is, your house's the hell of a place for anyone to leave a corpse, and no one in his right mind would do it if he knew you was at home. But with you away, this'd be a swell place to leave a corpse, because it's about the last place anyone would think of finding one. Now, if Jennie—"

"Hanson," Asey said, "you're not just wastin' time broodin' about Jennie, you're gettin' me mad! You're also tyin' yourself up into knots when there ain't no need to."

"Don't you think someone must've been here all the time?"

"If a murderer was lurkin' in here durin' Jennie's First Aid class," Asey said, "he must have been a man of steel. Lookin' in at it was a shatterin' experience. I should think that listenin' to it would have cracked the average murderer fresh from his kill, so to speak. Even if he understood the thumpin' an' arguin' an' groanin' that went on, he'd have to of kept hoppin' around in an invisible cloak most of the time, because the First-Aiders was all over the dinin' room, an' the hall, an' the livin' room, an' upstairs, too."

"Closets," Hanson said. "That's the answer to that. The First-Aiders wouldn't have gone into closets. That's where he hid. In a closet—isn't there one off here?"

"Uh-huh, an' it's full of packin' cases named 'Bundles for Bluejackets.' The icebox is full of blue wool. Closet in my bedroom is full of soap an' Kleenex. I hate to think what's tucked away in other closets. Machine guns for MacArthur, maybe. No, Hanson, just consider. When Cummings an' I see the dummy, it was lyin' on the livin' room floor. Someone—probably Jennie herself, must have taken it downstairs. Now that cellar's so small, you couldn't miss seein' a mouse down there. There's no place for anyone to crouch or hide."

"Well," Hanson said in exasperation, "what *do* you think? You think someone blew in through a crack? Think they squeezed in under the door frame? And then picked up the body and flew up the chimney with it? I don't see how else it was managed, if the doors and windows weren't touched!"

"You could do it much easier than that," Asey said. "All the doors was hooked on the inside except the front door. I just think that someone came in that way."

"Yeah," Hanson said. "Sure. Walked right through it, I suppose. Like a ghost in the movies."

Asey grinned. "I told you, you tie things into such knots, an' make things so hard! How do *you* usually get into places when you don't have a key, an' don't feel up to bustin' in a door?"

"Skeleton key," Hanson said promptly, and then looked surprised.

"Fine!" Asey said. "If the doc was here, he'd present you with one of them little gold stars he hands out to kids who take their medicine without any squawkin'."

"Well," Hanson said defensively, "well—well, you just don't *think* of skeleton keys down here in these parts! Who'd have a skeleton key to your front door, anyway?"

Asey shrugged. "I don't even know who's got the original. But as you said, my house is a nice place to park a corpse if I'm not home. An' if you planned to park one here, I dare say you might also go so far as to include a skeleton key in your plans."

Hanson got up and started to pace around the kitchen table.

"What I want to know is, where's that body now? Where's Cummings? Asey, I bet you we never find that body!"

"I bet we do."

Hanson stopped short. "Where?"

"Some place where someone wants us to find it," Asey said.

"What do you mean, where someone *wants* us to find it? Say, do you feel all right?"

"Uh-huh."

"But why? Asey, what would be anyone's purpose in wanting that body found somewhere else? It don't make sense!"

"Wa-el," Asey said, "I been tryin' to dope it out. Far as I could see, Mundy's bein' out there in my buttery was mystifyin' enough to confuse anyone. No clews kickin' around, except for that sugar-bag hood with the neatly cut slits. You'd think it was a setup that would suit a murderer fine. But apparently it didn't."

"But, Asey," Hanson's voice was plaintive and his forehead was wrinkled, "what would anybody *gain* by putting the body somewhere else and letting us find it there? It'd only mean murder, just like it did here. What would the murderer *gain?*"

"That's what I been askin' myself, an' the answer," Asey said, "is that he don't gain. He ain't either better or worse off than when he started. But—an' I think this is the real reason—someone else loses. See? Mundy's body in my buttery is confusin', but it don't incriminate anybody. Mundy's body somewhere else might turn out to be very incriminatin' indeed. Maybe his—"

"Maybe his what?" Hanson demanded as Asey paused.

"I was thinkin'. Huh, why in time didn't I consider that angle before! Huh!"

It had just occurred to him that Mundy's body found in a different place might create still another situation. It might just possibly turn up in some spot and under such conditions as to make the man's death look like suicide. Suppose, for example, that Mundy's body were found at the foot of a flight of steps!

"Oh, stop thinking, it's no use! *I* know where the body's gone!" Hanson said unhappily. "Those damn ponds! I can see myself out there tomorrow, grappling—what're you shaking your head for? What've you got against the ponds?"

"It takes a lot of doin' to dispose of anyone in a pond," Asey said. "You got to take the body there— an' that's bad. People will spot your car, or remember hearin' it, or else some young couple's parked off the road at the water's edge, or someone remembers you sneakin' around collectin' weighty objects. Nope, Hanson, I think I'm on the right track. Mundy here is a murder, yes. But you can't involve me. You can't involve Jennie—might as well try to involve the Statue of Liberty as her, an' you know it. Other places, though, they sort of open up vistas—wa-el, we'll see what turns up."

"Talk about tying yourself up in knots!" Hanson

said. "I sure think you're going a long way, to think someone would move a body to make someone else a suspect!"

"It's all guessin'," Asey said, "but it kind of rings a bell within me, as you might say. I wish Syl was home. He's a dabster at findin' things, an' I bet he could find Mundy for us. Remember his favorite lines, about the man that found the lost horse when everybody else give up? 'I thought, if I was a hoss, where I'd go, an' I went there, an' he was!' Syl would march out an' find—"

"Hey, listen!" Hanson interrupted. "Someone's knocking—hear 'em? It's about time Cummings got back!"

He rushed out of the kitchen before Asey could stop him.

Of course it wasn't Cummings, Asey thought as he slowly followed along the hall to the front door. It would be Kay Mundy, tired of waiting out in the Porter, and he wished she could have sat there quietly a few minutes longer until he could have planned with Hanson some phony scene where Hanson would start roaring questions at her in his best menacing manner. It was just possible that a good bullying might achieve more results with her than a sane, polite quizzing, and Asey wanted very much to know how Miss Mundy had occupied herself from the time he chased her down the lane until she appeared on the East Aspinnet short cut. She was a self-possessed young woman, and he had no reason to believe she had lied to him, but he had a hunch that she was going to hold a lot of things back, now that she knew about her brother.

"*Who* do you want? *Who?* Asey?" Hanson was saying to Kay, in the doorway. "How do you know he's home? What? What's that? Hey, Asey! She says you brought her here! You never told me you brought anyone with you!"

"You never give me a chance," Asey said. "Sorry to keep you waitin', Miss Mundy. Come in. This's Lieutenant Hanson, an'—"

"You bring *him*, too?" Hanson pointed beyond Kay to her companion on the doorstep, a sandy-haired fellow with glasses whom Asey recognized as the First-Aider he'd mentally named Blue Serge.

"No, I didn't bring him, but I'm glad to see him," Asey said. "Come in, Mr.—Corner, ain't it? He was at Jennie's class, Hanson, an' he may be able to tell us where—"

"Hey!" Hanson yelled suddenly. "Hey, Asey, look! Look what he's got in his hand!"

He pointed dramatically to the huge steel ring filled with keys which Corner carried.

"Yes," Corner said, "that's why I—"

"Keys!" Hanson's voice rose and drowned out Corner's attempted explanation. "See, Asey, keys! Skeleton keys! Say, mister, what're you doing with all those keys?"

"Dr. Cummings asked me to bring—"

"You seen Cummings? Where is he?" Hanson demanded.

"Over by Hell Hollow with two of your troopers. He asked me to—"

"What the hell is he doing *there?*" Hanson wanted to know.

"Well, he said he was hunting for Asey Mayo," Corner said, "and he wanted me—"

"How long ago did you see him?"

"Oh, ten or fifteen minutes ago. I bumped into him, and—"

"What you got those keys for?" Hanson prodded Corner with a belligerent forefinger. "Come on, now, what you been doing with those keys? What you got 'em for?"

"I'm trying," Corner said mildly, "to tell you. I met Cummings at the Hollow, and—"

"What were *you* doing at that godforsaken spot?" Hanson interrupted suspiciously.

"Hunting Mrs. Tuesome. And—"

"*Who?*"

"Mrs. Tuesome," Corner said patiently. "Mildred Tuesome. She—"

"Never heard of her." Hanson's tone insinuated that

Corner had obviously made Mrs. Tuesome up on the spur of the moment. "What were you hunting her there for?"

"She was lost."

Corner's simple statement really set Hanson going. Loudly and with feeling, he called on his Maker to witness the fact that he, Hanson, did his best, and was in there fighting all the time. But enough, Hanson felt, was enough.

"First Asey's lost! Then a body's lost. Then," he ignored Kay Mundy's startled question, "then Jennie, she's lost! Now someone else's lost! Why, I ask you? Why?" he glared at Corner. "Why was this Mrs. Dewsome lost, for God's sakes?"

"Tuesome, not Dewsome," Asey said, "an' calm down. I know she's lost, an' I don't honestly think it matters two figs."

"If you knew someone *else* was lost," Hanson said angrily, "why didn't you tell me so?"

"Look," Asey said, "I told you Jennie's class went rushin' off to a problem, didn't I? Well, Mrs. Tuesome was one of the class, an' she got lost, an' the rest of the gang seems to have gone off scoutin' for her. See? Now, for the love of Pete, Hanson, if you got to have details, let Corner tell 'em without your jumpin' down his throat so!"

"If anyone's lost," Hanson said, "I certainly think I

ought to know about it! It's my business. Now, what happened?"

"First," Kay said, "could you tell me if anything has happened to my bro—"

"Young woman," Hanson stuck his thumbs in his Sam Browne belt and glared at her, "if there's one thing I don't like and won't stand for, it's an interruption when I'm trying to get to the root of someone's story. Go on, Corner, what happened?"

"Well," Corner said, "Jennie gave us a problem, as Mr. Mayo told you, and we all showed up at the proper spot over by Silver Springs, except Mrs. Tuesome. But we've hunted her so often since she transferred to the class that Jennie's got it down to a system. We split up, and everybody takes an area, and tonight, Jennie told me to go to Hell Hollow. And eventually I met Dr. Cummings, and he said he was hunting for Asey Mayo. Said he'd lost him near Great Meadow, but he thought that maybe Asey might have cut across to the Hollow. I told him I doubted it, because I'd scoured the place and hadn't seen a soul, and then he asked if I happened to have my keys with me, and—"

"You *usually* have keys with you?" Hanson broke in.

"Quite often, yes. You see, I keep the hardware store over in East Aspinnet, and my predecessor made a habit of cherishing every stray, spare, duplicate, or

skeleton key that ever crossed his path. So anyone from
Weesit to Skaket who gets locked out of anything
comes to me, just as they always came to him, and I
rustle out the keys and get busy. I'd unlocked an old
trunk for Mrs. Cummings this morning, and the keys
were still in my truck, so I told the doctor I had 'em,
and he asked me to come here. Said something about a
front door being locked, and no one having a key. And
he asked me to tell you, Lieutenant Hanson, that he
hadn't found Asey. And as I was leaving, he yelled
out and suggested that I might make myself useful to
you. So I came, with the keys, hoping I could be of
some service—and hoping that what he told me about
Phil Mundy couldn't be true. But Kay's just assured
me it is—and I can't understand it! How does it happen that Phil was here? Why—"

"Before you ask them any questions, Bob," Kay
said, "won't someone tell me what's gone wrong? Lieutenant Hanson said something about a body being lost.
Asey, did he—does he mean Phil?"

"I'm sorry to say that he does," Asey told her. "For
reasons best known to himself, someone's seen fit to
move him from the buttery. Now, I'll go fetch the doc,
Hanson, an' tell him what's gone on, but first I wish
Mr. Corner'd set us straight on a few things. Did
Mundy—"

"Asey, I'm sorry to interrupt," Kay's voice was
tense, "and I know that the Lieutenant doesn't like it,

but Phil was my brother, and I really feel I have the right to know. Where is the body now? What did they do with it?"

"We don't know," Hanson said, "but Asey thinks he can find out. He's got a theory about a horse that got lost—"

His sentence stopped abruptly with the descent of Asey's foot on his instep.

"D'you mean he's not in this house, that he's been taken away?" Kay demanded. "Where d'you think he is? How can you find out by a horse? Aren't you going to *do* something about it?"

She was beginning to sound slightly hysterical, and Asey decided to nip her outburst in the bud.

"We'll do somethin'," he said crisply, "as soon as we get the chance, an' you're not goin' to help us by askin' a lot of things we can't give you the answer to. We're as anxious as you are to find your brother. Will you bear that in mind, an' try not to hinder us? Now, Mr. Corner, was Mundy at Jennie's class tonight? Did he come, did he leave early, or what?"

"He never came at all!" Kay answered before Corner had a chance to speak. "Not at all! I told you I didn't see him—"

"Miss Mundy," Asey said, "d'you mind goin' out to the car an' waitin' there for me?"

"But—oh, very well!" Biting her lip, Kay left the hallway, slamming the front door behind her.

"Aren't you rather harsh?" Corner asked Asey. "I mean, she's all broken up about this. When she hailed me just now, when I drove up, I noticed that she was pretty upset."

"Uh-huh, an' she might as well cry it out of her system," Asey said. "It may sound heartless to order her out, but there's somethin' astringent about a good cry. Now, what about Mundy, didn't he show up at all?"

Corner shook his head.

"That's why I couldn't understand it at all when Kay told me you'd found him here. When the class began, Jennie asked June where Phil and Kay were, and June said that they were coming, as far as she knew. So Jennie started class without waiting for them. Later, she phoned their house, but no one answered, and we all just assumed up to the class's end that Phil and Kay would be turning up."

"Say!" Hanson said, "did she start out with Mundy, I wonder?"

"No," Asey said, "Mundy went stalkin' off early this afternoon, after a tiff with his daughter. Kay told me about it. Corner, would you know where in time my cousin Jennie is?"

"I was just going to ask you about her, myself," Corner said. "I thought she'd surely be back home by now—do you suppose Mrs. Tuesome's still lost, and Jennie's still hunting for her?"

"Just where did Jennie aim to hunt, herself?"

"She didn't say. She sent the Hazards to Great Meadow, and June and Jonah to Silver Marsh—what did you say?"

"I said, they strayed," Asey told him. "Go on."

"Tiny went to Harding's Swamp—her car's so high, it can clear the tidewater. And I was ordered to go to Hell Hollow and to stay there till Mrs. T. was found. You see," Corner said with a grin, "last time I skipped home. I was tired. And—well, your cousin Jennie is a very firm woman. I didn't dare skip tonight."

"How do you folks know when Mrs. Tuesome's been brought to light?" Asey inquired.

"It's very ingenious," Corner said. "Whoever finds her phones Jennie's friend Sadie Hurd, on Pine Hill, and Sadie snaps on the light in her cupola. You can see it easily from any of the problem spots—but I was so excited when Cummings told me about Phil, I never thought to look when I left. But I'm sure it hadn't been on previously."

"If this woman keeps getting lost, why do you people waste time finding her?" Hanson asked. "If she gets to the wrong spot, she ought to know it when nobody else comes, oughtn't she? Then she could just go on to the next place. Why waste time on her? Why not let her find you?"

"We tried that. Just once. It was pouring cats and dogs," Corner said reminiscently, "and Mrs. T. sprained her ankle, and was found next morning by a milkman.

She nearly got pneumonia. You see, she can't tell compass points. We've done our best to explain about the Big Dipper, and moss on trees. Mr. Hazard even bought her a compass. But she's helpless. She just wanders off. Jennie says she's got to learn, and that we can't let any harm come to her while she does. Secretly, I think Jennie thinks these excursions are good for us. Hardening."

Asey chuckled. "For my part, I'd either excuse her from the problem department, or else tie bells on her. So you can't guess where Jennie is—oop!" The horrid thought crossed his mind that maybe Jennie and not Mrs. Tuesome, as he'd imagined, might have been a victim of the Army along with the Hazards. "Well, I guess she'll turn up. Corner, would you know who got to class first?"

"I think," Corner said slowly, "that either Tiny Hazard or Mrs. Tuesome went in first—but Mr. and Mrs. Hazard actually arrived first, if that's what you mean. They were waiting here when I came. They're always early."

"You say the Hazards was waitin' here? Where? Waitin' for what?" Asey asked.

"Waiting on your doorstep to go in. Jennie wasn't home, and they didn't think they ought to go in, even though they'd tried the knob and knew the door was unlocked." Corner smiled. "The Hazards are like that."

"Jennie wasn't here? Where does that woman spend

her time these days?" Asey demanded. "Ain't she ever home any more?"

"This is one of her Red Cross afternoons," Corner told him. "I know, because they were sending off a packing case, and I was called on to provide nails. In fact, I took pity on the girls and nailed the case up for 'em. Anyway, when I came here, the Hazards were on the doorstep, and I gathered they'd been there for some time. They looked frozen. They were delighted with my dummy, and we were exchanging pleasantries about it when Jennie came."

"*Your* dummy?" Hanson said. "Is that thing yours?"

Corner nodded. "It was left at my store by mistake this afternoon, and I thought that until the salesman who left it came back and retrieved it, it would be wonderful to practice First Aid on. You see," he added wryly, "I've been being class victim, and after you've been a victim, you get ideas like that. So I came a little early to show it to Jennie and see what she thought."

"You don't think the Hazards had gone inside at all?" Asey asked.

"I'm sure they hadn't. They wouldn't have looked that cold. I—"

He broke off as Asey swung around suddenly and opened the front door.

"Thought I heard the doc's car," he explained. "Uh-huh, you can always count on him hittin' the far pickets when he turns around."

Half way up the walk, Cummings stopped, stared at Asey, and then started to splutter.

"I am speechless!" he said. "Absolutely speechless! Why in the name of all that's holy didn't you let me know you were all right, Asey Mayo? What happened to you? Why d'you let me waste the best years of my life roaming through one damn swamp after another searching for you? Who d'you think I am, that fellow in the song who hunts Chloe? I've never been so speechless with rage at anyone in my life! Hello, Corner. Hello, Hanson, you called the ambulance yet? What d'you think of things?" The doctor set his black bag down on the hall floor and wriggled out of his overcoat. "What's your opinion of that bash? You called Reinhold? I'll want him. Well, speak up, Hanson, speak up, man, say something! What've you got done? What d'you think of him?"

"If I had him," Hanson said bitterly, "I might be able to think."

"If you had him? Had who? Reinhold? Good God, Hanson, don't you dare express yourself on the topic of a simple bash without Reinhold's advice? Asey, I'm so sore with you, I don't care a whoop what you think, but have you got any fresh ideas?"

"Can't say as I have, doc," Asey told him. "You come out an' take a look, an' you'll see what the problem is. Oh, Corner," he added as the doctor picked up his bag and marched out to the buttery, "do any of your keys fit this front door, do you think?"

"Probably, if you bought the lock here on the Cape." Corner walked over to the door and squinted at the lock. "Oh, yes. Yes, you did. That's one of our locks. At least, it's one of the kinds that we carry in stock. Yes, I'm sure I've got two or three keys that would open your door—look, would this have anything to do with—with this frightful business of Phil Mundy?"

"That's what I'm wonderin' about," Asey said. "Did you tell me your keys was on your truck all day?"

"Well, since I took them from the store to open Mrs. Cummings's trunk this forenoon, yes. But I greatly doubt if anyone could have taken 'em—that's what you're driving at, isn't it?" Corner asked. "I keep the ring hidden under the seat, out of sight. I have to. Everyone plays with 'em, otherwise. But even if anyone knew that the ring was on the truck and not in the store, it wouldn't do 'em much good to steal it, because it takes a little knowing to get the right type key without trying the whole lot. No, I'm positive that no one could have taken these keys of mine, or used 'em."

"I see. Catch Hanson up on Jennie's class, an' who was there, an' all, will you?" Asey said, and walked out to the buttery.

Cummings was staring at the empty floor with bulging eyes.

"I'm damned!" he said. "Asey, I'm speechless, by

George, I really am! Smacks of the supernatural, doesn't it? What happened, d'you suppose? And, by the way, what happened to you back there at Great Meadow?"

Asey told him, in full.

"Wow! I can just see the letter Hazard'll write to the Boston 'Herald'!" Cummings said. "With a carbon to the 'Herald-Tribune.' I can hear Grace Hazard dating things by this, in the future. 'Remember the first year of the war, Sterling dear, when we were taken by the Army?' Oh, that's terrific!"

"Didn't you see any trace of 'em, or of Mrs. Tuesome?" Asey asked. "Seems to me the Army ought to have found 'em an' let 'em loose by now."

"Probably the Army was awed to the point of convoying them home," Cummings said. "They're really awfully full of good will to the citizenry—the outfit that camped in our orchard last week presented us with a pound of sugar as a parting gift. Asey, where's this body been taken? To the ponds, d'you think?"

"That's Hanson's feelin', but I got a kind of different notion." Asey explained it, and when he finished, Cummings nodded slowly.

"Seems reasonable to me. Hm. In a sense, we've got the jump on someone, haven't we? That is, we would have if we knew where the body was. No clews around, eh?"

"None I can spot with the naked eye," Asey said.

"Yup, this was such a neat job here, I can't see any other reason for anyone botherin' to move him."

"What're we going to do about it?" Cummings inquired.

"Wa-el, if you moved Mundy away from an already good place, the assumption is you took him to a better place, an' sort of sat back an' looked forward to havin' him officially found there. I s'pose, in due time, someone'll find him."

"But, Asey, we can't just loll idly by and wait for him to turn up like—like a lost package or something!" Cummings protested. "We've got to find the man!"

"Uh-huh. Only if we go around screamin' to high heaven that we know there was a body here, an' it's been moved," Asey returned, "if we let everyone know we know, then it's just possible that the body might land at the nearest pond with a sudden splash. Tide's goin' out now, too. Huh. We know. Kay Mundy knows, Corner knows—did you tell anyone else besides Corner about this, doc?"

"I see your point," Cummings said. "If the murderer finds out we know, the possibilities are boundless—yes, Asey, I'm afraid I did tell people."

"Many?"

"My wife, when I talked with her over the phone —and that's as good as telling the town. And people I saw at the four corners while I was waiting for Hanson. I'm not much of a one to keep my big mouth shut anyway," Cummings said ruefully, "and there didn't seem to be any need for reticence or discretion. Too bad. It's probably a well-established news item, by now. Well," he brightened as he pointed to the buttery wall, "the spider's still there! That's something."

"So are the others." Asey told him about the spider that had disappeared from the Hazards' car seat, the one June had been burying, and the one Kay Mundy had bought.

"Pitchforks!" Cummings said delightedly. "Remember that pitchfork murder?"

"Uh-huh, an' I knew you would. Well," Asey started back to the kitchen, "I'd better take Kay Mundy home—did I tell you she's the one I chased? Said she'd worried about her brother's leavin' the house in a temper, an' she was tryin' to track him down—doc, I'm a dope! Shoes!"

"What shoes?"

"Mundy's brown sneakers was spandy new, an' if he went stompin' off to the woods like Kay said he did, they'd have been wet an' muddy. Huh! I think I'll look into that. An' I ought to check up an' see if the Army's let them others go. An' golly, what wouldn't I give to locate Jennie! Not that I think any of this business happened while she was home—"

"Why not? What do you mean?" Cummings interrupted.

"Wa-el, far's I can see, doc, the house was empty all

afternoon. Corner said Jennie was at Red Cross. Guess she must have grabbed a sandwich in town before comin' home."

"And what," Cummings said, "does *that* have to do with the issue?"

"Why," Asey said as they entered the front hall, "she hadn't time to get anythin' here before startin' her class, an' when you an' I first went into the kitchen earlier, it didn't look a bit cluttery or messed up. In short, Jennie wasn't home all afternoon, an' she didn't have any call to go out to the buttery for food after she came home. But Jennie can tell us more about Mundy an'—what you handin' out money for?"

"For you to give Kay. It's the half dollars she lost out of her pocket."

"Oh, so you got that." Asey put the coins into the pocket of his canvas coat. "I noticed it was gone from the floor—Hanson, I'm goin' to drive Kay Mundy home. I won't be long."

"That's just dandy," Hanson said. "And while you joy-ride, you expect me to stay here and twiddle my thumbs, and wait for someone to bring that body back, maybe?"

"You can't tell, they might," Cummings said cheerfully. "We can always whistle and see what happens. After all, I lost Asey on Great Meadow, but he came back."

Asey noticed a look of reproach cross Corner's face,

as if he disapproved of the doctor's levity. But before he could say anything, Hanson had turned on the doctor.

"Say, where are Daly and Mike? You leave them wandering around swamps?"

"I sent 'em to the lab. for some things," Cummings said. "Even without a body, there's still a bit of work I can do. Hurry back, Asey."

"Er—if you don't want my keys, or anything else from me," Corner said, "can I go along?"

"Of course," Asey said. "You'll be home, won't you, in case I think of anythin' I want to ask you? You're practically the only class member except Kay that's available, an' I don't think she's goin' to co-operate with me very amiably for a while yet. Doc, you an' Hanson try again to locate Jennie, will you? Comin', Corner?"

The two walked down the oystershell lane to where the cars were parked by the picket fence, and Asey opened the Porter's front door.

"If—what's the matter?" Asey swung around quickly as he heard Corner's agonized groan.

"My front tire! Oh, my God, both of 'em! I've been expecting something like this, but for both of 'em to pop at once!"

"Too bad," Asey said sympathetically. "Got spares? I'll help you change 'em."

"Spares!" Corner said. "They *are* the spares! I've

got nothing to replace these with till I finish dicker-
ing with a fellow in Pochet who smashed his truck
up last week, but salvaged the tires. Oh, if only—well,
I suppose it can't be helped!"

"I'll run you home," Asey said. "Get in."

It was a silent trip to East Aspinnet. Corner was visibly annoyed about his tires, Kay was visibly annoyed
with Asey, and Asey was too busy with his own
thoughts to be visibly moved by either of them.

As the Porter sped onto East Aspinnet's Main Street,
Corner spoke suddenly.

"Mrs. Tuesome! That was her buggy in front of the
Clarks'—did you see it?"

Asey stopped the Porter and backed up.

"Huh!" He leaned out and peeked into the empty
buggy. "S'pose she's visiting?"

"Probably. They're great friends of hers. I wonder
if—"

"Say," Asey got out of the car and peered curiously
in at the buggy's seat, "what's this thing here that looks
like a pig?"

"It is a pig," Corner said as he joined him. "A china
pig, covered with pink clover blossoms, and beware
of it! There's a slit in the back for contributions, and
you'll—here she comes. I thought I saw her at the side
door."

Mrs. Tuesome fluttered down the path toward them.

"Sterling? Grace? Oh, it isn't the Hazards! Oh, Bob!

Oh, dear, you all got lost again tonight, didn't you? I was—why, I declare, it's Asey Mayo! I met you years ago, but I'd know you anywhere, you haven't changed a bit! Not a day older, not a day!"

"Where've you been?" Corner asked as she paused for breath.

"I waited for simply ages at—er—simply ages, and then I just simply gave up and came home, and by the merest chance I met Sally Clark, and she needed a fourth—"

"Mildred," Corner said, "I think you're a fraud! You never even went to that problem!"

"Glass houses, Bob, glass houses!" Mrs. Tuesome shook her finger at him coyly. "You ran out the last time! And anyway, I'm putting my winnings right in Henry. A dollar and sixty cents!"

"Henry?" Asey said.

"He's head of the treasury!" Mrs. Tuesome told him with a tinkling laugh. "Oh, Asey Mayo, you've never met Henry, have you? Well, you shall!" She lifted the china pig off the seat and all but waved it under Asey's nose. "This is Henry, and he's going to buy us a mobile canteen—bring your wallet right out, Asey Mayo, because Henry always has to have a contribution when he's first introduced!"

The sudden recollection that his smallest bill was the hundred-dollar note he'd tried to change in the drugstore stopped Asey's hand en route to his pocket.

"I'm afraid," he said, "that the pleasure of Henry's acquaintance'll have to be postponed till I get some money."

But Mrs. Tuesome didn't seem to hear him.

"When Henry meets Asey Mayo," she crooned, "Henry's little sides will just *burst!* Men who make tanks *al*ways have *so* much money!"

"I'm sorry," Asey said, "but my wallet's at home."

"Oh, we don't believe it!" Mrs. Tuesome said. "Do we, Henry? Think of the famous Asey Mayo, driving up in his great big Porter, saying he hasn't any money! Why, Henry says your pockets are simply *lined* with bills!"

Asey was on the verge of telling her, a little desperately, that his pocket lining consisted of two half dollars that weren't his, when Corner came to his rescue.

"I'll contribute for him, Mildred. Here, hold Henry out. To Henry from Asey Mayo, to Henry from me."

"Why, Bob, you sweet thing!" Mrs. Tuesome exclaimed as the coins clinked somewhere inside the pig. "Isn't Bob the sweet thing, Henry? We always knew he was a dear boy—"

"Look, have you seen Jennie?" Bob said uncomfortably as he edged away from her.

"Oh, is *she* lost tonight? I'd be glad to help you hunt her!"

"No, thanks." Asey backed away to the Porter, and Bob followed.

"I'd be glad to," Mrs. Tuesome said eagerly. "It's only fair for *me* to hunt *her* for a change!"

"Thanks," Asey said. "Good night. Whew!" he added as he slid the car forward. "She's persistent!"

"I remember thinking she was mad when she first hauled out Henry," Corner said, "but now I'm not so sure that Henry isn't going to buy a canteen one day."

Asey chuckled. "I'm bettin' he buys a fleet of 'em —where can I drop you?"

"Why—er—the crossroads ahead will do," Corner said. "I live at Anderson's."

Asey left him, said good night, and sped on toward the beach. It occurred to him that he had been rather abrupt with Corner, but he wanted to have a talk with Kay before he returned home.

She didn't speak until they reached the fork of the beach road.

"First left, first right."

Asey drew up in front of a large new Cape Cod house.

"Thank you." Kay jumped out and shut the door.

"Wait a sec, please." Asey followed her to the front door. "I've been wondering about that iron spider you told me you bought. Think you could find it for me?"

"If you'll come in, I'll hunt it up."

She ushered him into a living room, and as she

snapped on two table lamps, Asey had a chance to see her features clearly for the first time since he'd met her. Her hair was dark-brown, her eyes were blue, and her cheeks were as red as the flannel shirt under her heavy tweed jacket. They grew a shade redder as she became aware of his scrutiny.

"I'll get the spider," she said, and departed.

Two minutes later, Asey heard her scream.

As he jumped toward the door, Kay rushed into the room, clutched at his arm, and clung to it.

"It's Phil! He—he's *here!*"

CHAPTER SIX

"HERE? In this house? Where?"

Asey disengaged himself from her grasp, repeated his question several times, and then finally gave her a little shake.

"Where? Miss Mundy, pull yourself together— that's better! Now, show me where he is!"

Kay, her face like chalk, led him across a hall, through a kitchen, and out to a cluttered, room-sized ell, at the far corner of which was an open cellar stairway, protected by banisters on the side nearest to them.

"I snapped on the light," Kay said in a dead voice, "and went over to the corner to see if I'd left the spider on that table by the wall, and I just happened to look down—this light puts on the cellar stair light. And there was his body at the foot of those stairs!"

Asey walked across to the banisters and stared down.

"Huh! So—"

He glanced at Kay, who stood clutching the door-jamb, and let the rest of his thoughts remain unspoken. What must have happened wouldn't sound pretty, but obviously someone must have carried Mundy's body half way down the stairs, and then let it drop. No one could have so posed a body, he thought, as to make it look so much like a genuine fall.

"They wanted it to look like an accident, didn't they?" Kay demanded tremulously. "And look—my bike!"

She pointed to the blue and white bicycle half propped against the banisters.

"*My* bike!" she said again. "That's mine!"

"Uh-huh."

"You don't understand, Asey! I moved it out of the way—but it was flat on the floor, with the stand and the rear wheel lying right across the top step! Don't you see? Don't you understand? Someone wanted to make this look as if I'd left my bike there on purpose, to trip him! They wanted it to look as if this were my fault! As if I—but—"

"But what?" Asey said as she paused.

"I just thought—won't there be fingerprints of who-ever brought my bike in and left it there? Won't there be fingerprints around, anyway? At your house, too? Can't you tell everything by fingerprints, Asey?"

"I wish," Asey said sincerely, "that it was as easy

as all that. But fingerprints've been subjected to enough
publicity so's the other fellow usually thinks of 'em
too. An' beforehand. From the looks of them handlebars, I got a good suspicion that someone's wiped 'em
off careful. Honest, I'd be sort of surprised if Hanson's
men found any prints on that bike except for yours."

With a quick motion, he stepped past the bicycle
and went down the stairs.

The sugar-bag hood had been removed from Mundy's head—another potential clew gone, Asey thought.
Otherwise—

"For Pete's sakes!" he said aloud, and his voice
echoed his amazement. "For Pete's sakes!"

Mundy's feet were no longer encased in brown
sneakers, but hip-length rubber boots whose tops had
been folded down.

"What's the matter? What's wrong?" Kay asked as
she joined him at the foot of the steps.

Asey pointed to the boots. "Are those your brother's
own rubber boots?"

Kay looked at him strangely. "Why, yes, I suppose
so. They look like his."

"Huh! Does your brother own a pair of low-cut
brown sneakers?"

"Asey, how *can* you stand here and look at him
and talk about boots and shoes!" She bit her lip. "Boots,
shoes—what do they matter?"

"I told you once," Asey said quietly, "that I was

just as anxious about all this as you are. But in the work I been doin' lately, time is what they call of the essence. Time's of the essence right now, too. I only got a day an' a half of my vacation left, an' I want to make the most of it. When I first seen your brother in my buttery, he was wearin' low brown sneakers, spandy brand new ones. Now, he's got on these rubber boots!"

"What! Oh, you must have been mistaken!"

Asey shook his head. "I'm sure of them sneakers. I noticed 'em particularly."

"But I don't think Phil owned any sneakers," Kay said. "I've never seen him wear any, brown or any other color. Usually he wears high leather boots that lace, and then strap just below the knee— I don't know the proper name for them," she added. "Hunting boots, maybe, or outdoors boots. Anyway, he has three pairs, and when one pair gets the least bit wet, he puts on another. He's always worrying about wet feet, and catching cold from them, and the kitchen stove always has at least two pairs of his boots thrust underneath, drying out. When all three pairs are wet, he wears these rubber things. Around the house, he wears moccasins. I'm almost sure he hasn't any sneakers. Of course, he could have bought some this afternoon, I suppose."

Asey refrained from making the obvious rejoinder, that even if Mundy had bought new sneakers, he could hardly have changed from them back to his rubber boots, under the circumstances.

"How did all this *happen?*" Kay wanted to know. "How did he get here? Who brought him? What's the reason for this shoe changing? Why would anyone have changed his *shoes?* It's—well, there's something awfully grisly about that part!"

"Wa-el," Asey said, "the shoe problem is somethin' I ain't even attemptin' to grasp at the moment, but the rest seems sort of clear. After the doc an' I left my house, someone must have come in by our front door, usin' either a skeleton key, or some key that happened to fit the lock. An'—"

"What d'you mean, some key that happened to fit the lock?" Kay interrupted. "I didn't know that keys ever fitted any other locks than the one they were intended for. They never have, in my experience."

"Corner said it was a local bought lock, so that part ain't too hard to understand," Asey said.

"I still don't."

"The lock on my front door was bought either from Snow's, which is now Corner's store, or some other hardware store in the vicinity," Asey said. "You might buy one, notice mine was like yours, an' get a skeleton key on the pretext that you was locked out, an' have the skeleton copied. Or you might buy one—this is likeliest—an' find your key fitted my door anyway. I remember one spring when all the rustproof, waterproof locks the fellows bought for their moorin's turned out to be twins. An' for years, my cousin Syl's key to his fish house was the one the savin's bank yelled for when they misplaced theirs."

"Never!"

"Uh-huh. It opened their rear door padlock. Anyway, the fellow come into my house an' went out to the buttery, an' there was the body just as he'd left it. Just by luck, Cummings put that bag on. Huh!"

"Bag?" Kay asked. "What bag?"

"A sugar bag, like a hood. It was over his head, but it's missin', now. So—"

"Look, Asey, I don't understand *any* of this! First you say he wore sneakers, but now he has on these boots! Then he had on a hood, but now he doesn't! What's it all add up to?"

"So this fellow," Asey seemed to be talking to himself, and Kay wondered if he had heard her question, "he hadn't any way of knowin' that the doc an' I had been there. Nothin' looked disturbed. Then—let's see. Then I think he unhooked our woodshed door, lifted the body out, hooked the door, an' walked back through the house an' out the front door. Yup, that'd be the sensible way."

"*Why?*" Kay almost shouted the word out, and Asey turned around and looked at her.

"Why? Because then if he was seen, he wouldn't be seen with the body. Then, after lookin' around an' assurin' himself that the coast was all clear, he walked around, picked up the body, put it into a car, an' brought it here. Probably he reconnoitered around to make sure the house was empty, an' then—your house wasn't locked up, was it? I thought not," he said as Kay shook her head, "because you walked right in just now. Anyway, he—uh—landed your brother down here, an' stuck your bike by the top step. Huh, I wonder if he draped this old car jack here by the bottom step to give the impression that maybe your brother's head hit against it when he fell. Where's that jack usually kept?"

"Over with those tools by the workbench," Kay said. "They were all things that were here when Phil rented the house. Asey, I feel so helpless and so confused! Sneakers, boots, sugar bags—how can you ever even guess what must have happened? And beyond anything else, why would anyone have wanted to kill Phil?"

"That was somethin' I meant to take up with you," Asey said. "Now, I already know that he an' June didn't get on, an' I've sort of gathered that your brother was able to rile people easy. Did he rile pretty easy, himself?"

"Well, he was impatient with anything he thought inefficient," Kay said slowly. "All his trouble with Sterling Hazard over these defense projects rose from arguments about red tape and paper work—did you say something?"

"I just coughed," Asey said, and coughed again to prove it. "Go on. He riled Hazard, did he?"

"Phil thought that if things were necessary, you should get them done at once, and then explain things later on a post card, if anyone asked for explanations. Sterling wanted everything authorized and signed and countersigned and notarized, and neatly typed in triplicate on the proper forms before anyone lifted a finger. Naturally they all but came to blows. And then Phil and your cousin Jennie didn't always get on, because she was impatient of his clumsiness and his questions, and she resented his habit of taking charge of things. Really, now that I think of it, Phil and Jennie were awfully alike."

"Quick on the draw?"

Kay nodded. "Yes. Yes, Asey, Phil was quick-tempered. But about June—wouldn't it be possible for you to erase the memory of that episode on the short cut tonight? It puts June in such a horrible light, and really, as I said, it's all because her mother spoiled her so, and put so many wrong ideas into her head."

"Usin' that for a justification," Asey said, "you could sort of excuse everyone from wife-beaters to dictators, couldn't you? Come along upstairs, Miss Mundy. I got to call Hanson an' Cummings."

"Wait!" Kay protested. "June hasn't any reason to kill her father! No one ever kills their father, except in a Greek tragedy or something! June wouldn't kill anyone!"

"If you remember, she kind of indicated tonight that

doin' away with you would be a pleasure," Asey returned. "What I was drivin' at, though, was somethin'· else. I know your brother'd been divorced for a long time, an' was a widower—did he happen to have any present candidates, as you might say?"

Kay smiled wryly. "In his present financial circumstances, a daughter was about all he could manage to support. And not very well, according to her. No, I think I can truthfully say that Phil wasn't tangled up with any prospective wives, or any affairs of the heart. Of course," she paused and then laughed. "Well, of course, they wouldn't count."

"Who wouldn't?"

"Well, Tiny Hazard—she's the Hazards' daughter, around fortyish—and Mrs. Tuesome, and—oh, three or four others all pursued him in a persistent, refined sort of way. There aren't many eligible males of their age group around down here. I think in a way it pleased Phil to have so many invitations, and so many people— well, not exactly fawning around, but at least hanging on his words. But Phil always joked about it, and I'm sure he never took any of them at all seriously—you want to phone, don't you? I'll show you where it is."

"So you don't think Tiny an' Mrs. Tuesome an' the others count, huh?" Asey said as he followed her up the stairs.

"Oh, my, no! We always laughed about his girl friends, Tiny and Mrs. Tuesome particularly. They were the leading contenders. You haven't met Tiny, have you?"

"I've seen her," Asey said. "Looks a bit like a mastiff, don't she?"

Kay giggled. "I've always thought of her as a cross between a Great Dane and an ox. Definitely not what you think of as a Glamor Girl. Without exception, she's the strongest woman I ever met. When Phil went snowshoeing with her and hurt his ankle, she actually picked him up and carried him home—and she wasn't even panting when she got here. Just a little redder in the face than usual."

"So!" Asey said. "That's very interestin'."

"Thirty-six holes of golf are just a brisk morning walk to her," Kay went on, "and she climbs the Matterhorn at intervals—at least I think it's the Matterhorn, but it may be Everest. Once I was unwise enough to hike with her, and I simply gave up and had to be driven home, and since then, Tiny keeps berating me for being so soft. It's *so* hard to explain to people like her that when you work for a living, and sit cooped up in an office pounding a typewriter all day, you're inclined to lose both your zest and your stamina for the rugged life. The phone's in the living room, over on that table."

"You mentioned age groups," Asey picked up the receiver and gave his number. "I wondered," he added as he waited, "about Ives an' Corner. Why ain't they in the Army—what's that? No answer? Will you ring again? Okay."

"What's the matter?" Kay asked as he replaced the receiver.

"Probably Hanson an' the doc stepped out. Maybe Daly an' Mike came back. I'll call again in a minute. Why aren't Ives an' Corner in the service?"

"Bob has a bad heart. He never suspected it until the draft doctor turned him down, and I think it's distressed him terribly," Kay said. "He's so healthy-looking, I think he feels silly explaining about his heart, and although he's never said so, I suspect that he moved here to get away from his home town and the people he knew because of it. Sometimes at the movies, when the newsreels get awfully patriotic, and that Newsreel Voice shouts out 'Pearl Harbor,' Bob digs his nails into his palms, and gulps, and then shrivels down into his seat, and looks so crushed and thwarted. I've felt so sorry for him."

"Takes it hard, hey?"

"I think he tries to make up for it by working twice as hard at everything," Kay said. "He rushes around helping with the heavy work at Red Cross—he's always baling, or packing, or crating—and he donates blood, and takes First Aid, and he's an Auxiliary Fireman, and he donates things from his store, and he's always getting equipment that people say can't be got. He simply works like a beaver all the time."

"What about Jonah Ives? How old is he, anyway?" Asey asked.

"Thirty."

"An' all that beard!"

"It's rather startling, isn't it? He's rather a mysterious figure to the town, you know. He likes old maps, and maps of any kind are pretty suspect down here these days."

Asey got the impression that Kay was falling over backwards in her effort to make Jonah Ives sound like a proper citizen.

"Instead of explaining that maps are a hobby of his," she went on, "and photography another, he just grins and says nothing."

"Why does he wear that beard?"

"I asked him, and he said he thought it went with his biblical name."

Asey chuckled. "Why isn't he in the service? Didn't you ever ask?"

"Well, yes," Kay said hesitantly. "Once he told me he was the sole support of eighteen female dependents, and another time he said the Army thought he was mentally unfit. I suppose he was joking, I don't know. Asey, about Phil—I still feel so distraught and discouraged. How can you make a start when there aren't any motives for anyone to have killed him?"

"Aren't there?" Asey picked up the telephone again.

It seemed to him, although he didn't trouble to say

so, that quite a number of people in Phil Mundy's circle of acquaintances might possibly have had a motive for killing him. June's apparently ingrained dislike of her father might have needed only the added stimulus of believing that he really was stealing her mother's money to spur her on to murder. And if Mundy had angered Sterling Hazard, at whose frown bank presidents had been known to raise their office window and jump out! And if Tiny Hazard and Mrs. Tuesome had been competing for his affection!

"Certainly," Kay said, "you couldn't believe that—well, I simply cannot bring myself to refer to them as The Women in His Life! But you couldn't believe that either Tiny or Mildred Tuesome had any motive for killing Phil! That would be the height of absurdity—what's the matter this time?"

"Line's busy. Didn't you," Asey asked with a grin as he set the phone down again, "ever hear tell about hell havin' no fury like a woman scorned?"

"Whoever penned those words meant women," Kay retorted. "Not Tiny Hazard! Not Mildred Tuesome!"

"Aren't they women?" Asey asked gently.

"Yes, but—but—well, you know just what I mean! Asey, think of that pair! Think of Tiny leaping over Alps, and wrestling steers on dude ranches! Think of Mildred Tuesome, fluttering and cooing around! They certainly aren't what I think of as women scorned, or *femmes fatales!*"

"I wonder," Asey said, "if maybe you ain't makin' the error of thinkin' that only the emotions of your own age group matter much, or have any particular violence. You figure June's too young an' too misled to realize how she sounds, an' then you discount Tiny an' Mrs. Tuesome because they're older than you, an' you're kind of amused by 'em. But when you come right down to it, their feelin's matter considerable to them, an' right now, they count considerable. So do their wills. June's got a will of cast iron. Tiny sounds like a strong, firm-minded soul, an' from my five minutes with Mrs. Tuesome, I'm willin' to wager that Mrs. Tuesome's the match of either of 'em. An'," he grinned at Kay, "I wonder if maybe all three of 'em aren't one up on you."

"Oh, dear!" Kay said wearily. "June tells me I'm prying and bossy, Phil says I'm too pliable, Jonah says I'm too much of a worrier, Bob says I'm too complacent and take things too lightly, Tiny says I'm flabby, and now you as good as call me weak and spineless! And last week the Hazards insinuated I was impertinent!"

"So? Why?"

"Oh, I casually remarked that I didn't see any great saving of tires ensuing from their walking to the post office if they had the chauffeur pick them up there and drive 'em home. Isn't it odd, what people think of you?" Kay added. "Somehow, I always thought of myself as a capable, bright-eyed secretary, like the ones in office-furniture ads—aren't you going to call Hanson again?"

"Uh-huh. Just one thing more. Have you any enemies?"

"Me? Of course not!"

"Er—you're quite sure?" Asey persisted.

"Well, people find fault with me—I just covered that angle. But I haven't any enemies! I may have annoyed people—I'm sure I have—but I don't think anyone's chewing their nails to get revenge—oh. Oh, I see now why you ask that. You mean, is there anyone who dislikes me enough to try to implicate me in Phil's death, what with my bike across the stairs, and all? But, Asey, that's not really anything to worry about now, is it?"

"Wa-el, no," Asey said. "In one way, no. Not now. On the other hand—"

"But it wouldn't really have mattered under any circumstances, would it? I was frightened to death at first," Kay said honestly, "but no one would actually have suspected me, would they, even if you hadn't found Phil at your house before? It never could have worked out so as to implicate me! It just proves that someone has a warped mind."

Asey smiled.

"I venture to say that if the doc an' I hadn't found your brother, if you'd found him an' called Hanson, in the ordinary course of events, you'd have had a pretty tough time. Uh-huh, I mean it," he added as Kay made an exclamation of unbelief. "Consider, now. Hanson's first question would be, 'Whose bike is that?' An' can you see yourself gettin' any forrader in explainin' to Hanson than Bob Corner got tryin' to explain about them keys? N'en, consider this. S'pose June found him there, an' s'pose June was in the same mood as she was earlier tonight. What'd she say about your bike bein' there? Consider that one rather careful-like."

"But—"

"S'pose," Asey went on, "that June told Hanson you done it on purpose. S'pose she started talkin' wild about your askin' your brother for money. You seen enough of Hanson to guess his reactions. Can't you picture him stickin' his thumbs in his belt an' glarin' at you? Can't you see the act June'd put on? Can't you imagine the sort of things she'd say?"

Kay sat down suddenly in a chintz-covered armchair.

"Asey, that cod line!"

"What cod line?" Asey noticed that her face had that chalky look again.

"Last week I had a cod line rigged up out in that back entry to hang wet woolen socks and mittens on— the blizzard melted into an awful drip. And the end of the line I tied on the banister out there slid down, and when Phil stomped in without putting on the light, he tripped. It was simply luck that he didn't fall down those stairs then. If June told Hanson about that!"

"Just so," Asey said. "I see you get my point. 'Course, things would've got sorted out ultimately, but you'd have had a bad time till Cummings an' his boys got down to some serious work. Now, be honest. You may not look on June as an enemy, but won't you admit she may consider you one?"

Kay nodded slowly.

"Uh-huh. One more thing," Asey spoke very casually. "When did you get that coupe you was drivin' on the short cut? Did you have it off my lane when I chased you? Did you come back here from my house an' get it? When?"

His barrage of questions didn't seem to disturb Kay.

"I walked back here and got it," she said. "I don't know what time it was. I meant to go see Jennie and ask her advice—Asey Mayo!" her voice suddenly quivered with indignation. "Are you insinuating—yes, you are! You think I had the car hidden by your house, and that *I* brought Phil's body back here! Well, I didn't, and I can prove it! We've made a fetish of car saving, and I can show you what the car mileage was when Phil brought the coupe home this noon, and you can prove by the speedometer and the gas and everything that I only drove it from here to where you met me on the short cut! I'll get the chart!"

She rushed out of the room before Asey could point out to her that chart or no chart, it didn't matter a whit now that June had taken the car.

Two seconds later, Kay rushed, empty-handed, back into the living room.

"Asey, come quick!"

"What's wrong?"

"I was going to grab the chart from the kitchen shelf, and something moved outside—Asey, someone's peeking into the cellar! Quick, go see who it is!"

Asey darted past her, all but dove to the kitchen, and peered cautiously out.

"Can't you see?" Kay whispered breathlessly over his shoulder. "Back near the garage, by the bushes, see? Go get him, quick! Maybe it's the murderer coming to see if his plan's working out—go on, get him, Asey, quick!"

Asey glanced toward the back entry, where the light was still burning, and then dashed for the front door. To start after someone from that lighted ell would be the same, he thought, as announcing his intention over a loud-speaker. But if he could creep around the house, he stood some chance of grabbing that shadowy figure in the bushes.

He circled stealthily around the porch, grinned when he found the person was still standing by the bushes, and paused to set himself for the flying tackle he intended to make.

"Asey!" Kay's voice rang out with a plaintive clarity. "Asey, can't you find him? Where'd he go? A-sey, where are you?"

The figure melted from sight at her first word, and Asey, gritting his teeth, started out in pursuit.

If, he thought bitterly as he raced along, if that was Kay's conception of being a bright young secretary, or a bright young anything else, she was sadly mistaken! Of all the dumb gestures!

He lengthened his stride. It might well be that Mundy's murderer had only just discovered that his victim had been previously found in another place, and that he had returned to see what was going on. Certainly there was no valid reason for any innocent bystander to peer into the Mundys' cellar at this hour.

"I'm sure," Asey muttered, "he wasn't no meter reader!"

He lifted his head and listened to the footsteps rhythmically pounding along through the woods ahead of him, and forced himself on at a quicker pace.

It had been his feeling when he'd chased Kay earlier that he would get her sooner or later, in spite of his slippery, leather-soled city shoes, and the handicap of his long overcoat. Now, as he dashed along, he had a premonition that he was going to be left behind. And he hadn't any alibi except a lack of speed. Being cooped up in the Porter plant, he suspected, had something to do with it.

The footsteps ahead suddenly ceased, and Asey grabbed out at a pine tree to stop himself without plunging headlong.

So Superman was getting winded too, was he? That was all right with him, Asey thought. When it came to playing a brisk game of hide-and-seek in the woods, he'd match himself against anyone. The fellow would stand there like a statue, hoping Asey would give up and go home, and then, if that failed, he'd carefully tiptoe off.

"Okay," Asey murmured. "I can wait, too! An' when you start your tiptoein', I'll be tiptoein' right behind you!"

He leaned back against the pine tree, and waited, and listened, and listened, and waited.

His reward came ten minutes later in the form of three shots that cracked out and echoed over the woods.

"No, sir, it's backfires!" Asey said. "Golly, it's a car! For Pete's sakes, it's that old Buick, that old tourin' car, startin' up! Huh!"

So it hadn't been Superman, but that Superwoman Tiny Hazard who'd outrun him and outfoxed him and left him flat-footed there, the Lord only knew where, in the East Aspinnet woods!

And what, he asked himself, had she been doing, peering into Mundy's cellar?

He walked thoughtfully ahead to where he figured the beach road should be.

Where had Tiny been all night? Why should she have parked her car so far away? If Mrs. Tuesome hadn't been the Army's third victim over by Great Meadow, could it have been Tiny? Or Jennie?

Asey shook his head. If only he could locate Jennie! Jennie was not a gossip, but she had a masterly grasp on local undercurrents. The middle-aged romancing of Phil Mundy and Tiny Hazard and Mrs. Tuesome that had seemed so hilarious to Kay had probably been followed with eager interest by the natives of East Aspinnet and the surrounding towns, and there was no doubt but what rumors would have seeped over into Wellfleet and Jennie's ken.

He found the road, turned dejectedly back toward the Mundys' house, and shivered as the east wind whipped around his ears.

For all that had gone on, this whole business was still something that you could mercifully boil down and mull over. Someone had bashed Mundy, put on that silly hood, put him in the buttery, put on brown sneakers. Then, after an interval, someone had removed the body, removed the hood, put on Mundy's rubber boots, and taken him home. And there, with the single, superbly simple gesture of placing Kay's bike on the top step, someone had made Kay Suspect Number One.

That brown-sneaker angle was odd, he thought. But the murderer must have put them on Mundy's feet, otherwise he wouldn't have had the rubber boots in his possession to put back on again. Maybe Hanson's boys could find out something from those boots, but

Asey doubted it. The sand and clay of one part of the East Aspinnet area was very much like the sand and clay of another part. Anyway, Hanson's boys and Cummings could find out about the spider problem!

Asey pulled his coat collar up around his neck, and sighed.

What with one spider being interred by June, and one disappearing from the Hazards' back seat, and one being purchased by Kay, he rather fervently hoped that Hanson's boys and Cummings would decide that the blunt instrument was a Ming vase, or a railroad tie, or almost anything except an iron spider!

"Pitchforks!" he muttered.

A car sped up the road, passed him, then stopped and backed up.

"Hullo, Asey, what're you doing here?" Cummings seemed curiously restrained, Asey thought, and then he realized that the doctor had two passengers with him. "Meet Mr. and Mrs. Hazard," Cummings went on. "They've—er—just recently been found and released by the Army, Asey."

"How do you do? Who was the third?" Asey asked promptly. "Was it Jennie?"

"No, Roland Higgins. That was the first thing I asked 'em, too," Cummings said. "Rolly was taking a short cut home, and I gather he was good and sore till he found out that one of the fellows who jumped him was a cousin of his from Brockton. They got Ives, too, as you guessed. Asey, what in thunder are you doing here?"

"Wa-el," Asey decided there was no tactful way of explaining that he had been chasing the Hazards' daughter over hill and dale and pine woods, "I been out for a sort of rapid stroll. I found Mundy, doc."

"No! Where, in the woods?"

"At his house. I been tryin' to get you an' Hanson on the phone. S'pose you could squeeze me in an' drive me along there, an' then the Hazards could get their car an' drive along home—p'raps," he added, "the doc explained to you how I happen to have your car, Mr. Hazard?"

"We understand perfectly the position into which you were thrust," Hazard said, "and it is our desire that you keep the car and use it as if it were your own. Grace and I feel it's the very least we can contribute to the solution of this frightful business, don't we, dear?"

"Indeed we do, and we really must thank you," Mrs. Hazard said, "for telling people about us. I don't think that even that Major—he was a Major, wasn't he, dear? That tall man with the moustache? I don't think even he quite understood how you knew about us, or how you managed to convey the information to him through so many channels, but it was most kind and thoughtful of you, and Sterling and I think you're just as clever as your cousin Jennie has claimed."

"I hope," Asey said politely, "that you didn't—uh—suffer too much?"

"It was a most interesting experience." Hazard spoke in a detached sort of way, rather as if he were giving his opinion of some play he'd seen. "I must confess that Grace and I have felt rather relieved by it. We had heard so many rumors about our Army that it is a pleasure to be able to state categorically that our Army is definitely alert."

Asey knew from Cummings's vigorous nose-blowing that the doctor was with difficulty restraining himself from pertinent comment.

"Such nice boys!" Mrs. Hazard said. "So—no, Mr. Mayo, you're not crowding us at all! Do drive on, doctor, I know we'll manage beautifully. Sterling, perhaps Mr. Mayo would know what they might like for dinner."

"Dinner?" Asey said.

"The Hazards," Cummings explained as he started the car, "have invited the whole da—the whole outfit to come to dinner, en masse, the first opportunity they have."

"We've been wishing we knew someone in the Army," Mrs. Hazard said. "We knew so many in the last war—if only I knew what they liked to eat!"

"That problem," Cummings said, "was foremost in their minds when they came back to your house—that's probably why you couldn't get us, Asey. Hanson and

I were out talking with them. They were returned in a jeep."

"I must remember that name," Hazard said thoughtfully. "Jeep. Jeep. That was quite an experience, too, wasn't it, Grace?"

Mrs. Hazard agreed with something more than casual politeness that it had indeed been an experience. "I'm so surprised," she went on, "to find that no one else of our class group reported back to Jennie's."

"They should have," Hazard said firmly. "It's the new rule, and Jennie must insist on it in the future."

"I don't suppose," Asey said, "that either of you knows where Jennie is, do you? No, I almost didn't think you would. Nobody does. Turn here, doc, an' then to the right. If the Hazards don't honestly mind my usin' their car, s'pose you go in an' take over at Mundy's, an' call Hanson, an' I'll drive 'em on home in this. I'd like to ask 'em about some things."

"We'd be only too happy to co-operate in any possible way, wouldn't we, Grace? We find this affair of Mundy very distressing. Mundy was a most able man, a successful organizer, and his only fault was his impatience with anything or anybody he suspected of hampering direct action." Hazard sounded, Asey thought, like an obituary notice. "I had intended to find a place for him where his talent for action might have been of service. I feel sure that this terrible situation is the result of his quick temper—I'd warned him that someday, when he flared up, he might inspire someone to—er—"

"Take a sock at him?" Asey suggested.

"In a nutshell, yes. Isn't that your opinion, Mr. Mayo?" Hazard asked as the doctor stopped the car in the Hazards' driveway.

"Could be." Asey wriggled out of the car, and, after extracting his black bag, Cummings followed him and grabbed his arm.

"My God," Cummings said in his ear, "don't you have to hand it to the old school? I've nearly bust! They get jumped on, tied up, dumped like sacks of meal out in the woods—and they're so pleased to find the Army's alert, they ask the whole damned outfit to dinner! They're jounced home in a jeep, they're told of a murder, and they say that while it's distressing, how fortunate it happened while you're home, and what should they feed the soldiers! You can't faze 'em. Will you be right back?"

"Uh-huh. Look after that bash as soon as you can, will you?"

Asey got into the coupe, backed out of the driveway, and started along the beach road.

"Did you really find poor Mr. Mundy there?" Mrs. Hazard asked. "How—"

"I feel, dear, that Mr. Mayo wishes to ask questions of us," Hazard said.

"Oh, I'm sorry—could I just ask him what he thinks

the boys would like for dessert? D'you think that something simple, like Baked Alaska, would do? My cousin Edgar, who's a Major General, always compliments Emil on his Baked Alaska."

Asey chuckled. "I should think it might go over big. Most anything'd go over big, if you had enough of it. You sure it's all right for me to keep your car over night? Golly, I forgot to take Ives's bike off the back seat. I hope it don't mark up your upholstery!"

Both the Hazards, in unison, assured him that he was to think nothing of it.

"Anything we can do, anything at all, we're only too happy to," Hazard said.

"I noticed," Asey said casually, "that you had a fine iron fryin' pan on your back seat, too."

"Oh!" Mrs. Hazard said. "Oh, that's our bomb pan. It's for bombs."

"Bombs?"

"In the village today, I asked if the bomb scoops had come—Harrison, our butler, has been most anxious for us to have some bomb scoops. He's our warden," Mrs. Hazard explained. "And Sterling and I saw those iron pans, and we wondered if Harrison might not be able to concoct some sort of temporary scoop from one, just to tide us over until the real scoops arrive. Mr. Mayo, who *could* have killed Mr. Mundy?"

"Grace, dear!" Hazard said.

"I know, Sterling, dear, I shouldn't ask. But you know he didn't affect everyone the way he affected you! Tiny said that most of the people here *liked* his outspokenness and direct manner! Tiny said people were thinking of asking him to run for some town office, and you know Tiny and I never minded his—" she broke off abruptly, and Asey had a feeling that she had been rather firmly nudged. "This is the turn, Mr. Mayo."

"Uh-huh. I knew the Standin's," Asey said, "I been here often to take old Jim Standin' out for a fishin' trip. Tell me, who came first to Jennie's class this evenin'?"

"We did," Hazard told him. "As I explained to the police officer at your house, we are not ordinarily—er—considering dinner at the time Jennie's class meets, so we have a high tea on those days, and this afternoon we finished earlier than we realized."

"Did you happen to see anyone lurkin' around?"

Hazard shook his head. "No one at all. The officer asked us that, too."

"No car? No vehicles?"

"No," Mrs. Hazard said. "I remember looking all around to see if Jennie's bicycle was there."

"I see." Asey stopped in front of the vast, rambling white house. "Didn't hear any noise?"

"None. We didn't enter the house, but I'm positive

no one was in it." Hazard got out of the coupe, and turned around to help his wife. "It was good of you to bring us back, Mayo."

"And do keep the car as long as you want to," Mrs. Hazard added. "Maybe, Sterling, dear, since Mr. Mayo knows so much about Porters, he might be able to locate that little squeak that's bothered me so."

"Really, Grace dear! Mr. Mayo has more on his mind than little squeaks! Good night, Mayo, and thank you."

"Good night," Asey said, "an' if I find your squeak, ma'am, I'll stop it."

"You're very kind." Mrs. Hazard started away from the car and then stepped tentatively back. "I'm sure you'll find out who killed poor Mr. Mundy—my daughter and I enjoyed him, and I know she'll be very distressed, too, when she hears what has happened to him."

"Good night," Hazard said again, with finality, and took her arm.

Asey drove the doctor's coupe along down the semicircular driveway, and then braked quickly just before swinging back on to the tarred road. Someone had tossed a beer bottle out from a passing car, and he didn't want to subject Cummings's precious whitewalls to the jagged pieces of glass that littered the turn.

He jumped out, kicked the glass into a clump of bushes, and then, before returning to the car, he casually turned and looked up toward the house.

He found himself blinking.

Mr. Hazard, the polite, silver-haired Sterling Hazard, had just smacked the face of his fragile, white-haired wife—and even at a distance, it looked like a hefty smack.

"For Pete's sakes!" Asey said.

He watched while the front door opened and the Hazards went in. Then the outside light was snapped off.

Asey shrugged, got into the car and continued on his way.

"I wonder, now!" he murmured to himself, "I wonder if dear Sterlin' ain't bein' less of the polite old school than he is bein' considerably careful! He tried to steer dear Grace from sayin' a word about Mundy, an' when she spoke of him, an' brought up Tiny, that didn't sit a bit well. Huh! I wonder, now!"

He drove back to the Mundys' house at a clip which would have thrown Dr. Cummings into one of his more de luxe speechless rages.

Hanson's car wasn't there, but the coupe which June had swiped from Kay was parked with its front wheels in an empty flower bed, and as Asey got out, he saw Jonah Ives pass by the living-room window. The fellow, Asey thought, hadn't wasted much time getting here after being loosed by the Army.

He was greeted, as he opened the front door and stepped into the hall, by a series of wild staccato shrieks coming from somewhere in the rear of the house.

At once June appeared, on a dead run, and following her was Jonah Ives.

He was yelling, and she was screaming, and both of them rushed out the front door past Asey, without seeming to notice him at all.

"So!" Asey said, and strolled leisurely after them.

Jonah grabbed the girl as she got into the coupe, and pulled her out with a fine disregard for her kicking heels and flying fists—and also, Asey suspected, her biting teeth and scratching nails.

Then he sat down on the running board of the car and proceeded to administer one of the most competent spankings which Asey had ever witnessed.

When it was over, and June had run sobbing into the house, Jonah took out his pipe, filled it, and lighted it with the air of a man thoroughly satisfied with himself.

"Sooner or later," Asey said conversationally, "I think I'd have done that myself."

Instead of giving any start of guilty surprise at Asey's presence, Jonah merely turned around calmly, surveyed Asey, and nodded.

"She asks for it, doesn't she? Duck coat, yachting cap—you're on Jennie's mantel. Asey Mayo, isn't it? I'm Jonah Ives, and I learn your exploits along with incidental intelligence on First Aid. To me, the four-tailed bandage for nose problems will always be inextricably mixed up with a corpse you once found in a phone booth."

Asey chuckled. "June's been actin' up, I take it?"

"She's been making an awful stink! I've yearned to beat that chit for a long time, but tonight she went too far. She came rushing in—apparently she'd heard about this uptown—and started howling invective at Kay. She—you say something?"

"I was wondering," Asey said, "how she happened to know enough to rush here. If she'd heard what the newspapers call the first unconfirmed reports of this action, she'd ought to have scurried over to my place, not here."

"I thought of that," Ives said, "and asked her about it. She went to your house and talked with some cop—"

"Oh—oh," Asey said. "Oh—oh!"

"That's what I said, too. And while she was there, Cummings phoned the cop and told him about Phil being here. So June larruped over and started howling invective at Kay."

"Claimed Kay done it, I s'pose."

"Oh, yes. With trimmings. When I tried to shut her up," Jonah said, "she yelled that Kay and I were in cahoots, and had undeniably murdered Phil between us —for God's sakes, what goes on now? Hear that rumpus inside? If she's after Kay again, I'll horsewhip her!"

He rushed indoors, with Asey following him, and

both came to a quick stop at the threshold of the living room.

Armed with a carving knife, June stood by the desk in the corner, brandishing a paper in her left hand.

"Don't come near! Don't any of you dare come near me! I've got it! I've got the will she made father sign, the one that gives all his money to her, and I'm going to take it straight to the police!"

CHAPTER SEVEN

"JUNE!" Kay said desperately. "June—"

"Don't you move a step, Kay Mundy, or I'll stab you! If any of you move an inch," June's eyes were glinting dangerously, "I'll stab her, d'you hear! Don't any of you dare move!"

"Somewhere along simple fractures," Jonah spoke calmly and reminiscently, "a situation like this came up, Mayo. Was it simple fractures? Yes. 'Once traction has been started, it should not be released until splints are in place. Do not attempt to set a bone. Do not transport the patient, even for a very short distance, before splints have been applied—' what's the matter, Kay? Have I got it wrong?"

"Matter! Can't you *see* what the matter is? Aren't the two of you going to *do* anything?"

"Hush," Jonah said. "We're making a preliminary survey. As I said, General Mayo, along around simple fractures, Jennie told me how you once set upon

and erased from further action three evil men, all over
six feet six inches tall, all heavily armed with Tommy
guns—or was it machine guns? Anyway, you did it
all with your bare, honest fists. Maybe my details are
garbled, but the point I make should be clear. Just
how the hell do we cope with this brat?"

"Men are one thing," Asey returned in equally non-
chalant tones, "an' women are somethin' else again.
Now, if we rush her," June was listening intently,
he noted, "if we rush her, she really might hurt Kay."

"I'm going to!" June said. "That's just what I'm going to do, if any of you moves a single inch!"

"Or she might hurt herself," Asey went on, "which
wouldn't distress me none. Or, she might just possibly
hurt us."

"Jonah! Asey!" Kay said. "*Do* something."

"We are stymied," Jonah said sadly; "there are
more of us to get hurt. Er—it's a nasty defeatist out-
look, Mayo, but would you suggest appeasement, at
this point?"

"Wa-el," Asey said, "no. Her strategy ain't bad, but
her tactics are punk. Thinkin' we'd thrown all our
forces into the fray of this room here, she went an'
left her flank unprotected. When Mack comes in that
window behind her—"

June fell for it and turned her head, and five seconds later, Asey presented the carving knife to Jonah
with a bow.

"Thank you, sir," Jonah said ceremoniously. "I only did what any other right-thinking, clean-living, red-blooded First-Aider would have done. I kept cool and didn't lose my head. But I shall treasure this always, as a memento of this occasion—d'you think if we gave it back to her, she'd commit hara-kiri?"

"I doubt it. Now, Miss June Mundy, fork over that paper, an' go sit down on the couch, an' keep still!"

"Or what?" June demanded belligerently.

"Jonah used his hand," Asey said. "I'll use my belt. You won't like it."

"Who *are* you?"

"Asey Mayo. Sit down."

"*Asey* Mayo? Oh. Well, let me tell you, *I* know who killed my father! Kay did it! Kay—"

"Now you listen here," Asey said. "I've seen your acts before tonight! I seen you when you swiped Jonah's bike in the woods. I seen you bury that iron spider. I seen you swipe the car!"

"June Mundy!" Jonah said, "did you take my iron spider out of my bike basket and *bury* it? Did you? You low thing! After my landlady and I spent the morning seasoning it, and it cooked like a charm—what the hell did you do a thing like that for? Kay, why did she do that? Asey, can you guess?"

"All I know," Asey said, "is that she was interrin' it under a pine tree."

"Oh, I get it, I think!" Jonah said. "I'd told her

while we were hunting Tuesome how much time I'd spent on that pan—you were going to say, 'Yah, yah, if you want your old spider, go dig for it!' And then come watch me burrow over half of Cape Cod, and just roar with laughter? Weren't you? Yes, I thought so! That's just the sort of nasty kid trick you'd love!"

"I know who killed my father!" June characteristically changed the subject. "I know who killed him! Kay did!"

Asey walked over to the couch and stood in front of her.

"That'll do!" he said. "Understand? Now, Kay, what's all this business about a will, anyway?"

"I don't know!" Kay said helplessly. "Apparently June does, although I don't know why she should, unless she's been prying into Phil's private papers in the desk there! She must have been, because she knew just which pigeonhole that sheet was in—look at it, Asey, and see what it is."

"Well?" Jonah asked a few minutes later when Asey, with a frown, tossed the folded paper down on the desk top. "Well, what's the story? What is it, anyway?"

"Seems to be just about what June claimed," Asey said slowly. "It's a will that Mundy made, an' signed this mornin'. Leaves everythin' he has to you, Kay."

"To *me?*" Kay sounded dumbfounded. "Signed this *morn*ing?"

"Uh-huh. An' this will shall supersede all previous wills, an' so on, an' so forth. An' his daughter, for good an' sufficient reasons, an' one thing an' another, shall receive the sum of one dollar, to satisfy any claims she may have on him, an' so on, an' so forth. It's all full of legal words, but that's about the gist of the thing."

"I don't know what to say!" Kay said. "I—I can't understand it! But it isn't valid, is it? It won't stand?"

"Seems as if. There's a notary's seal on it, an' witnesses' signatures. Seems all legal an' proper."

June broke the little silence that followed.

"Now," she said triumphantly, "now will you listen to me, Mister Smartypants Mayo? I tell you, Kay's been wringing money out of him for weeks! *Or*dering him to give her money! I've heard her. I've seen father writing checks for her! She must have taken every cent he had left, and more besides, because father hasn't even given me my own allowance, that comes from mother's bank, lately! When I asked him why, he said for me not to worry, that everything would come out all right in the end—don't you see? Don't you understand, you fathead? Kay got everything father had; she blackmailed it out of him, and then she got him to make this will in her favor, and chuck out the one that left everything to me!"

"An' how," Asey inquired as June paused for breath, "how d'you know that such a will existed?"

"Then she killed him so she could collect!" June ignored his question. "If father's body hadn't been found first at your house, if he'd been found here, then it would have seemed like an accident! And she'd have collected and—"

"How do you know that there was a previous will that left everything to you?" Asey interrupted.

"Well, I saw it." June avoided Asey's eyes. "I just happened to see it. It just happened to—to be on the desk one day when I was writing a letter, and I glanced at it. And, anyway, it doesn't matter how I know! What matters is that she blackmailed him, and then forced him to make this new will, and then she killed him—for his money! And if you want to know, she'd tried to kill him before! Last week she stretched a cod line across those cellar steps, and father nearly broke his neck then! I'm going to tell the police about that, too!"

"I suppose," Jonah said thoughtfully, "it's useless to point out to you in your present hysterical condition that if Kay had actually been attempting to kill your father last week, you would have been the one to gain, not Kay? If this new will was signed only today, you can hardly claim that an accident last week was any attempt at murder for profit."

"She just wanted to kill him, last week," June said. "They'd been arguing, and fighting like cats and dogs. Then I suppose when her cod line failed, she thought it over and decided that if she was going to kill him, she might as well make some money out of it!"

"June!" Kay said. "June, how can you?"

"Oh, you can stand there looking hurt and innocent!" June retorted. "But you're clever! You wanted money, and you got it!"

"D'you think it would make matters worse," Jonah asked Asey, "if I spanked her again?"

"You can't make matters any worse for yourself!" June said. "I'm going to tell the police a lot about you, too! How you prowl around and make maps of roads, and send long telegrams to people in New York, and how you pry around the Army, and how you watch planes, and how you were out on the beach the day that torpedoed tanker burned! I've watched you plenty! People call you a spy, but I know you *are* one!"

"No, Jonah," Asey said. "Restrain yourself!"

"Just let me take a little crack at her!" Jonah's voice was still calm and bantering, but his eyes had narrowed to slits. "Just let me knock out a tooth or two!"

"No, she—"

June burst suddenly into tears, and rushed from the couch to the doorway, where Hanson had suddenly appeared.

"Oh, thank God you've come, thank God!" she clung to Hanson. "They've been persecuting me! I know who killed my father, and they're persecuting me!"

Putting her head on Hanson's shoulder, she sobbed as if her heart were breaking.

Hanson patted her head. "Come, come!" he said soothingly. "Come, come!"

"Something tells me," Jonah said to Asey, "that he is a sucker for blondes, and if anything brings out his protective instinct more than a blonde, it's a blonde in tears!"

"What's the matter, little girl?" Hanson asked solicitously.

"Kay made daddy change his will," June said brokenly, "and leave everything to her! And when I said I'd tell you, they threatened to beat me and knock out my teeth—and he *did* beat me!" She pointed to Jonah.

"You poor kid!" Hanson glared at Jonah, and patted June's head again. "You come right into the other room and tell me all about this, kiddie!"

"Kiddie!" Jonah said. "Kiddie, yet! I'm going to be sick!"

"You wait till I find out what you've been doing to this poor kid," Hanson informed him coldly, "and you *will* be sick! Good and sick! Come, kiddie."

"Go on, kiddie, tell papa all, kiddie!" Jonah said. "Lay it on with a nice trowel, kiddie. Have fun, kiddie. But remember that Jonah's only biding his time, kiddie, and you'll have every last damned lie taken right out of your little hide, kiddie! Kay," he added as Hanson put a protective arm about June's shoulders and led her into the dining room, "I hope to God you're not going to take this sitting down! Mayo, you don't intend to sit idly by and let June drag Kay headfirst into a mess like this, do you?"

"The problem," Asey said, "is that there's the will! An' if there's one thing Hanson's more partial to than a blonde, it's what he calls a good, sound money motive. Kay, don't you know anything about your brother's wills, or about this new one? Did he ever mention wills to you? D'you suppose he changed it after that fight with June, or before?"

"It must have been before," Kay said. "He told me when he went to town this morning that he had some papers to be signed, and he went straight to his desk after he came home. Phil has spoken about wills several times lately, but I just thought he might be considering his in the light of his business problems."

"Look, Kay, never mind what you thought!" Jonah said. "Concentrate, and tell us just what Phil actually *said* about wills!"

"Well, I thought—I mean, in my opinion—well," Kay said desperately, "one dismal gray day last week, during the postblizzard rain, Phil got an awfully morbid streak. He was worrying about bills, and fussing about defense things going wrong, and damning everybody—"

"Includin' Hazard?" Asey interrupted.

"Yes. Phil had begun the day by having another fight with him. Anyway, from all that, Phil got on to the topic of wills, and he discussed wills interminably. He asked if I'd made one, and how much money I had, and what plans I'd made for cushioning myself against a postwar depression. When I told him that my cushioning consisted of four small Defense Bonds, he moaned and groaned and began to brood about my future—look, I do want to explain about my asking Phil for money. I'd withdrawn my account in New York, and he was keeping my money for me until I found out what I was going to do and where I was going to be permanently. There were problems about subleasing my apartment, and I had a batch of small bills, and I had to ask Phil to write more checks than I'd expected. But you can tell from his checkbook that my bills were paid with my money—there's nothing sinister about that at all, though June makes it seem so."

"You ain't got any idea why he changed wills?" Asey asked. "Did you get the impression that he was goin' to make changes?"

"He said June was his first consideration, but God knew he ought to do something about me," Kay said. "I told him I didn't see why he felt that way. I mean, I've always managed to get along, and besides, I had what little the family had left, and Phil started out from scratch. I said there was no reason for him to consider me at all, and he said the two of us, June and

I, were driving him bats, and he slammed out and had another row with Sterling Hazard. He was still jumpy that night at First Aid—remember, Jonah, when he argued so with Jennie about pressure points, and demonstrated on June, and all but dislocated her hip? But he hasn't mentioned wills since. Except once, and then just sort of in passing."

"Speaking of First Aid," Jonah said, "where in blazes were you tonight?"

"Hunting Phil." Kay told him all about it. "So," she concluded, "I suppose I might as well face the dismal fact that I don't know where I was at any given time."

"Oh, no! God, no!" Jonah said. "Don't tell me you're wide open to any accusations June might feel like making! You must have been somewhere, some time, where someone saw you!"

"Only at Asey's, when he chased me, and I thought he was Pete Melrose," Kay said. "And Asey's already insinuated that I had ample time and opportunity to have driven Phil's body here, and driven back to the short cut where he met me."

"I've got it, Phil's chart!" Jonah banged his fist on the couch arm. "That's it. I never could see any damned use to that thing, but that chart'll prove everything!"

"It might have," Kay said. "I thought of it, too. But June grabbed the car from me, and if I know her, she's driven every drop of gas out. And probably driven as fast as she could, over the worst roads, just for sheer spite. That's what she did the last time she stole the car, when Phil forgot to hide the keys. Remember those speeding fines he had to pay, Jonah? Anyway, if Asey could have seen the car mileage when I met him on the short cut, he'd have known I'd only driven a mile or so. It would have been all right then, but it's all wrong now—oh, what a frightful mess!"

Cummings bustled into the room, beaming from ear to ear.

"Hullo, everybody, I'm—good God, but you three look dour!"

"We feel dour," Jonah said. "We've got reason to. Where've you been? Haven't you heard what's been going on?"

"You did seem to be making a terrible racket," Cummings said, "but I've been being too busy to pay any attention. What's wrong?"

"In there," Jonah pointed to the dining room, "our little buttercup, June, is telling that cop—what's his name, Manson? Hanson? Well, she's telling Hanson how Kay killed her dear daddy for his money. With tears, floodlights, and what amounts to festoons of neon trimmings. And there *is* a new will, it seems, and he *did* cut June off and leave everything to Kay. And Kay doesn't know where she was this evening. That is, she knows, but nobody can prove anything. That's what's wrong. At least, it's part of it."

"Don't let it worry you," Cummings said cheerfully.

"All the circumstantial evidence in the world isn't going to matter a whale of a lot, because I've just found out something that will occupy Hanson's mind—and yours too, Asey—for some time. Remember that pencil-like mark on Mundy's head?"

"Uh-huh."

"I'm now willing to stick my neck out to the extent of telling you that I think it was the result of contact with the rim of an iron spider—mind you, I won't swear to it on any stack of Bibles until Reinhold double-checks. But that's my impression."

"How in blazes did you find that out?" Jonah asked blankly.

"I did it," Cummings said, "with my little hatchet—as you might say. Come along, Asey, I want you to figure from there."

"Wait! How did you know? Whatever made you think of an iron spider?" Jonah demanded.

"The thought occurred to Asey and me over in his buttery," Cummings explained. "There was a spider hanging on the wall there. I thought of it again when I looked at Mundy just now—by George, Asey, whoever planted that jack there did a masterly job! If I hadn't seen Mundy before at Asey's, I think I might just possibly have been tempted to say that after he pitched down the stairs, his head had bounced off it."

"How?" Jonah said. "I should think he'd have hit head first."

"Ever have your feet go out from under you when you stepped on an icy sidewalk?" Cummings returned. "Usually you smack down on your hip or your fanny, and then your head jerks back and you get a good crack on the cranium. Plunging down those steps in the dark, you'd be as likely to crack the back of your head as not. Anyway, I thought of that spider again, and then when I spotted that dandy new one under the stairs, I picked it up, and by George, the mark on my thumb where I touched the rim was just that same pencil-like smudge!"

"Spider? You mean, that's what someone used to hit Phil with, and then left it behind down there?" Jonah asked.

"It's the dandy new spider," Kay said, "that I bought today. When I carried the kerosene can down, I took it along. I completely forgot. I intended to hide it away —you see, Jonah, I bought it for Phil's birthday present. He's been wanting one to make pancakes in."

"I know. He talked so glowingly about his mother's iron spider, that's why I bought mine today. Don't look so sunk, Kay! Be of good cheer and stout heart. If the possession of an iron spider is going to have any sinister connotations, then I'm right there in the swim with you. *I* have an iron spider—wherever June buried it."

"I dug it up," Asey told him. "It's out in the Porter's back seat, along with your fancy bike."

"So you salvaged that? Thanks a lot. I was afraid June might have dumped it into a pond, or left it on the railroad tracks for the fast freight to play tag with. You know," Jonah said, "something told me during that seasoning process that I was enduring a lot for a lousy little iron pan, and now I see I should have obeyed my original impulse and given the damned thing to my landlady, who obviously craved it."

"Did you use your spider?" Cummings asked.

"I cooked my supper in it, on the beach. Very tasty."

"Then yours doesn't count," Cummings informed him. "You see, that spider down there is an old-fashioned, old-style iron spider, and it's brand new. Never been used. After it was made, it got given a protective coating of—well, grease or fat, I don't know which. Then, later, some cautious person smeared it with vaseline and rubbed it in, to ward off rust. There's some of that in Mundy's hair, by the way, that I thought was some sort of hair dressing when I first saw him. Well, to sum it up, that protective coating, plus rubbed-in vaseline, plus years of inactivity and dust-catching, all combined to give that unused spider the ability to leave a smudge almost like a pencil mark. I don't say that your pan won't make a smudge mark too, Ives, but it wouldn't be the same sort of smudge if your pan has been seasoned and used. See?"

"No," Kay said. "I don't. Not at all."

"I get it," Jonah said. "I assisted at the seasoning

process of mine, and Mrs. Nickerson commented at length on the toughness of the pan's outer coating. I thought at the time that she was just griping on principle, as she usually does, but now I understand. Point is, a spider rim made a certain mark on Phil's head, but it had to be a new spider. And if a spider rim made a mark, I conclude that the spider struck the blow. Right, doctor?"

"You mean," Kay said as Cummings nodded, "someone used *my* spider to kill him?"

"I won't go so far as to say that someone actually used yours," Cummings answered. "An unused, old-fashioned spider is as far as I'll go."

"But after you've given it an examination in the laboratory," Jonah said, "you can tell for sure if Kay's spider was *the* spider, can't you?"

Cummings shrugged. "You can find out many interesting things in a laboratory, but you don't always discover facts that are of any particular use or value to you. For example, Reinhold will probably be able to tell you in detail what fat was used as a coating. He'll find fingerprints. My own, say. D'you wear gloves when you shop, Kay?"

"Usually. I did today. And I kept my gloves on when I came home, because I had to carry that kerosene can down cellar—I've been thinking about that," Kay said, "and I'm almost sure that I never touched that spider with my bare hands."

"Well, then, that's that!" Jonah said. "If your prints aren't on it, you couldn't have used it! Right, doctor?"

"You may well find," Cummings said, "that Hanson will argue that she is therefore guilty as hell, because otherwise her prints would have appeared. In Hanson's bright lexicon, a glove-wearer is a low and cunning crook who wishes to conceal his fingerprints from the authorities."

"By the same token," Jonah said, "I suppose a person who leaves fingerprints is a low and stupid crook who didn't know any better?"

"Exactly!"

"In short," Jonah said, "you can't win?"

"With Hanson," Cummings said, "it's sometimes hard sledding. Not that the fellow hasn't his good points, mind you. He's magnificent with traffic jams and drunks and lady drivers and petty larceny, and he hits the nail on the head pretty often in bigger things. And he's honest as the day is long. He simply has certain mental limitations."

"That," Jonah said, "is what I call being charitable with lemon sauce."

"I know Hanson well," Cummings returned, "and I try to be philosophic. Anyway, Ives, Reinhold may pick up my prints, or those of any Tom, Dick, or Harry who's happened to caress that spider in the last year or so. But I wouldn't kid myself that he'd find a lock of Mundy's hair, or even a spear of it. And assume that he did, and that we could say without qualifications, 'This is the spider that bashed Mundy!' You still wouldn't know who held the spider, would you? That's why I said that Hanson and Asey had a job ahead of them."

"D'you really think my spider was the one?" Kay asked.

"I hate being pinned down," Cummings said. "I don't know. Frankly, I don't think so. If he was killed at Asey's, why wouldn't the murderer have used the spider already there in the buttery—if he was so crazy about spiders? Only, of course, that one is aged and timeworn, and couldn't have left that mark. I can't think why anyone should kill him there with a spider taken from here, either—Asey, what do you think? You must think something; you've been sitting there like a sphinx. D'you think someone set out to kill Mundy with Kay's spider over his shoulder, like a musket? You think someone took it from here, and then brought it back?"

"Wa-el," Asey said, "there's always the purloined-letter angle, to leave it here so's nobody'll think anything of it. But as you say, cartin' a spider around seems sort of silly. Seemed silly to find one in the Hazards' back seat."

"*They* had one?" Jonah said. "Oh, no! They never did!"

"That was my reaction, too," Kay said. "I thought

that was fantastic! But what d'you think Hanson will think, Asey?"

"That's what *I* worry about, what *he* thinks," Jonah said. "Or what he will think, after Little Buttercup's finished telling him her life story—look, I've got an idea! Let's tell Hanson that the spider in the cellar is mine!"

"You'll do nothing of the sort!" Kay protested.

"I'm not offering myself up as a martyr," Jonah said. "It can't incriminate me any, and it may save you a lot of to-do. See, Kay, if Hanson voices any base suspicions about me, I have what the books call a perfect alibi. June and I left Jennie's together and proceeded to Silver Springs, the problem spot. At Jennie's orders, June and I hunted Tuesome the hell and gone over the Silver Marsh, and then we drifted over to Great Meadow, where the Army stepped in and took charge of me. So Hanson can't claim that I had any time or opportunity to move Phil—oho! Oh, brother!"

Jonah sat back in his chair and gave an ecstatic little hoot.

"What's come over you?" Cummings wanted to know.

"Brain wave—funny how the most obvious things fade out of your mind in this sort of thing, isn't it? Kay, where'd you get that spider?"

"At Bob Corner's."

"I bought mine from him, too," Jonah pulled out

his pipe and filled it. "And while we are not seven, like the old poem, sugar, we're certainly six!"

"What're you talking about?" Cummings demanded. "You feel all right?"

"When I went to get the mail this morning," Jonah said, "I looked into Bob's store window, and there were six iron spiders displayed therein. A fine, symmetrical array, with cold chisels and blackout lights and axes and Sterno stoves neatly arranged around 'em. On my way back from the post office, I dropped in and bought one. You bought one. The Hazards bought one—why, for God's sakes, I wonder?"

"They hoped it would make a nice pro tem bomb scoop," Asey said. "They told me so."

"Oh, those poor lambs!" Jonah said. "They try so hard! First they had sixty buckets of sand in their attic, then someone told 'em incendiaries would burn right down to their cellar, so all sixty pails got taken to the cellar at once. Then they felt so unprotected, they took half the pails back up to the attic again. Then they read a book on home defense and decided to line their attic with four inches of loose sand, and three ceilings fell in under the weight. Then they dispersed buckets of sand all over the house—frankly, it's the tiredest-looking sand I ever saw!"

"Have you seen it since they mixed it with that Kelly-green chemical?" Kay asked. "It haunts you.

You simply can't take your eyes off it. But, Jonah, even if there were six spiders at Bob's, that doesn't get us anywhere!"

"Oh, yes, it does! When I pedaled along to Jennie's tonight, I noticed that the spiders had all gone from Bob's window, and that six corn poppers had taken their place. So that leaves you three spiders to track down, Asey."

"Four," Asey said. "The Hazards' spider up an' disappeared. Huh!"

"Three or four, what does it matter? Point is, Kay's isn't the only new and unused old spider that could have been used to kill Phil," Jonah said. "It doesn't seem possible that every spider purchaser could have been sufficiently whimsical to sit right down and season their respective spiders the instant they got home. If Br'er Hanson—"

"If Hanson what?" Hanson himself loomed in the doorway.

"If Br'er Hanson," Jonah said calmly, "wishes to make anything of Kay's new and unused spider being in the cellar, then Br'er Hanson has to take into account the fact that other and potentially lethal spiders are at large, also. To catch you up with current events, when we refer to a lethal spider, we don't mean that a spider bit Phil—"

"It hit him. I know." Hanson said. "I been listening

to you for some time, out in the hall here. He was hit with an iron spider, and Kay Mundy bought one to-day."

"Oh, come, come, Hanson!" Cummings said. "You don't have to say that in quite such ominously fateful tones! You sound like the Voice of Doom in a drama-tized news broadcast! After all, this seems to have been Spider Day in East Aspinnet. Everyone bought one. Kay's having a spider doesn't—"

"Where's that will?"

"On the desk." Asey handed it to him.

Hanson read the will, tucked it away in his inside pocket, stuck his thumbs in his belt and started teeter-ing back and forth on his heels.

Cummings and Asey exchanged looks. They knew what that teetering meant.

"Hanson," Asey said, "I don't know as I'd go leapin' into anythin' without a lot of due thought."

"Hanson," Cummings said, "I second that motion and hurriedly offer a little amendment that hasn't as yet been aired. You'd better see Mundy—"

"I been down and seen him," Hanson said. "I looked him over."

"Well, go look again," Cummings retorted, "be-cause—"

"Has she got a motive?" Hanson said. "Yes. Was she seen near Asey's? Yes. Did she have a car? Yes. Did she have the time and the opportunity to bring the body back here? She did. Did she have an iron spider in her possession? She did. Anyone else have a motive? No. So there you are."

"How d'you know nobody else's got a motive?" Asey asked.

"June says her father hasn't an enemy in the world," Hanson said. "June says—"

"Look, did it ever occur to you that June might just possibly not be the ideal informer?" Jonah demanded. "Did you ever stop to think that that brat—"

"Listen, I don't want any cracks about that poor little kid!" Hanson said. "She's been through a lot, and she's sure kept her chin up and done her best to help track down her daddy's murderer. Now, Miss Mundy, you might as well come along with me right now. June's put a few things together for you, and there's no sense wasting any more time. Come on!"

Cummings shot a questioning look at Asey, and then sauntered over and stood behind Jonah's chair.

Five minutes later, when the front door had closed behind Hanson and Kay, Jonah jumped up and indignantly turned on Asey and the doctor.

"Why'd you let him get away with that? Why'd you keep me from saying anything? What'd you hold me down in that chair for? What the hell is the matter with you two? What're you thinking of? Are you crazy?"

"Calm down!" Cummings said. "We know Hanson.

I told Kay not to worry, we'd take care of everything. She understands."

"But can Hanson *do* a thing like this? *Can* he snatch her off?"

"He already has," Cummings said. "Bear in mind, Ives, that Hanson's had a hard time with an up-Cape blackout this evening, and he's cross and sleepy. We could have wasted the rest of the night talking his ear off, and we wouldn't have changed his mind. He's sending an ambulance here, and Reinhold will see to things, and now we can sit back and go to work in peace and quiet—where'd June go?"

"I hope," Jonah said, "that she's got sense enough to stay out of my way! Where'd she go, d'you know, Asey?"

"I suspect she took that coupe," Asey looked out of the window. "Yup. It's gone. I thought I heard it— doc, what was it you found out besides about the spider rim an' the smudge mark?"

"Come see. I could have shown it to Hanson, but he wouldn't have cared."

"When was Phil killed?" Jonah asked as they went down the stairs to the cellar.

"Somewhere between—oh, five-thirty and seven, I'd say," Cummings told him. "Not much earlier, not much later. Now, Asey, take a good look at that spider, and then look at his head."

"Huh," Asey said. "Before I met up with Kay an'

June on the short cut, I had it in mind to do a little practical experimentin' with the Hazards' spider. I'd come to the conclusion that some of my first-thoughtin' didn't jibe, an' just lookin' at this spider, I can see how I went wrong. How do you figure he was hit, doc?"

"From above," Cummings said. "As if—well, say that someone was standing on your back doorstep, and Mundy stood on the ground in front of him, back to. I think Mundy turned just a fraction of an inch before he was hit, and that helped cause the rim mark. He wasn't hit with a full swing—that spider's heavy, and he could have been more badly damaged. But he was hit hard enough, God knows."

"Explain the little cut, will you?" Asey's drawl was drawlier than usual.

"I never made the slightest attempt to explain that," Cummings returned. "I don't intend to. That's your department."

"Didn't that come from the spider?" Jonah asked. "From contact with the rim?"

Asey smiled. "You're makin' the error I made. If you aimed to bash anyone with a spider, how'd you hold it, so you'd hit with the bottom first, or the rim first?"

"You'd hold it to hit bottom first, of course," Jonah said. "Bottom down, rim up, as you would if you were putting it on a stove—though I suppose you'd grip the handle with the back of your hand up. That sounds terribly involved, but I can visualize it very clearly."

"That's right," Asey said. "Now, holdin' it that way, how could the rim cause a cut? The rim made that mark. The cut's somethin' else again."

"I say, maybe that's just the clew you need! Maybe there was a roughness—a projection, rather—on the spider that would have made the cut! Then you could tell which spider out of all the spiders was used!" Jonah said enthusiastically. "Then you'd—"

"Whoa up, an' look at that spider of Kay's," Asey said. "Nice smooth cast iron. You won't find any projections on it. Or on any other."

"Then how *was* the cut made?" Jonah demanded. "If the rim didn't make it, or the pan—I've got it. Look, if you swung sideways, you might have made a cut, Asey!"

"You'd also have made a glancin' blow, which wouldn't have killed him. To be killed like he was, he had to of been hit a good bash," Asey said. "Look at his head, man! That wasn't any glancin' blow!"

"Maybe he was hit twice, then," Jonah said. "First a glancing blow—no, that wouldn't ever do. If someone hadn't killed him at once, Phil would have been at his throat. Well, suppose that he was bashed first, and then hit a glancing blow—no, damn it, that won't work either! Phil would be down on the ground, in that case, already dead. You wouldn't have anything to gain— oh, I give up! I always thought I'd make such a swell detective. I solve those little Minute Murders like clock-work every day in the papers—how do you explain it, Asey?"

"Wa-el," Asey said, "one's fact, an' one's fiction."

"I don't mean how do you explain my shortcomings in the detective world, I mean how do you explain the cut?"

"Come on, Codfish Sherlock," Cummings said. "Give us the benefit of your second thoughts."

"Elementary, my dear doctor, easy as pie," Asey said. "If the cut wasn't made by a spider, it was made by somethin' else."

"But what?" Cummings said. "*What?* That cut bled a bit—remember the stain on the sugar bag? Well, that cut had to be inflicted practically simultaneously with the bash, or very soon after. Damn, I wish I hadn't put that hood back! I wish I'd stuck it in my pocket! I'm sure we could have told something by the cutting of those slits—Ives, what do you First-Aiders get taught about bandaging for the face or the back of the head?"

"Um," Jonah said thoughtfully. "Um. For burns and scalds, usually. One of those triangle things. Tie a knot at the point, beginning knot down about six inches from the point. Stick the knot at the crown of the head, put the base down over the face and chin to the neck—d'you know, I'm impressed with myself! Bring the ends around back, cross 'em, bring 'em forward and tie under chin. Cut slits for eyes and nose if same are not injured.

A very eerie effect. We frightened each other to death."

"Ever use sugar bags?" Cummings asked.

"Some supervisor or other, a strapping veteran of World War One, clumped in one evening and showed us a lot of variations on different things," Jonah said. "She told us in France, they'd sometimes used bags, like sugar bags, for head problems—did they?"

"There were times in France," Cummings said, "when funnier things than sugar bags were put into use. So she showed you about bag hoods?"

Jonah nodded. "She showed how they'd keep certain types of dressings in place. We were delighted with that bag idea until after she left, and Jennie acidly pointed out that our future chances of having any vast supply of head-size sugar bags were virtually nil."

"Did this supervisor come just to Jennie's class?" Asey asked.

Jonah grinned. "No, she visited around—we heard the repercussions. Some of the instructors got sore because she wandered so far from the textbook, but we all thought she made a very useful point in suggesting that occasionally you'd have to use some ingenuity."

"Well," Cummings said, "then anyone in this area might have known about sugar bags. That doesn't help. Asey, who came to Jennie's class first?"

"Corner said the Hazards got there first, but didn't go in. He thinks either Mrs. Tuesome or Tiny Hazard went in first—you know, Ives?"

"I came last—Asey, d'you mean that Phil was killed *before* class, that he was out in your shed all *during* class? Why—why, all of us—say, I never thought of that when I was so cocksure of having a perfect alibi! It would matter as much what people did before class as what they were doing afterwards!" Jonah sounded dazed. "Hey, someone must have known about class time, and our being there!"

"Uh-huh," Asey said. "That's why they left Mundy there, an' come back later, I think."

"But what a chance they took! Suppose Jennie'd found him!"

"Suppose she had," Cummings said. "What of it? We found him, and he confused us."

"Someone must have known all about Jennie's comings and goings, and her plans—no, when you think it over, I don't suppose they were taking so much of a chance at that. If you were awarding a medal for violent activity on the home front, Jennie would get it hands down, and there wouldn't be a dissenting vote from Weesit to Pochet. It's a local legend that she's home only to sleep."

"She's not even botherin' to do that, tonight," Asey said.

"But look, you can assume that the person who killed Mundy brought him here, can't you? Well, June and I hadn't any chance to bring him here, and the Hazards were tied up—where was Bob Corner?"

"I found him wandering around Hell Hollow for Tuesome," Cummings said.

Jonah laughed. "He skipped the last hunt, and Jennie tongue-lashed him to a pulp. I had a feeling he'd never dare skip again. Where was Tuesome, did anyone ever find her?"

"She skipped and spent the evenin' playin' bridge," Asey said. "Winnin' thereby a dollar an' sixty cents for Henry the pig."

Jonah shook his head.

"Tuesome'll regret that!" he said. "Jennie'll probably make her knit ten sweaters for bluejackets, or give umpteen pints of blood to the Red Cross for penance—well, that leaves only Tiny Hazard, and heaven knows she'd never kill Phil!"

Asey wanted to know why not.

"Why, she's definitely smitten with Phil! Kay's only admitted lately that she thinks so, too, but I guessed it long ago," Jonah said. "Just after Christmas, Tiny was reproaching me for not being in the service, and she told me then that Phil was her idea of a true patriot, tireless in his efforts for his country, and so on. I guessed then that the glow in her eyes when she mentioned his name wasn't all love of country."

"Why *are*n't you in the service?" Cummings asked bluntly.

"I was born in Canada," Jonah said, "although my family moved to the States shortly afterwards. It worked out fine, at first. I served as a photographer with the Canadians, and then I got invalided home—"

"Oh, so that's why you wear that fool beard!" Cummings said. "Scars, eh?"

Jonah nodded and went on quickly. "Now I'm waiting while people make up their minds as to my status, whether I'm a friendly alien, or a near citizen—I've got first papers, and I rather hope to get into our Signal Corps, after I've discussed the situation with thirty million more people and waded through several more thousand yards of red tape."

"Why in thunder didn't you tell people, instead of letting us call you a spy?"

"Oh, I was just contributing to morale," Jonah said with a grin. "People enjoy a good spy. Takes their minds off their troubles. Besides, everything's so balled up, there's nothing much to tell. And," he paused, "well, it kept Kay thinking about me."

"What about the eighteen female dependents?" Asey inquired.

"Oh," Jonah laughed. "One mother, four sisters, two horses, ten dogs, and a Persian cat. I thought that one got under her skin—Asey, it can't be any of us, of Jennie's class! In my maddest dreams I couldn't picture the Hazards bashing anyone or anything! Why, the other day I heard Sterling Hazard automatically say 'Sorry! I beg your pardon!' when he bumped against Tuesome's horse!"

"Could you," Asey said, "picture Sterlin' smackin' his wife in the face?"

"Smacking Grace? On the day he did a thing like that," Jonah said, "the oceans will dry up, and the sky fall!"

"Wa-el," Asey said, "without any rumblin' accompaniments from nature, he did just that tonight."

"I don't believe it," Jonah said flatly.

"Me, either," Cummings added.

"But he did, an' I seen him do it," Asey said, "an' it should ought to go to show you that you can't always sometimes tell."

"I suppose you speak the truth," Jonah said, "but it —well, it shatters my faith in human nature. And you said they got to your house first—no. No, I can't think that of them! Those dear, fine people!"

"There was once a pitchfork murder which I attended—in a purely professional capacity, of course," Cummings said. "And following it, twelve men appeared at intervals, all bearing pitchforks. All of 'em were deacons in the church, or otherwise godly and reliable citizens. Very interesting case. One of my favorites."

"Who did it?" Jonah asked.

"The pitchforked man's dear old white-haired grandmother," Cummings said. "Since boyhood, he'd refused to wipe his feet on the mat before coming into her clean kitchen, and one day she said if he didn't wipe his feet, she'd kill him, and he didn't, and she did. What're you going to do now, Asey?"

"Call Bob Corner an' ask him about the spider situation."

Corner, finally brought to the phone by an irritated landlady, sleepily said that he had sold two iron spiders.

"One to Kay, one to Jonah Ives. The others went like hotcakes, the clerk said, but I don't know whom he sold 'em to. Look, if they were charged, I could tell—want me to open up the store and get the slips? I'd be glad to."

"Simpler to ask the clerk," Asey said. "Who is he?"

"Willard Thomas. He lives in your town, on Briar Lane."

"Thomas?" Asey couldn't remember any family named Thomas.

"T-h-o-m-a-s." Corner spelled it. "In that house with the gingerbread porch. Briar Lane."

"Oh, the old Fuller place. Okay, I'll go see him right away. What's that? How are things going on? Wa-el, Hanson's taken Kay Mundy off, but—"

Asey waited while Corner, now thoroughly wakened and aroused, expressed his vigorous indignation.

"No," he said when Corner finally stopped for breath, "I don't think she did, either. No, I wouldn't worry about callin' in lawyers an' such, right now. No, I don't think you can do a thing to help, thanks. What? Oh, well if I want to look at your records, I'll follow your suggestion an' bust that little windowpane right in. Okay. Sorry to have bothered you. Good night."

"What's the story?" Cummings asked, as Asey joined him and Jonah in the kitchen.

"I'm goin' to interview his clerk," Asey said. "Come get your bike an' spider, Jonah. I'm takin' the Porter."

"Can I go with you?"

"Better stay with me." Cummings caught the flicker of Asey's eyebrows. "Then if I have to leave on a hurry call before the ambulance comes, you can hold the fort."

"Where is this ambulance, anyway?" Jonah asked.

"Oh, probably it was at its blackout station," Cummings said, "and there's been some hitch or other getting it here. Asey, you won't be long, will you? Then you come back here, and if I've gone, I'll leave a note for you. By the way, aren't you pretty tired?"

"Funny thing," Asey said, "I'm not as tired as when I come!"

"Hm. Well, remember the speed limit!"

Asey dutifully put the Porter along the shore road at a snail's pace.

What bothered him most of all about this business of Mundy was something he found difficult to put into so many words. It was a feeling that the background mattered as much as the method; that the backdrop against which he had been killed was as important as the iron spider that killed him.

Here was Mundy who had lost everything he'd

worked to get patriotically steaming around trying to get things done, not caring two hoots whose toes he stepped on in the process. And all around him people were steaming, like Jennie. What with practically being imbedded in the Porter plant, Asey thought, he hadn't begun to realize to what extent things had changed, how many extra things people did, or in how many ways their lives had been touched, or curtailed.

There were the Hazards, transplanted from the city, wistfully trying to do the right thing and act the right way, moving their overworked sand around, trying to improvise bomb scoops, being ordered around by Jennie—it was a far cry from prewar Beacon Street, Asey guessed!

There were the bicycles, the horse and buggy, Tiny's old car with its unrationed, obsolete tires. And Jennie's slacks, the blue yarn in the refrigerator, the mileage chart for Mundy's car, the secretiveness of the phone girl, the darkened lanes, the casual talk of blackouts, of ships torpedoed offshore, the speed limit, and all the rest of it.

Adding it up, Asey thought, it would be hard to plan a murder, and harder to commit one after you'd planned it. You couldn't ever quite tell where your victim might be, what he might be doing, or how many people might be watching you from a spotter's station, or how many people might suddenly fly to the scene on a problem of one sort or another.

A bash suggested a spur-of-the-moment killing.

There was nothing premeditated about a bash. Suppose you had a spider, though, Asey thought. What an ideal time to use it—not only Jonah would have had the opportunity of noting that the six spiders in the store window had given way to six corn poppers!

"All right," Asey said aloud. "Say it was some brilliant spur-of-the-moment thinkin'! But from then on, he planned well!"

Putting Mundy in the buttery, moving him later—that had been well planned. And nobody had been dumb enough to show their hand.

What puzzled him was that pair of brown sneakers!

Why should anyone take off Mundy's rubber boots, put on brown sneakers, then put the rubber boots back on again?

"Let's see, now, why does anyone take off rubber boots? Why do I? Oh, golly, I'm dumb! Because they're wet!"

The answer was almost startling in its simplicity, but it seemed logical enough. Mundy's rubber boots had been wet, and the murderer hadn't wished to leave any trail of incriminating drip over Jennie's spotless floors.

But why had anyone bothered to put on a pair of new brown sneakers in place of the boots?

Asey shook his head and dismissed as quickly as it came his inspiration to call on the local drygoods stores in the morning. You could have bought sneakers anywhere, months ago, and still possibly happened to have had them with you. Those brown sneakers weren't anything he could track down, certainly not on the basis of what he remembered of them after a brief glance.

He slowed the Porter down to a standstill as he spotted a dangling red light in the middle of the road ahead.

"For Pete's sakes!"

The light came from a red lantern hanging from the rear of a buggy.

"It can't be Tuesome's!" Asey got out, peered inside, recognized the china form of Henry the pig, and whistled softly to himself.

It was Mrs. Tuesome's buggy all right, although why Mrs. Tuesome should be wandering around the beach at three in the morning, Asey couldn't imagine.

He walked quickly across the road to the beach grass, stood there for a moment, and then strode on along toward the water's edge.

He had left the Porter in such a position that its headlights slanted across the sand and gave him just enough light to make out the figure of Mrs. Tuesome, to see her throw something a few feet, run after it and pick it up, and then throw it again.

As he neared her, Asey found that what he suspected was quite true.

Mrs. Tuesome was laboriously attempting to cast an iron spider into the sea!

CHAPTER EIGHT

AND, FURTHERMORE, Mrs. Tuesome was so occupied with her chore that she neither heard Asey nor apparently had any inkling of his presence until he lunged forward and grabbed the iron spider out of the teeth of the undertow.

But once she caught on to the idea that she had an active and participating audience, Mrs. Tuesome made up for lost time by screaming wildly at the top of her lungs.

"Stop it!" Asey said firmly. "Turn around and march back to the road. What's the meanin' of this, anyway?"

At the sound of his voice, Mrs. Tuesome turned off her screams as if they were controlled by a faucet.

"If it isn't Asey Mayo!" she said cordially. "I must say, I'm so glad to see you! I've been frightened to *death* down here, but it was absolutely the only way I could think of!"

"Just what," Asey demanded, "was your underlyin' thought?"

"Why to get rid of that ghastly spider, of course! It was simply *haunt*ing me!" she shivered elaborately. "Oh! I almost called you to ask what you thought I ought to do—it isn't a very easy thing to dispose of, and of course *you* know all about disposing of things. Men," she added with a little sigh, "always seem to know *so* much!"

"Why were you tryin' to throw it away?"

"I tell you, it was haunting me! And it's such a *permanent* sort of thing! You can't burn it up! And I couldn't bear the thought of giving it to anyone else, and I couldn't endure keeping it—I mean, it would always *stab* me every time I looked at it, and of course, I think it's a horrible thing to use. So hard to keep it *smell*ing clean! And it would have been blatant sacrilege to give it for salvage. After all, you can't buy a present for a very, *very* dear friend, and then have someone phone you that he's been *killed*, and then callously give the present for salvage. *Can* you? I mean, not even for Victory!"

"Do I gather," Asey said, "that you bought this spider as a present for Phil Mundy?"

Mrs. Tuesome nodded, and then blew her nose with a wisp of a handkerchief.

"He's been wanting an iron spider for *so* long! The

poor dear, dear! He used to tell me about his mother making him—"

"Pancakes. I know. Were you at the Clarks' all evenin'?"

"I must confess it," Mrs. Tuesome said, "I really *was!* I know it was *dread*fully wicked of me to run away from the problem, and I do wish," she put her hand on his arm, "I really do *hope* that you'll explain to Jennie about my neuritis? I simply couldn't face that east wind tonight, I *knew* it would bring on my neuritis! Of course, Jennie's *so* vigorous, she simply can't understand what it is to suffer!"

"An' you never left the Clarks all evenin'?"

"It was just so cosy there in front of their fire, I just stayed and stayed. They simply had to *push* me out! Even when Sally and Joe and Albert Morris all rushed to a test call, I just stayed right in front of that perfectly lovely fire and played solitaire. I have the *grand*est new solitaire," she said as they came to the buggy. "You put down eight cards—"

"Uh-huh. How long were they gone at this test?"

"It was an Auxiliary Fireman thing," Mrs. Tuesome said, "and the Austins' truck wouldn't start, it was loaded with so much equipment—oh, it took them *simp*ly ages! I got this new solitaire twice, they were gone so long, and it takes *hours!* You put down eight cards, then six, and then—"

"I'm sure it's a mighty fascinatin' game," Asey said. "Was you alone two hours, say?"

"It must have been all of that, I'm sure. Because I listened to six different commentators on the radio, from Peter Paul Bray to Marvin G. Rouser. Now tell me, *you*'re in a position to know about such things, *is* our Navy—"

"Jennie's husband Syl is the naval expert in our family," Asey said. "Now, you get into your buggy, an' you an' Henry jog right along home. Good night!"

"Oh, you dear thing, *you*'re going to keep the spider and dispose of it for me, aren't you? What a *load* off my mind! I'm *so* relieved—do you think that if I promised never, *never* to skip again, and really to *learn* the problem spots, Jennie wouldn't scold?"

"The least you can get off with," Asey recalled Jonah's prophecy, "is six sweaters for bluejackets an' a couple pints of blood for the Red Cross. Good night!"

He could hear her fluttery little moans as he got into the Porter, put the spider on the seat beside him, and drove off.

Both Hanson and Cummings had assumed that Mundy's body must have been moved in a car, but a buggy would have done just as well. It would have been no trick at all, he thought, for Mrs. Tuesome to have jogged back to his house while the rest of Jennie's class were assembling at Silver Springs, and then to have jogged over to Mundy's in East Aspinnet while the class searched for her. Then, too, she had a couple of hours later in the evening during which she might have jogged anywhere, reasonably secure in the knowledge that the class would probably still be scouring the swamps and meadows, as they invariably did.

But it was Asey's impression that if the woman couldn't manage to manipulate a spider well enough to throw it into the broad Atlantic, she could hardly be expected to swing it, accurately and soundly, against the back of Phil Mundy's head!

"No," Asey said to himself, "I don't think so! If she couldn't hit the ocean, I don't think she could have hit him. She never—"

He gave an exclamation of triumph as his headlights picked up the figure of a broad-beamed woman pumping a bicycle up the road ahead.

Slacks, leather jacket, handkerchief wound around her head!

At long last, Jennie herself!

Asey drove the Porter past her and turned so that the car blocked the road, then jumped out, ran up to her and planted a hearty kiss on her cheek.

"Where in time have you been? It's—it's—it's—"

Asey took a hurried step backward and swallowed hard.

The woman wasn't Jennie at all!

"It's—I'm sure," he had seldom felt much sillier, "I'm

awful sorry. I beg your pardon. I thought you—uh—"

"You thought what?" the woman was rigid with indignation.

"I thought you was my cousin Jennie. Jennie Mayo. I'm sorry."

"Isn't it enough for you to go around practically assaulting a perfect stranger," the woman said coldly, "without insulting me, too? Jennie Mayo weighs twenty pounds more than I do, and she's fifteen years older if she's a day!"

"I'm sorry," Asey said, "but from the r—but as I seen you, comin' up from behind—uh—wa-el, ma'am, at night all cats are black."

"I should not think you'd have the arrant audacity to be frivolous!" the woman said. "Allow me to inform you that I am Miss Pease of the Aspinnet Township High School, and I'm not a cat—at night, or any other time! We have, moreover, a law in this town about hindering or obstructing Civilian Defense workers, and if you don't get on your way, you're going to get *this*," she drew something from her pocket, "right in the *face!* And in case you can't see what it is, allow me to inform you that it's a water pistol filled with ammonia! And if I hear or catch sight of your annoying any more women, I shall have you arrested and prosecuted to the fullest extent of the law!"

"You won't, ma'am!" Asey told her with deep sincerity. "Good night!"

He all but scurried back to the Porter, and the big car shot out of sight just as fast as Asey could make it shoot.

He was less than half a mile from his goal of Briar Lane and the house of Corner's clerk when the headlights revealed what seemed to be a wrecked car, pulled off to the side of the main road.

He craned his neck and looked as he went by, and then he braked, and backed up.

It was Tiny Hazard's old Buick, apparently abandoned, but no more of a wreck than it had appeared to be when it had been parked down by his picket fence.

"I say!" a muffled voice came dimly to him. "I say, there!"

Asey leaned across the seat, opened the right-hand front door, and looked out.

The light from the Porter's interior showed a grubby face peering up at him from underneath the Buick.

"I say, d'you have a flashlight, or would you be willing to aim your headlights so I could see for just a second? I say!" Tiny Hazard wriggled out and got to her feet. "Isn't that Mr. Hazard's car? Oh, were you sent to hunt me up?"

"No, your father just lent me this for the time bein'," Asey said as he got out. "My name is Mayo. Asey Mayo."

"Oh, really? How do you *do?*"

Asey found his hand gripped in what felt like an iron

vise, vigorously shaken, and he barely resisted the temptation, when his hand was finally dropped, to see if it had been returned with all five fingers intact. He couldn't feel even one.

"I'm glad to meet you," Tiny went on. "If that's father's car, there'll be a flashlight in the glove compartment—mind holding it for me?"

Asey turned around and fished out the flashlight with his left hand.

"If you'll tell me what you think is wrong, I might maybe be able to fix it for you."

"Oh, I've just finished driving a joint pin into the universal," Tiny said casually. "I want to take a look at the other—my light gave out, and I hadn't any matches. Just hold that while I see."

Asey bent down and watched her while she squirmed underneath the car, glanced around professionally, gave a couple of experimental taps with the head of a wrench, and rolled out.

"It's okay," she said. "You know, I've been intending to write and ask if you had any place for women in tanks—don't waste that light, put it out. I think tanks would be rather fun."

"If," Asey obediently snapped out the light, "you went at tanks as easy as you seem to've gone at this, I feel sure you'd have fun. How come this car goes?"

"I drove it to the Coast last year on a bet, and I had so many extra sets of tires made, I thought it was only right and practical to drive the car and use the tires. They aren't any good to anyone else, and after all, every ounce of rubber is a national trust." She paused. "Well, thanks a lot."

"Takes somethin' to drive, don't it?"

"I prefer it to being in that!" Tiny pointed a scornful finger at the Porter. "I can't breathe in that effete thing—I'll be all right now, thanks. Don't bother waiting till I get started."

"Glad to crank her for you." Asey wondered if it was her intention to try and ease him away without ever mentioning Phil Mundy. He was sure she had been the person he'd pursued through the East Aspinnet woods, and if she'd looked into the window of that lighted cellar, as Kay said she had, then she knew about Mundy. Even if she didn't know he had been killed, the briefest glance would have been ample to assure her that he was dead. After all, June had learned of her father's murder, Mrs. Tuesome had been informed of it by telephone— it certainly seemed as though Tiny should have picked up somewhere the additional information that Mundy had been killed.

"Can I crank her for you?" he asked again.

"No, thanks. I can manage very nicely, thank you."

"You're quite a mechanic." Asey decided to see what would happen if he kept the conversational ball rolling. "Take a course?"

"I went to Tech," Tiny said. "I always think a

woman should be able to do everything a man does, just as well as he does, if not better. Well, I won't keep you. If you happen to hear of an opening for women in tanks, I'd be glad to know about it. Good night!"

She reached past him, picked a crank up off the front seat, and walked rather quickly toward the front of the car.

"Here, let me give you some light, then." Asey snapped on the flashlight. "Might as well have a little light on what you're doin'."

"I can crank this car blindfolded," Tiny said. "And do turn off that light! I hate to see people wasting batteries. They're scarce!"

That made twice, Asey thought, that she had ordered him to turn off the light. Was she really being thrifty, or was it just possible that there was something she didn't want him to see?

Turning around, he flashed the light over the front seat, and then ran it over the cushionless back seat.

"Are those—er—iron spiders," his voice was purring a little, "that I see in back there, on the floor?"

"Yes. Salvage," Tiny said. "Well, I'm going to crank her now. Good-by."

"First," Asey sauntered up to her, "tell me about those spiders. How come you happen to have two, Miss Hazard?"

Tiny straightened up, put her hands on her hips, and looked down at him.

"Why shouldn't I give two iron spiders for salvage, if I wish to?"

"Miss Hazard," Asey said, "there's somethin' in your tone that sort of insinuates that before you break down an' tell me the truth about these spiders, or anything else, I've got to prove I'm a better man than you are. Now, do you honestly think we're goin' to gain anything by prolongin' this fencin', or by turnin' it into a rough-an'-tumble? You know about Phil Mundy's bein' murdered, don't you?"

Tiny hesitated. "Yes," she said at last.

"An' you know, or at least you ought to be able to guess, that I'm tryin' to do somethin' about it. You did guess, didn't you? Yes, I thought so. An' you was a friend of his. You liked him, didn't you?"

"I intended to marry him," Tiny said.

"Oh," Asey said. "So you was engaged?"

"No, but I intended to marry him."

"I see." Perhaps, Asey thought to himself, it might be wiser not to comment on that. "Now, why did you come to Mundy's house a while ago? Don't say you didn't, please, because I chased you, an' I know you was there."

"Oh, I say, was that *you?*" Tiny said interestedly. "You run awfully well! Very well indeed! I like men in condition—so many men are soft, don't you think?"

"Uh-huh. Why were you there?"

"Oh, at the hardware store this morning, I noticed

they had some iron spiders," Tiny said, "and I knew Phil wanted one. His mother used to—"

"I know." Asey was beginning to get a little tired of those pancakes that mother used to make. "So you 'bought him a spider for his birthday. Er—what impelled you to deliver it tonight?"

"Well, there were six spiders in the window this morning," Tiny said, "but I noticed tonight when I drove past that they were all gone, and from something Mildred Tuesome said at class this evening—I suppose you know we go to your cousin Jennie's for First Aid class?"

"That fact," Asey said, "has got driven home to me. Go on."

"Well, from something Mildred said, I rather suspected she'd bought one for Phil, too. So—" Tiny hesitated, "so, when I went past Phil's tonight and saw lights, I thought I'd just give him mine and get ahead of her."

"That sounds fine," Asey said, "except that you wouldn't see the lights there, drivin' past, an' furthermore, your car was parked way up back of the woods."

"I say, you *are* smart, aren't you!" Tiny sounded impressed. "I mean, it's so unusual to find a man who can run also having brains. Actually, I parked my car way up on the road because I wanted to leave the spider on the back doorstep with a little birthday note—just casually telling what time it was, of course."

"Why?" Asey wanted to know.

"Well, I decided that the spider Phil got first would mean the most to him, and because I rather think that Mildred Tuesome intended to marry Phil, too, I wanted *my* spider to be there first. Then I saw father's Porter, and the cellar light was on, and I couldn't imagine what father might be doing there at that time, and then I looked in, and saw Phil."

"Why'd you run when Kay called out?"

Tiny hesitated. "Well, I suppose I might as well tell the truth. I always think honesty is really the best policy. Half the reason I parked up the lane and came through the woods was that I didn't want Kay to see me or know I was there. She's the—well, the smart, sophisticated type, don't you think?"

"To be honest," Asey said, "I hadn't thought of her that way."

"Well, you know how New Yorkers *are*. Not that I don't think some New Yorkers are quite nice," Tiny added hurriedly, "but of course most of them are soft, and really rather effete, and they talk so flippantly. Kay is quite flippant. I was afraid she might think it was funny if she saw me coming there with a spider. I don't really see how people can laugh the way she and Jonah Ives do, over nothing at all! *I* think things are serious, don't you? And particularly now, with the nation's very existence at stake, it doesn't seem they should laugh so much!"

"Wa-el," Asey bit his lip. "As long as they don't impede the war effort, I don't think it matters if they laugh an' sing from morn till night, like the Miller on the Dee. Let's see, now. You parked up the road because you was afraid Kay might see you an' make some wisecrack. Go on."

"When I first saw Phil, I thought he'd fallen, and then I had the most awful feeling that if father was there, he and Phil might have had another fight," Tiny said. "You see, father threw an inkwell at Phil last week, and mother has been nervous about the two of them ever since. Sometimes father really loses control of himself —I simply can't get him to take enough exercise, that's the real trouble. I always say that a soft body makes for a soft mind. Don't you think so?"

"I'm not much of a hand," Asey said, "for generalizin'. Uh—does your father often strike your mother?"

He felt that he was asking the equivalent of the old "When-did-you-stop-beating-your-wife" question, but with Tiny, you couldn't broach a subject tactfully. You had to jump right in.

"When he's really angry, he either throws something, or strikes the first person who's handy," Tiny said. "I tell him that regular exercise makes for self-control, but he says that men of his age only exercise to keep their weight down, and his weight *is* down."

"Uh-huh. So you saw Phil lyin' there, an' was worryin' about maybe your father might have fought with him. That right? Then Kay called out, an' you got panicky, an' run—did you have the spider with you durin' that sprint?"

"I used to be rather good in the Olympics," Tiny said modestly. "I say, are *you* married?"

"No," Asey said quickly. "So now you aim to give the spider for salvage, do you? Uh—without any tears?"

"I always say you might as well be practical about things," Tiny said. "After all, you can't cry over spilled milk. You have to keep your chin up. And it isn't as if we were really engaged. One's country comes first, anyway. It needs iron. I say, didn't you ever find the right woman?"

Asey drew a long breath. On the whole, he thought, he preferred quizzing Mildred Tuesome, even at the risk of contributing to Henry the pig. Or June, even if it involved the brandishing of carving knives.

"You're a director of Porter Motors, aren't you?" Tiny said absently. "Mm. Father couldn't possibly disapprove of Porter Motors. He's always had a Porter or two. He couldn't call *you* a common garageman!"

"Was that what he called Phil Mundy?"

"When he was annoyed with him. Father," Tiny said with a little sigh, "is so particular, and of course it's only practical to think of the trust fund, and his consent, and all. D'you do much mountain climbing?"

"High altitudes," Asey decided that Miss Hazard

should be nipped in the bud, "affect me somethin' awful. I can't take an elevator in the Empire State Buildin'. I can't even climb Cannon Hill without gaspin'. What about that second spider you got in back there? Where'd you get that?"

"Oh, that's the family's. At least, it was on the seat of the Porter. You see, I noticed the car parked outside the drugstore, earlier, and I stopped to ask mother if Mildred Tuesome had been found. And when I opened the door, the light went on and I saw a spider, and of course I thought mother must have taken mine from the Buick when it was parked out in front of your house—that's really quite a nice house of yours," Tiny almost sounded pensive. "With a tennis court and a good pool—"

"Is your mother," Asey interrupted firmly, "in the habit of swipin' things from your car?"

"She and father are both so afraid someone will suspect they're hoarding something!" Tiny said. "Why, we were using saccharin and honey months ago, because they felt they should set an example and not buy sugar! Now I always say that if you know things are going to be scarce, it's only practical to stock up. You can't tell, in these trying days, what may lie ahead, can you? I bought five dozen spark plugs and some batteries and odds and ends like that, and mother and father took them right back! They sent back the blankets, and the suits, too—I think it was only practical to buy a dozen suits, don't you? After all, I shouldn't have to buy any suits for years. Wool is wool. And—"

"Look," Asey said, "let me get this straight. You seen the spider in the Porter outside the drugstore, an' you took it, thinkin' it was yours an' that your mother had taken it from your car, because you think she might've thought—golly, this gets hard!—that you'd just bought the spider to hoard. Is *that* the story?"

"Why, yes," Tiny said simply.

"So you took it an' left—without botherin' to track down your mother, or to look an' see if your spider was in your car?"

"I was annoyed," Tiny said, "because I wasn't hoarding. I'd bought the spider for Phil. I thought mother and father had gone too far. So I put the spider in my car and drove off. I didn't know there were two until I found them when I stopped over by Phil's."

"How long did you hunt for Mrs. Tuesome at the swamp?"

"Until the tide came in—why do you want to know about the spiders?"

"Because," Asey said, "Phil Mundy was killed by a bash from one. What was you doin' this afternoon before you come to class?"

Tiny didn't answer, and Asey repeated the question rather sharply.

"I suppose honesty is the best policy," she said at last. "Father and I had rather a row."

"About Mundy?"

"Well, yes. I mean, whenever he's been provoked lately, he's always managed to bring in Phil's name," Tiny said. "But mostly it was about shoes. Well, not exactly shoes, either. Sneakers."

"So?" Asey said. "Just why?"

"The East Aspinnet Drygoods Store," Tiny said, "was having a sale of sneakers, and of course I wear through a pair of sneakers in no time at all, so I felt it was only practi—"

"I know. You went in," Asey said impatiently, "and bought up a few dozen pairs, didn't you?"

"Well, while I was at it, I thought it was only sensible to buy some for mother and father and all the servants. Father was very provoked," Tiny said, "when I brought the cases home—they really weren't cases, exactly. Just those large cardboard carton things. Anyway, he and mother decided that since it was a sale, the drygoods man probably wanted to get rid of them. And because there were all sizes and all kinds—"

"Includin' brown, I suppose?" Asey interrupted.

"Oh, yes, all colors. Anyway, father and mother decided that instead of returning them to the store, which might hurt the drygoods man's business, I should present them to the Red Cross. So I took them over to Jennie at the main workroom."

"So!" Asey said. "So! Was there anyone from Jennie's class there, by any chance?"

"Phil was there, and—"

"Phil was *there?*"

"Oh, yes, he often stops in and lends a hand with the harder work. And Mildred Tuesome dropped in to ask Jennie something about the Fireman's Drag and the Fireman's Carry."

"What'n time would she be wantin' to know about them for?" While such inquiries from Mrs. Tuesome would sound a little amazing under any circumstances, Asey thought, they took on a suspicious tinge when you considered the moving of Mundy's body.

"I can't imagine," Tiny said. "I suppose she's been reading in the back of the First Aid book again. I don't think it's sensible to read the back of any book till you come to it, do you? I mean, I think you should take things as they come. Father always reads the ends of mystery stories first, and I don't think it's *fair*."

"So Mundy an' Tuesome were there," Asey said. "Huh. An' Corner said *he* went there."

"Oh, yes, he came as I was leaving. He brought some nails. And I think probably mother and father came, later."

"Why d'you think that?"

"They told me," Tiny said, "that they meant to check up and see that the sneakers got to the Red Cross. You see, they found out that I'd kept a few spark plugs and batteries and suits and things, and now they insist on checking up."

"I see." Asey was beginning to understand how, after life with Tiny, the Hazards would have been quite able to take the Army in their stride. "Tell me, why didn't you give Phil his birthday spider when you seen him at the Red Cross?"

"I didn't suspect then that Mildred Tuesome had bought him one," Tiny said. "I didn't see until later that all the spiders were gone from Bob's window—are you getting cold?"

Now that he stopped to think of it, Asey realized that the east wind had become pretty bitter.

"Why, I—"

"Rather a coldish wind," Tiny went on. "I thought we might sit in the Porter. It would be much cosier."

"Why," Asey made a swift recovery, "I don't feel it a mite. Guess you must be—uh—out of condition, Miss Hazard. Now, I'm goin' to take the two spiders you got here," he reached over into the back seat of the Buick, "an'—ouch!"

"What's the matter?" Tiny asked solicitously.

"Cut my finger on some of your lattice-work floor— no, guess it's only a splinter. No matter. I'll just—"

"*Don't* put your finger in your mouth!" Tiny said severely. "Hold the flashlight in your other hand so I can see—oh, I'll fix that right up with my knife!"

From a lanyard around her neck, Tiny removed the largest and most murderous looking Scout knife that Asey had ever seen.

"Now," Tiny said brightly, "I'll have that out in no time!"

With lusty enthusiasm, she brought forth a reamer, a corkscrew and a screwdriver, and finally she managed to locate and open the big blade.

Instinctively Asey started to draw his hand away, and then stopped when it became apparent that he could get out of her clutches only at the price of leaving his finger behind in her iron grip.

"Hold still!" Tiny said, and set laboriously to work.

He could have removed forty splinters while she toiled and tugged, Asey thought, but he was afraid that any movement or any helpful suggestions on his part might unnerve her sufficiently to turn his simple splinter into a major laceration.

"There!" Tiny said. "I think I did that rather well, don't you? Now I'll bandage it!"

"No," Asey said hurriedly. "No, Miss Hazard, I don't need no bandage!"

"Hold still, and turn the light over to the front seat!" Tiny kept a firm grip on his finger while she rummaged around in a string bag. "There, I've got it. Now, I'll show you how good I really am!"

Five minutes later, Asey quizzically surveyed the bulbous, misshapen mound which had formerly been his hand.

"There!" Tiny glowed with pride. "I guess that will

prevent any further injury or infection—did you say something?"

"No," Asey said. "Uh—no."

"You did, too! Something about Egypt!" Tiny insisted.

"I just remarked," Asey said, "that this would do credit to a mummy."

"Well, maybe there's a wee bit too much bandage," Tiny looked judicially at her handiwork, "but I always say you shouldn't do things halfway. I mean, better a good bandage and enough of it than some skimpy thing that wasn't enough. Don't you think so?"

"I see your point." Asey decided he should be thankful that she hadn't taken it into her head to apply a small traction splint. "I—uh—understand now why the doc wants a tag. Tell me, do all the people in Jennie's class go around armed with bandages, an' knives—that knife's got a pair of scissors, I noticed."

"It did have," Tiny said, "but they don't work. They were such tiny little things, I broke them the first day. Yes, Jennie likes us to carry knives or scissors. Mother and father had Sherlton's make them up an alligator case to match their First Aid kit—it's probably in the Porter's trunk, if you'd like to see it. I think Sherlton's are frightfully good with leather, don't you?"

"Guess so." Asey had never heard of Sherlton's. "What about the rest of the class?"

"I don't think they take their equipment seriously

enough," Tiny said. "Phil has rather a nice jackknife with a platinum handle that I gave him, but he often forgets it, and Kay usually forgets, and June always does. And Mildred Tuesome carries embroidery scissors—fancy that! But she says they're the only kind she can get her fingers around. I don't know what Bob Corner carries. Some little gadget or other. He was turned down by the Army, you know."

Tiny's tone indicated that under those circumstances, neither Corner nor anything he might care to carry could interest her very much.

"Huh," Asey said. "Who do you think killed Phil Mundy, Miss Hazard, bearin' in mind that honesty's the best policy?"

"June," Tiny said promptly. "I don't think father would have minded so much about my marrying Phil if it hadn't been for June. Father said she was a horrible, rapacious child, and of course, she was most unpleasant to me. She was pretty unpleasant to Mildred Tuesome, too."

"It's rather a personal question, Miss Mundy," Asey said, "but did Phil Mundy ever ask you to marry him?"

"I suggested it to him—I always think it's only sensible to let people know where you stand, don't you? But Phil said his prospects weren't rosy enough for him even to contemplate marriage. I'd guessed that was what had been holding him back, so I assured him that father would take care of things—do you know it's getting on towards four in the morning? I wonder," Tiny said brightly, "what people will ever think if they see us here, talking so intimately!"

"Let me," Asey said hurriedly, "crank her up for you. I didn't know it was so late. Give me the crank, quick!"

"You might hurt your poor hand," Tiny said. "I can do it. I *like* to crank."

A minute later the Buick, after a preliminary barrage of backfires, roared away.

Asey deposited the two iron spiders in the Porter's back seat along with Mrs. Tuesome's, and then he sat down behind the wheel and set to work freeing his hand from the serpentine maze of Tiny Hazard's bandage.

At least, he thought, he had five of the six spiders, and he would find out about the sixth just as soon as he could unearth his hand and drive on. That Corner might have six, sixteen, or even sixty more new, unused, old-fashioned iron spiders tucked away was a possibility he couldn't bring himself to consider.

He bit at one of the bandage knots. The trouble with this business of Mundy was that there were so many little odds and ends. Almost anybody at Jennie's class had ample opportunity to have killed the fellow before the class gathered. Most of them carried a knife or scissors that could have cut the slits in that sugar-bag hood. The Hazards, Tiny, Mildred Tuesome, Corner, and even Mundy himself, all had a chance to grab a pair of sneakers from Tiny's hoard. And there was nothing that would have prevented either June or Kay from buying a pair at the drygoods store's sale, as far as that went.

But Jonah Ives had no chance to move Mundy's body, nor had he any vehicle in which to move it. Neither had June, for Hanson would have been at his house before the time June swiped the coupe on the short cut. Mildred Tuesome? Asey gnawed through another knot. She had asked about the Fireman's Drag and Carry, she could scream at will, and her honeyed fluttering made a fine smoke screen. And she had embroidery scissors. Suppose, Asey thought, that Tiny had told Mildred that she intended to marry Phil. Would Mildred have killed him rather than let Tiny have him? That spider-casting might well have been an act—if only Mildred Tuesome had known in advance that he was in the vicinity and likely to discover her in the casting process.

"Whoa up!" Asey paused before tackling the fourth knot. "The beaches are probably patrolled there along by the harbor mouth—s'pose Tuesome sort of expected someone to find her, an' was deliberately bunglin' the castin' away of that spider so's she could tell someone—if not me, anyone at all—how she had to get rid of that pan before she got haunted to death by it? Huh, I wonder if I was foxed!"

The Hazards? Dear Sterling seemed to be a bit of a martinet in his own house—but neither he nor dear Grace could have taken Mundy's body away. Or could they have accomplished that before they went to Great Meadow?

Tiny?

Asey sighed.

She'd been wandering around before the First Aid class, she'd had her pick of practically all the sneaker stock of East Aspinnet, and from what he had seen of her, Asey judged that Tiny probably could have run all the way to East Aspinnet, bearing Mundy's lifeless body in her bare hands, and been fresh as a daisy at the finish. It was the first time he had ever met up with just such a combination of Girl Scout innocence and Amazonian prowess and predatory directness, and he frankly admitted to himself that the mixture left him puzzled.

And then there was Bob Corner. Kay Mundy had talked more about him than she had about Jonah. He seemed to know the Mundys well. But he had gone to Hell Hollow and stayed there—and what could have been his motive in killing Mundy, even if he'd had the chance?

He considered the problem of motives as he untied what he hoped was the last knot.

June apparently hated her father, and thought that he had been withholding her money. She knew about the new will. Kay entered the money angle, too, except that she genuinely didn't seem to have known about the will, or to have cared much about money, anyway. Hazard, in one of his tempers, might have struck out and bashed Mundy, and succeeded thereby not only in relieving his feelings, but also in erasing from the scene his daughter's choice of a husband. Mrs. Tuesome might have felt she was being jilted, or double-crossed, and that worked two ways. Tiny might have felt she was being cut out by Tuesome. That spider episode proved she was jealous.

"S'pose," Asey said to himself as he started the car, "s'pose Tiny suggested marriage to Mundy, an' when he headed her off by pleadin' poverty, s'pose Tiny said blandly that her father'd get him a job. Then Mundy, bein' an outspoken fellow, says nothin' doin', not even if dear Sterlin' got him a hundred jobs. If Mundy had turned her down hard, I wonder, now! Would that have touched her off, or would she just have started lookin' around for another likely candidate?"

In any case, it still didn't seem possible to him that Tiny could ever have cut such neat slits as there had been in the hood on Mundy's head! After that bandage job, Asey felt he could recognize Tiny's handiwork almost anywhere!

There were motives all over the place, when you stopped and thought about them, and they were motives that ought to be good and sound, like money, and love, and jealousy, and revenge. But somehow, Asey thought as he sped along, it almost seemed as if someone had been more interested in involving Kay Mundy than in anything else. More pains and trouble had been taken, more chances had been run in the process of removing Mundy's body from his buttery to the fellow's own cellar than had ever existed in the actual act of committing the murder.

And once Mundy had been moved, the murderer had just simply sat back. No one had trailed him to see what he was up to, Asey thought. No one had presented him with any false clews, no one had tried to lure him off into any merry chases.

It occurred to him suddenly that no one had been in any position to challenge him to a chase—he had more or less commandeered the only modern car in the vicinity!

He drew up in front of the house with the gingerbread trim, got out, and beat a hearty tattoo on the door. If only this clerk could cast a little light by telling him that someone—say Mildred Tuesome—had bought two spiders!

The porch light went on, and Asey had a feeling that he was being scrutinized by someone inside.

"I'd like to see Mr. Thomas," Asey called out hopefully. "It's Asey Mayo."

The front door opened, and the middle-aged man in the red and green striped dressing gown yawned and asked him in.

"Mr. Thomas?" Asey said. "Sorry to rouse you. Bob

Corner said you might give me some information about the iron spiders you sold today at the store. I'm Asey Mayo, an' I'm tryin' to—"

"Find out who bashed Mundy with the spider. I know. Come in and sit down."

"Er—how'd you happen to know about that?" Asey inquired.

"My daughter's the phone girl. I always pump her when she gets home. Mundy tell you that getting out them spiders was my idea?"

"No. So that girl's your daughter?" Asey said. "An' the one at the drugstore too? Huh. Mind my sayin' you ain't like 'em?"

"Take after their mother. Close-mouthed. You ought to see my son, though. Hail-fellow-well-met. He's in the M'rines. Nothing close-mouthed about *him!*" Thomas said. "Takes after his old man."

"I see. Now, Corner said he sold one spider to—"

"One to Kay Mundy, and one to Ives. I sold one to Tuesome, and one to Tiny Hazard, and one to the Hazards to make a bomb scoop of—not that they could, but they got money enough to waste on foolishness. Yes, sir, that was my idea, bringing up them spiders. Corner wouldn't of thought of getting that old stock up and getting rid of it, not in a thousand years."

"Who'd you sell the sixth spider to?"

"Say, you know I been tryin' to remember that ever since Beryl—she's the one at the phone office—told me

about listening in to Doc Cummings talking to someone up-Cape. Far as I can remember, I sold that last
pan to Mundy himself—no, sir, I been in hardware all
my life, and I tell you, he's going to go broke without
me!"

"You mean Corner?" Asey asked. "You leavin' him?"

"Listen, last week he says I'll get a raise, this week—
today—he tells me I'll get through next week! Now
you take that nail jar. That's why so many folks keep
dropping into the store anyway. *Corner* never thought
of that nail jar. *I* did!" Thomas said with pride.

"Nail jar?" Asey said. "What nail jar?"

"Why, every week I fill a jar with different size nails,
you see? You pay a quarter, guess how many there is in
the jar, and after we got seventy-five quarters, we buy
a War Bond and give it to the one guessed the nearest,
see? That brings 'em in! I said to Corner last fall, you
buy a good truck with good tires, quick! Buy what you
can get, quick! Buy anything you can get, only be sure
it's quick! And what did he do? Bought new showcases.
Got tied up with a lot of fancy stuff that's all froze—
that's why I went down cellar and dug up them old
spiders!"

"You got any more?" Asey asked.

"No. But we could sell a carload if we had 'em. Seems
as if everybody wants a good sturdy spider to fry their
way through the war. I said to Corner, sell 'em the old
stuff! Let 'em keep it in their cellars for a change! All

the time he's rushing around being helpful; and mind you, I don't say he isn't as hard-working and patriotic as anyone in town, and it isn't his fault he ain't in the service—but what he don't know about hardware is a sin!"

"An' you're sure," Asey got up, "that you sold that pan to Mundy?"

"Far as I can remember. He was crooning over it for an hour, talking about his mother—"

"An' pancakes," Asey said. "I know, I heard a lot about them. Thanks, Mr. Thomas, an' good night."

"Don't suppose," Thomas said, "you could tell me anything about tanks? My boy wants to get into tanks."

Asey grinned. "All I can tell you is they're mighty nice tanks, an' if he ever gets in one, he'll like it! Good night!"

He hesitated at the East Aspinnet crossroads, and then turned toward home. Cummings would certainly have left Mundy's by now, and by this time, Jennie certainly should be home!

He parked the Porter next to Corner's truck by the picket fence, and started wearily up the oystershell walk.

He stopped short as a muffled scream broke the stillness.

Asey stood like a statue, trying to locate the direction from which the scream had come. Not very near, he decided. Perhaps down by the lane.

He turned, and listened, and waited.

Strange noises occasionally issued from the Melroses' lane, but this was nearer. And it wasn't any exaggerated squeal that might have come from a parked car. That was a good, solid scream of terror. Unmuffled, it would have made one of Mrs. Tuesome's yelps sound pikerish by comparison.

At the sound of a car starting up, Asey raced for the Porter, started it, listened again, and nodded.

The car must have been parked on the Melroses' lane, and now it was speeding down the shore road at a frantic clip which suggested that its driver never meant to be seen—or caught—this side of the Rockies.

Asey jammed his foot down on the accelerator, shot the Porter down his lane, and caromed off onto the tarred road. No parker or joy rider would tear off like that! This, at last, looked as if someone were showing his hand!

The car had too much of a head start for him to attempt any direct pursuit, Asey decided as he swung off on the Pond Road. He would short-cut to the main highway and catch it at the intersection beyond. If the car beat him to it, he still had a vantage point from which to pick up the headlights and carry on the chase.

He was going to make it, he thought with triumph as he approached the highway. Not with any time to spare, but—

He never knew afterwards just what he did during

that fantastic split second when someone, waving a red lantern, stepped unconcernedly out into the middle of the highway ahead; whether he yanked on the hand brake before he stood on the foot brake, or the other way around.

But the Porter stopped!

To be sure, it was heading up-Cape instead of down-Cape, but it had stopped!

"Just where d'you think *you*'re going?"

The lantern-bearer, Asey saw as she walked past the headlights, was a woman in slacks and a mackinaw.

"Lady," Asey said severely, "don't ever stop no more cars like that! An' when you say your prayers from now on, bless Bill Porter. Them brakes was his brain children—now, look out of my way! I'm in a hurry!"

"The *nerve* of you!" the woman said indignantly as she jerked open the door.

"Lady, get—"

"Who d'you think you are?" The woman reached past him, and before Asey suspected her purpose, she had grabbed the keys from the ignition.

"Hey, gimme those! Listen, lady, I'm chasin' what I suspect may be a murderer!"

"Is that so?" The woman returned acidly as she slammed the door shut. "Well, you can sit right here and dream about it till the chief comes!"

"Look, you can't do this to me—look!" Asey opened the door, and the interior light flashed on again. "Look at me! I'm Asey Mayo—what's the big idea, anyway? What's that arm band you're pointin' to?"

"Auxiliary Police. I'm substituting for my husband. He was tired. And—"

"You're *what?*"

"I told you! And we're having a test. And I was told to stop all cars, and I intend to do what I was told! And besides, you were exceeding the speed limit by about a hundred miles an hour—and that's the Hazards' car, too. Stole it, did you?"

"No, they lent it to me! Now, gimme them keys! I'm not kidding you, I'm chasing—"

"You're not chasing anybody! You're sitting right here till the chief comes!"

Asey got out. "See here, I'm Jennie Mayo's cousin, Asey Mayo—you know Jennie, don't you? Now, if you don't gimme them keys, I'm goin' to take 'em by force! I mean it!"

"Do, do you?" The woman suddenly pulled a flashlight from her pocket, snapped it on, and aimed it at a blue light that had appeared on the crest of the hill to the left of them ahead on the highway.

"If you want a scuffle," Asey said, "all right! But there's still maybe a chance I can locate that fellow, an' I mean to have them keys! You—"

He broke off abruptly. The blue light was a bicycle headlight, and as the woman's flash played briefly over the rider, Asey recognized her. It was Miss Pease of the

Aspinnet Township High School, and he didn't care to have her witness what was going to amount to a good rough-and-tumble.

Miss Pease blinked a flashlight twice, the woman blinked hers twice, and Asey maintained a discreet silence until the bicycle had disappeared from sight.

"Now," he said, "gimme them keys!"

"You say you're Jennie Mayo's cousin?"

"Yes! Hand them keys over!"

"If you're Jennie Mayo's cousin," the woman said coldly, "why didn't you speak to her just now?"

"Was *that* Jennie?"

"That was Jennie. And there," the woman added, "are your keys!"

Asey saw her arm go out, and heard the keys clink dismally somewhere in the pitch darkness to the left.

"What—no, I won't ask you," Asey said. "Let me guess. You got one daughter works at the drugstore, an' Beryl works at the phone office. Right?"

The woman nodded.

"Uncle," Asey said. "Uncle!"

At a quarter to seven that morning, he drove the Porter back to his house. The Auxiliary Police chief was his own cousin, and between them they had finally managed to find the Hazards' car keys.

He would quietly get some breakfast, Asey decided as he wearily went up the walk, and then he'd take a cat nap on the couch. No use disturbing Jennie, if she had only got back herself at five.

After absent-mindedly opening the wool-packed refrigerator, he went out to the buttery and opened the door.

For several minutes he stood silently on the threshold, looking in bewilderment down at the floor.

June Mundy lay there lifeless. In the corner beyond her limp body was Jennie's old iron spider. Apparently it had been used to kill the girl in just the same manner that her father had been killed.

CHAPTER NINE

AN HOUR later, Cummings returned from the buttery to the kitchen, slammed his black bag down beside the table, and shook his head.

"I'm speechless!" he said, and seemed to mean it.

"How long do you think she's been dead?" Asey asked.

"Oh—let's see, you heard that scream around five, or just before, didn't you tell me? Well, she was killed around then. Not any earlier. How d'you figure it, Asey, that someone grabbed her in the woods by the lane—but what would she have been doing over here, anyway? You don't suppose she suffered a stroke of conscience and came to see you and to repent, do you? Or d'you suppose she'd been threatened, and was rushing to you for safety? Or was she just nosing around?"

"The situation's obscure," Asey said. "Huh, I've always wondered what the communiqués meant by that, an' now I begin to understand. June left Mundy's be-

fore Hanson an' Kay went—did she come back while
you was there? No? Then she must just have been wan-
derin' around, an' finally come here. I s'pose you can
assume she wanted to see me. Only she met up with
someone else just before I come, an' they grabbed her.
Then they put her into the coupe, an' beat it—it must
have happened like that, otherwise the coupe would've
been in the vicinity, an' it ain't. I looked while I was
waitin' for you. To think I might've caught 'em, if
Mrs. Thomas hadn't butted in! I s'pose—"

"What?" Cummings asked as he hesitated.

"Wa-el, I was thinkin', doc, it wouldn't have taken
a lot of reconnoiterin' for someone to find out what'd
happened to me, an' that I—what's the phrase they use
when armies get stymied?"

"Last time," Cummings said, "they used to laugh-
ingly call it All Quiet on the Western Front. Now,
I think it's a Period of Stalemate. But how could anyone find out that Thomas had you temporarily stale-
mated without being stopped themselves?"

"If someone knew where the Auxiliary Police posts
were," Asey said, "an' if they knew there was a test
goin' on, all they had to do was to avoid 'em. I think
this fellow knew, an' deliberately cut off along the
shore road—it's the long way around to anywhere, an'
Cousin Ben said there was no posts on it. Now, this
fellow must of guessed I was after him when I set out
in the Porter—if he didn't hear me start up, he could

of spotted the headlights. Then when I never appeared, he could reasonably assume I'd got caught. A few minutes of quiet creepin' around, after he'd doubled back on his trail, would have confirmed it. He'd have known then that I was out of the way for a spell, an' he had time enough to kill June—if he hadn't killed her already—an' bring her back here."

"So you didn't fall for Jennie's spider!" Cummings said with a grin. "He left it there on the floor, but there's the same rim mark on her that was on her father. He used the same spider he used before, the sixth spider —Asey, I've just thought of something! If this fellow made off in the coupe, then he didn't have a car of his own. Would he have been carrying that spider, on foot? It doesn't seem sensible!"

"Tiny ran a race with a spider clasped to her bosom," Asey returned. "Tuesome was tryin' to shot-put hers into the ocean. Jonah carried his in the basket on his handlebars. If there's one thing I've learned since I come home, it's that you can't tell what anybody's likely to do with an iron spider! Besides, doc, the fellow might not have been on foot at all. He might have had a bike that he picked up after he returned an' left June in the buttery. He might have had a horse that he gave a good slap to, an' sent runnin' home. Might've been in a rocket ship. You can't tell."

"Go back a bit, now." Cummings got up and started to pace the floor. "If June came here to see you, and if she met someone she knew prowling around outside,

she wouldn't be afraid, but she would have been curi-
ous. Suppose—"

"I've been supposin' just that," Asey said. "S'pose
she let loose with one of them quick, dramatic flurries of
hers, an' said, 'What're you sneakin' around here for?
I bet you're the murderer! I bet you killed my father!
You're the one!' "

"Think she really knew?" Cummings asked.

Asey shrugged. "You can't tell. She might have
guessed. The point is, she's got a way of sayin' things
that makes what she says sound as if she knew. If she
confronted someone with a lot of dramatic accusations,
I don't think they'd be likely to assume she was bluffin'.
You or I would have laughed her off an' told her to
calm down an' act sensible. But if we had a guilty conscience, I think we'd probably have grabbed her quick
an' swung the spider an' put her out of circulation before she got a chance to tell anyone on us."

Cummings shook his head. "I still can't see why anyone should have a spider with 'em!"

"Maybe," Asey said, "they aimed to leave it on my
doorstep. Or out in the shed. Or the garage. It'd be a
nice idea. I'm sure I'd never think of huntin' for or even
findin' that spider around here. Maybe someone was
carryin' it as a sort of decoy, doc."

"I've heard of decoy ducks," Cummings returned,
"but I never heard of a decoy spider! What do you
mean?"

"Wa-el, if the prowler was spotted by you or me or

Hanson, all the person had to do was to wave the spider excitedly around an' say what do you know, he'd found it—see? That would explain why they were here, an' it wouldn't get us any forrader. I think someone aimed to leave it here, doc, an' I'm sure June got killed because she made someone think she knew all about 'em. 'Course, we're doin' an awful lot of fancy cuttin' out of whole cloth," he added thoughtfully.

"I'm sure the murderer isn't going to favor us with the whys and wherefores, and June can't, and I must say, I think it sounds rather well," Cummings said. "It's sensible—hey, I see Ives! He's getting off his bike down by the fence."

"Don't mention June to him," Asey said quickly. "I told you I called up an' left a message for Hanson to come as soon as he got in. Well, don't let's mention this till he gets here. It might be interestin' to see if anyone's sort of huntin' June." He raised his voice as Jonah knocked on the front door. "Come on in!"

Jonah whistled a Sousa march as he strode along the hall.

"Hi!" he said cheerfully. "Enter a bearded messenger, bringing good tidings. Heard about Kay? The girl's loose!"

"She break jail?" Cummings asked.

"No, she was loosed. Seems that when she and Hanson got there, whoever took her name asked if she was any relation to the blonde brat he'd picked up a while back for speeding, and went on at a great rate about what a little liar she was. Hanson began to look green, Kay said—"

"I bet he did! Oh," Cummings said wistfully, "I wish I'd been there!"

"Well, to do the fellow justice, apparently he'd begun to have qualms on the trip up," Jonah said. "Kay told me he kept muttering about how Mayo was always right, and how after all a fellow made mistakes. Anyway, after this other lad's comments about June, Hanson began to stall, and kill time, and give Kay magazines to read. And then June called up and asked to speak to Hanson, and said it was all a lie, and Kay'd never asked Phil for any money that wasn't hers, and she'd never fought with Phil, and so on and so forth."

"June did?" Cummings said. "She really did?"

"Amazing, wasn't it?" Jonah said blandly. "And then something told me to borrow a car and dash up there—you know, just to show the girl she wasn't forgotten by the outside world—and if Kay wasn't just starting to be driven home! So I saved Hanson's tires and brought her back."

"So," Asey said. "So! An' did you have much trouble forcin' June to make that call?"

"Now how in God's name," Jonah demanded, "did you know that I inspired the call?"

"Oh, I sort of guessed. It was so pat. How'd you do it?"

"After the doc left, I hung around, and June came back—really, I think she'd begun to be awfully afraid of what she'd done with her loose talk. I didn't lay hand on her. I just suggested in a firm manner that she'd better call and tell the truth, and she seemed almost glad to."

"Then what?" Asey asked.

"Then she reverted slightly to her usual self," Jonah said. "Reaction from her good works, no doubt. She called me a few names, refused to give me the car keys, and slatted off upstairs—where I thought it was wiser not to follow her. So I wheeled over to the Hazards and borrowed one of their fleet, and went up and fetched Kay. When we got back, we noticed the coupe wasn't there, and Kay worried, and I told her to forget the child. But just now, on my way over to see Kay, I found the coupe on the East Aspinnet road, out of gas, and no June! Kay's nearly mad with worry."

"Well, well!" Cummings said. "What d'you think could have happened?"

"Kay thinks she may have run away, and ordered me to come tell Asey and have him find her—is Jennie back?"

Asey shook his head. "She passed me like a ship in the night," he said. "That's all I know about her. An' to think she used to carp about Mrs. Roosevelt never bein' home!"

"In the Victory Monument to come," Jonah said, "I hope Jennie's name leads all the rest. It ought to. What'll I do about June? Think she'll turn up?"

"No doubt about it," Cummings said. "We'll tell Hanson, anyway."

"But shouldn't we do more?" Jonah asked. "Shouldn't we seek her out, or scour the vicinity, or make a house-to-house canvass? Frankly, I'm a little worried. I mean, suppose the brat roamed around, shooting her mouth off, and happened to shoot it off to the wrong person?"

"I see your point," Asey said, "but hadn't you better make inquiries first of all?"

"Well, all right." Jonah hesitated. "Well, I'll ask about, and see you later. So long."

Cummings went to the front door and watched him leave.

"Pretty reluctant," he reported to Asey. "Kept turning back. I think he wanted to ask a lot more. What d'you think about him?"

"He got June to do what he wanted," Asey said. "I can't see where he'd anythin' to gain by killin' her."

"He borrowed one of Hazard's cars. Hm," Cummings said. "Suppose June ran out of gas over there in East Aspinnet, and walked here, and suppose it was Jonah in that car? No, I don't think so either. I found out a lot about him while we waited for the ambulance. He was in France and in Norway. Asey, someone's taking a big chance on Jennie's being here. Or rather, on her not being here."

"You got any idea where she might be?" Asey inquired. "I've stopped askin' if anyone knows where she *is*."

"My wife guessed she was mixed up with some business of changing spotters' schedules, but she said she wouldn't know where to put her finger on Jennie— and if she doesn't know, I don't see how anyone else could. I don't see how they'd dare take the chance of coming here—say, here's Mildred Tuesome! Funny— first Ives, and now her. And she's running to beat hell!"

Ignoring the formality of knocking, Mrs. Tuesome rushed out into the kitchen, excitedly calling out Asey's name, and wildly waving two slips of pink paper.

"Sit down, Mildred!" Cummings said. "Get your breath, woman! What's the matter?"

"I can't sit down—Asey Mayo, read these slips! Read them! I went to Red Cross early to—to appease Jennie, and look! Look what I found! Read what these say!"

Asey took them from her shaking hand. One slip said, "Finish Mon.," and the other said, "Finish Tues."

"See, someone meant to kill Phil—finish Mon.," Mrs. Tuesome said. "That means, finish Mundy! And finish Tues.—that's me! Someone means to kill *me!*"

"An' that," Asey asked gently, "is what you're so worked up about?"

"Well, wouldn't *you* be worked up, if someone had written 'Finish Mayo'!"

"I shouldn't give it a thought," Asey said. "Now,

you pop along back to the Red Cross an' put these slips back where you found 'em, on the piles of sweaters, or whatever it was."

"How *can* you be so *cal*lous! Someone means to finish me—"

"Come, come, Mildred!" Cummings said. "One means finish on Monday, and the other on Tuesday!"

"Oh! Oh, why I *nev*er thought of that! Oh, Asey Mayo, you're simply marvelous! I never was more relieved, never! Is—er—have you made any of your marvelous deductions about poor dear Phil?" she added solicitously. "Has anything *hap*pened?"

Cummings took her by the arm. "We were plump in the middle of some dandy deductions when you dropped in, Mildred. Now, you scoot along back to your knitting!"

He ushered her out, and returned to the kitchen.

"She is simply dancing off with an uplifted heart," he told Asey. "At least, that's what she told me. I think we can write her off, don't you? I could sooner picture Mundy and June being killed by a charlotte russe. Or a fruit salad with whipped cream. Asey, from the looks of that buttery floor, I'd say that the fellow worked in his stocking feet. There's no trace of shoe marks or heel marks. That being the case, why in blazes did he do all that rubber-boot and brown-sneaker changing on Mundy's feet? I don't *get* that! I don't—by George, isn't this incredible! Here's Hazard. Think you ought to render proper homage, and receive him in the living room? I'll stay here."

Hazard, wearing gray tweeds and a Burberry, and an incongruously gay Alpine hat with a jaunty feather, politely accepted Asey's invitation to enter.

"But, thank you, I won't sit down. I know you're busy, and I don't want to bother. Mr. Mayo, I want to apologize to you for several things. First, that you should have had to witness my unfortunate display of temper last night—er—I believe you did witness it?"

Asey nodded.

"I regret," Hazard said, "I most sincerely regret that. I can only say that Grace and I had—er—rather a try-ing evening after a very trying afternoon, and frankly, my nerves were on edge. I was, furthermore, very surly about your very natural and very proper questions. I tried to eliminate all mention of Phil Mundy, and I must explain why—I very nearly came here last night to explain. You see, my daughter had decided that she wished to marry Mundy. After I learned of his unfor-tunate murder, I worried that she might mention her attachment for him, or that it might be brought to light. I didn't want our name involved. Our name has never been involved in such a—a situation."

"I see," Asey said.

"And to tell you the truth," Hazard drew a long breath, "this attachment existed very largely in my daughter's mind. I am sure Mundy suspected it, and I am equally sure he did not reciprocate. I did my best to portray Mundy in an unfavorable light, in my daughter's presence, because I wished to discourage her—although actually, as I told you, I recognized Mundy's ability, and I respected it, even though he and I occasionally had words as to method. This situation of Mundy and my daughter is—er—one that her mother and I have—er—met with before."

"I guessed that," Asey said with a grin.

"Oh, dear!" Hazard sounded worried. "I do hope she hasn't trans—ah, well, one mustn't cross bridges, must one! But I will confess, Mr. Mayo, that I have set up a number of athletically inclined men in various healthy and useful occupations in distant corners of the globe. Tea plantations, rubber plantations, all that sort of thing. Of course, it's harder these days to pack—ah, Fido, good morning!"

Asey looked with surprise at the black and white cat who strolled along the hall and wove around Hazard's legs.

"Huh! We got a new cat?"

"Yes, I'm very attached to Fido. He often plays with me—I see that the name puzzles you?" Hazard asked with a smile. "Your cousin Jennie named him Fido so that if she became nervous, alone here, she could call 'Fido, Fido!' and people would think she was calling a dog. I won't bother you further, Mr. Mayo. I simply wanted you to understand. Er—everything is going properly, I presume?"

"As well as can be expected," Asey said, "under the circumstances."

"No new developments?"

"None to mention," Asey told him honestly.

"Please don't hesitate to call on me if I may be of service." Hazard bowed, patted Fido, and departed.

"Listening to that man," Cummings said when Asey returned to the kitchen, "always leaves me with the feeling that I've dropped in on a lecture by mistake— he peeked toward the woodshed. I watched him. He ask any leading questions?"

"Asked if there were any new developments—come on, Fido. I'll get you some breakfast if I can find any in our bare larder. The last incumbent used to get hot oatmeal cooked in Jennie's best manner."

"Give him an egg," Cummings suggested. "There's one left in the wire basket—well, who d'you think'll drop in on us next?"

A series of backfires from the old Buick answered his question, and Asey sighed as he saw Tiny Hazard loping up the oystershell walk.

"She's waving slips of pink paper, too," Cummings observed. "Suppose she wants you to diagnose 'Tape Selvage' or 'Cut Bias'?"

"You go see," Asey said hurriedly. "It's your turn. I got to feed Fido."

Cummings was grinning when he returned from the interview.

"She found the slips in the gutter outside the Red Cross—what in the world did she mean when she said she intended to spend the day working there to keep a stiff upper lip, I wonder? Amazing woman! Anyway, one slip said 'Get Mundy,' and one said 'Get Corner,' and the third said 'Get Tiny.' I suggested she take 'em back to the Red Cross and find out what they wanted her got for. She was terribly anxious to know how you were—what were you doing with her last night?"

"What," Asey countered, "did she lead you to believe I was doin' with her?"

"She leered," Cummings said with a chuckle, "in a most suspicious manner. She never asked about Mundy, or June, or anyone or anything else, and I'm sure she knew perfectly well that those slips had either blown out or been swept out of the Red Cross—why d'you suppose she came?"

"I'd hate to guess," Asey said. "Gee, what backfires! Doesn't seem as if it could have been her Buick this mornin', anyway!"

"Didn't you hear Jonah say he borrowed one of the Hazards' fleet? They've a dozen cars handy, if Tiny chose to use anything but that battered wreck. Asey, we ought to take another look at June! I keep feeling thwarted. We're not getting anywhere!"

"So?"

"Well, are we?" Cummings retorted.

Asey smiled. "I think we are," he said. "There's just so many loose odds an' ends you got to get settled, an' this Grand Central Station atmosphere has cleared up a lot of little things that's been botherin' me. Tell me, have Kay Mundy an' Jonah Ives always been such great friends?"

"I didn't know it," Cummings perched on the kitchen table. "But apparently Ives was quite taken with her. Guess that she never gave him much of a chance, what with his spy aura. She's been quite the belle, you know. I've seen her around with Bob Corner a lot, and my wife's mentioned seeing her with boys from camp."

The doctor hitched himself back further on the table, and Asey's duck coat slid onto the floor.

"Asey Mayo!"

"What's the matter?"

"Look!" Cummings pointed to the two fifty-cent pieces which had rolled out of the pocket of the duck coat. "I was so careful to give you those to give back to Kay, and you never did!"

"Oh, them," Asey said. "I forgot all about 'em. To tell you the truth, I had high hopes of that one on the buttery floor bein' a clew, sort of, till I found out you'd dropped it."

"*I* dropped it? What are you talking about? I never dropped any fifty-cent piece in the buttery!" Cummings said indignantly. "Whatever made you think I did? *I* never said I dropped anything in there!"

"Looky here!" Asey said. "There was a coin in the buttery by Mundy's body when I first seen it!"

"*I* never saw it! Why didn't you mention it?" Cummings demanded.

"I took it for granted it was one of the two fifty-cent pieces you'd found outside that dropped out of Kay's pocket when she run away from me!" Asey said. "I figured it'd dropped out of *your* pocket when you bent over to look at Mundy!"

"I can't think why you should have!"

"But I asked you about it!" Asey said.

"You never did," Cummings retorted. "When?"

"Listen, when you came back here, after Hanson'd arrived, you went steamin' out to the buttery while I stopped to ask Bob Corner somethin' about our front-door lock. When I went to join you, you was returnin' from the buttery. An' we talked a few minutes, an' then you give me them two coins to give to Kay. Right?"

"I remember giving them to you, yes."

"Uh-huh. An' I said, 'So you got it, I noticed it was gone from the floor,' or somethin' like that—but you didn't contradict me!"

"I don't," Cummings said plaintively, "understand a word of this!"

"Look, there was a coin by Mundy's body. I saw it.

I thought it'd dropped from your pocket—you'd stuck them coins in your pocket. When I showed Hanson the buttery, an' found the body was gone, I noticed the coin was gone, an' I thought of course you'd picked it up before you an' I left. Now, d'you understand?"

"All I know," Cummings said, "is that I never dropped any coins anywhere, in all my life. I've hung on to every last one—look, what *are* you getting so excited for? Suppose there was a coin there? What earthly good will it do you? I don't know how many fifty-cent pieces are minted per annum, but I'm willing to wager it's a staggering total. What is there about this to make you look like Fido eating his egg? Sometimes I think you're stark raving—here's Jonah back, Asey. He's got Corner with him."

Jonah's forehead was wrinkled.

"Asey, we can't find June anywhere! No one knows anything about her, no one's seen her! We've phoned virtually every house in East Aspinnet, and run through all the people she knows here in town. Kay and Bob and I think you ought to call Hanson."

"I'll tell him," Asey said, "when he comes. He said he'd be down this morning."

"It's swell about Kay, isn't it?" Corner asked as he picked up Fido. "But what now?"

"Oh, I don't know." Asey's tone and manner were so completely different from what they had been a half minute before that Cummings looked at him sharply.

"We got some gaps an' crevasses—doc, you got my knife?"

"*Knife? Your* knife? No! Why should I have your knife?" Cummings said. "I don't know what you did with it. I haven't seen it."

"I want to cut this linoleum on the workledge so's it's even," Asey said. "Either of you two got a pocket-knife?"

Jonah's hand went to his pocket and Corner's went to his vest. Both smiled weakly, and then looked at each other and laughed.

"Jennie would lay us out in lavender," Jonah said. "We're supposed to be equipped at all times to tear the best bed sheets into bandages. I lose on the average of a knife a week. You lost yours, too, Bob? Sorry, Asey —listen, isn't someone knocking?"

Cummings went to the front door and returned almost at once.

"It's that Thomas girl that works in the drugstore, and she wants you, Asey. It's something about her mother being sorry, but what with First Aid problems, and the stove not working right because it had to be converted from oil to coal, and cutting her foot on a bullrush at the Hollow—you'd better go talk with her. I can't understand!"

Asey grinned when he came back.

"Boiled down," he said, "mother's sorry she stopped me. I think father gave her an earful—hey, Fido, lay off! Sorry, Corner, did he scratch you? I think the poor cat's alone so much, company sort of confuses him."

"Hazard and I are rivals for his affection," Corner said. "Look, is that dummy around? The salesman who left it called and says he's coming for it today—I thought he was on his way to Boston, and we'd have it to practice on for two weeks, but he was on his way down the Cape to Provincetown."

"I'll get it," Asey said.

He went down into the cellar, and his face, when he reappeared, was a study in bewilderment.

"Doc, didn't you think that dummy was down there?"

"I'm sure it was. Hanson said so."

"It's gone," Asey said simply.

"Gone? Gone where?"

"I don't know. It just ain't there. Maybe Hanson took it—sorry, Corner. We'll have to do some ferretin' on that. Tell me, are you two fellows overburdened with work this mornin' an' forenoon?"

"Well, I told Kay I'd find June," Jonah said. "What about you, Bob?"

"There's plenty I ought to be doing," Corner said, "but until I hear from that fellow about his tire, there isn't much I really can do. None of it matters, much, anyway. Except those Red Cross cases. I ought to find someone to take those. They're important, and I promised I'd look after 'em."

"Commandeer the idle rich," Jonah said. "The Hazards would love to send a lackey with one of the beachwagons. What can we do for you, Asey?"

"Wa-el, it's goin' to sound a mite odd, but will the two of you," Cummings looked at Asey and then looked away. Asey was improvising, "will you go to Hazard's, an' sort of insinuate yourselves on 'em, an' hang around 'em until—let's see. Till about two? If they split, you split an' string right along with 'em. If they try to shake you, just don't let yourselves be shook. Would you do that?"

"Of course," Jonah said. "But what about June? Will you do something about finding her?"

Asey nodded. "I'll try."

"And when do you want us back?" Corner asked.

"Say, at two."

"Anything you want us to watch out for, or guard against, or anything like that?" Jonah asked.

"No, just stick around 'em, an' keep on stickin', no matter what. Then come back here. Okay?"

Cummings watched the two leave on their bicycles, and then he swung around from the window and faced Asey.

"All right!" he said. "What's up?"

"Wa-el," Asey said, "I got an idea that's sort of been brewin', an' now I want to see what I can do with it."

Cummings marched over to the cellar door, opened it, and peered down.

"That dummy's still there!"

"I know it." Asey closed the door, locked it, and pocketed the key. "An' your part in this is to sit here an' see that no one goes down there an' finds it, see? Not even Hanson. You're to sit here, an' hold the fort!"

"All I do is hold forts!" Cummings said irritably. "I'm sick and tired of holding forts!"

Asey grinned. "You hold this one, an' maybe you won't have to hold any more."

"Where are *you* going?"

"Oh," Asey said, "hither, thither, an' yon."

"When'll you be back?"

"I told 'em two o'clock, didn't I?"

"Why," Cummings asked suspiciously, "did you send that pair off on a fool's errand?"

"Maybe it ain't," Asey said gently.

"Did that girl, that Thomas girl, give you a clew? What did she tell you? She *did* tell you something, didn't she?"

"Maybe so," Asey said.

"I think," Cummings said, "that you are the most annoying individual I know!"

Asey chuckled. "If Jennie turns up, tell her I called, will you? And show Hanson what's happened."

He picked up his duck coat, and wriggled into it as he strode off down the lane toward the Porter.

It was just a few minutes past two when he returned,

and the assortment of vehicles parked in the yard by the picket fence brought a smile to his face.

Tiny's Buick, Tuesome's buggy, Kay's coupe, Jonah's bike, Corner's bike, the doctor's car, Hanson's official sedan, and a dark-blue Porter touring car that looked as fresh as the day it had left the factory three years before—doubtless, Asey thought, one of the Hazards' fleet.

"Asey!" Hanson ran down toward him. "Gee, say, I'm glad to see you! They been pesterin' me to pieces!"

"They know about June?"

Hanson nodded. "Say, what *about* her? I don't get this! Why your buttery? Why *your* house? You don't suppose Jennie's gone haywire or anything, do you?"

"Ain't she back yet? No? When I get through with this business," Asey said, "I think I'll collect me a posse an' hunt her in earnest. Now—"

"What you mean, when you get through with this? You mean," Hanson asked excitedly, "you *got* it? Honest?"

"I sort of think maybe perhaps. They all in the house? Then let's go see if this'll work."

"What you got that *pig* for?" Hanson demanded as Asey picked Henry up from the Porter's rear floor. "What's that for?"

Asey grinned. "An awful lot," he said, "hinges on Henry. Come along."

The group in his living room eyed him, Asey

thought, as if he were the Gestapo agent who was going to send them all to a concentration camp.

"We are shocked," Hazard said, "to hear about June, Mayo. I—"

"Henry! Oh, you've got Henry! How did you *ever* get Henry!" Mrs. Tuesome interrupted. "How did you ever *find* him? Why, I *hid* him—"

"Don't I know it!" Asey said. "It took me the better part of an hour to locate Henry."

"But the *trunk* he was *in!* I *locked* it! With a *key!*"

"I'm afraid," Asey said, "that trunk is sort of goin' to be in the market for a new lock."

He put Henry down on the brick fireplace hearth and almost absent-mindedly picked up the iron poker.

"Oh! Oh! Oh! Somebody *stop* him!" Mrs. Tuesome screamed. "Oh, he's going to *break* Henry! I simply can't *bear* to have—stop him, *stop* him before he—*ohh!*"

The poker descended, and Henry dissolved into a thousand china fragments.

Asey knelt down and started gingerly to fish around among the coins, and then with a smile of triumph, he picked one out, and stood up.

Jonah leaned forward and stared curiously at Asey's choice.

"Why, that isn't a coin at all!" he said. "That's Corner's gadget knife that looks like a coin—isn't that yours, Bob? How'd it get inside Henry—hey, Bob!

Where is he? I thought he was right here beside me!"

"Mr. Corner left," Mrs. Hazard said. "When Mrs. Tuesome started to scream, he went out—"

"Hanson!" Asey said. "Come on, quick!"

They reached the front door just in time to see Corner shoot Cummings's car out of the yard and down the lane.

"Come on, Hanson, hurry!" Asey ran to the Porter town car, got in, and as quickly jumped out. "Never mind, we'll take the tourin' car—golly, he swiped them keys, too! Let's see if he—"

But in addition to taking the keys from both Porters, Corner had also removed Tiny's crank from the front seat of the old Buick.

Jonah and Cummings panted up.

"Whyn't you get him?" Cummings demanded. "He's got *my* car—oh, God, my *tires!* Go *a*fter him! Take a car and go—what's the matter, did he swipe all the keys? Asey Mayo, you're not going after him on a bicycle, are you?"

"Better a bike than that tired-lookin' horse! Come on, Jonah, we can only try—Hanson, you an' doc send out a call to have him stopped, an' round up some cars. Get some of Hazard's."

"Which way?" Jonah asked as they pedaled down the lane.

"To the big hill on the main highway. We maybe might be able to catch sight of him—"

"Wouldn't he be likely to make for a back road, ditch the car, and lay low? He knows East Aspinnet like a book. He's often gone through the lanes with me —he knows 'em all."

"We'll try the hill. If we can't see him, we can maybe pick up a car—hustle!"

Five minutes later, Jonah stopped beside Asey on the long hill, and mopped his forehead.

"We're licked, Asey!" he said. "By this time, he's driven the car into a thicket in those woods, and tonight he'll creep out—hey, what's the matter? D'you see something? What d'you see? *Where? I* can't—hey, be careful! You can't keep up a pace like—hey, Asey, wait! Wait for me!"

Seven minutes later, Jonah dismounted beside Asey, looked at Cummings's car lying drunkenly in the shallow ditch by the side of the road, looked at the earnest group of busy women in slacks who scurried around and looked finally at Corner, flat on the ground.

Then he reached out and touched the elbow of a woman hurrying past.

"I beg your pardon," Jonah said politely, "but did the gentleman in the car break his leg?"

The woman turned a glowing face toward him.

"We don't really think so," she said, "but we put on a traction splint anyway—we were right here and waiting when he skidded, and we had a splint handy. Wasn't that *won*derful?"

"Are you," Asey asked in a choked voice, "the head of this outfit?"

"Yes. We're from Weesit. Group Two—what's that?" she asked, as Asey held out something toward her.

"That," Asey said, "is my wallet, with my compliments. Will you take it, an' buy whatever Group Two needs in the line of First Aid equipment? It'll salve my conscience for some of the cracks I've made. An' thought. You couldn't have done a better job of immobilizin' him if you'd had a gun, an' handcuffs, an' leg irons—how'd he happen to skid here?"

"Well, Annie was having trouble backing the beach wagon around," the woman said. "She stalled. And he was going *so* fast, he simply skidded right off the road when he tried to swerve around her—he should have *known* better than to go so fast!"

"He should, indeed," Asey said. "An' I suspect he knows now—for Pete's sakes!"

Mrs. Tuesome's buggy, with Cummings at the reins, precipitated itself almost into the group.

Ignoring Asey and Corner, and everyone and everything else, Cummings jumped out, rushed over to the ditch, and made a critical circuit of his car.

When he turned around, he was beaming.

"The tires are okay!" he looked at Corner and shook his head slowly. "I'm speechless! Absolutely speechless! All I can say, Asey Mayo, is that you've chased a lot of criminals in your day, but this is the first time, to my certain knowledge, that you ever caught one with a traction splint! Is his leg *really* broken? No, I suspected it wasn't. Well, girls, we'll let you have the fun of loading him into the buggy—I'll return the splint later."

"You mean, you want our victim?" the group leader asked.

Asey grinned.

"I sort of hate to snatch him from you," he said, "but we got triple-A priority, ma'am. We want him for a couple of murders."

"What I don't understand," Jonah said an hour later in Asey's living room, "is how you guessed about him in the first place!"

"What *I* don't understand," Kay said, "is how—"

"Let him," Cummings said, "begin at the beginning! Give him a chance! Go on, Asey. What *I* don't understand is how you guessed that the fifty-cent piece wasn't a fifty-cent piece! How'd you know it was a knife? That was what really started you going, wasn't it?"

"Wa-el," Asey said, "it was you yourself suggested we ought to hunt for little scissors, doc. Tiny said Corner had a 'gadget' knife. When I asked him an' Jonah for a knife this mornin', Jonah reached for his pants pocket, but Corner's hand went toward his vest, like he was gropin' for somethin' danglin' from his watch chain. But there wasn't nothin' there. I sort of got to broodin' about that. So, after I left here, doc, I went up to the Red Cross workroom an' chatted with Mrs. Tuesome. She give me a fine description of Corner's little round medal knife that he most always usually wore on his watch chain, an' how it had one stubby little hooklike blade that pulled out from one side, an' this pair of—uh—wee scissors that pulled out from the other. Mrs. Tuesome was very helpful."

"But how did you know the knife was in *Henry?*" Mrs. Tuesome demanded. "When you asked me about it, you never *told* me it was inside Henry, or that you meant to *break* him!"

"I was sort of afraid to, for fear you might just possibly let the cat out of the bag," Asey said. "I guessed it was in Henry, because I seen Corner put it in there—don't you remember how he contributed to Henry for me, last night?"

"Yes, and it simply amazed me!" Mrs. Tuesome said. "Because I'm sure I've asked Bob a thousand times for contributions, and he's awfully—well, I wouldn't say he was exactly *sting*y, but I've had to wear myself to a perfect frazzle, usually, just getting him to give a *dime!*"

"Uh-huh. I sort of gathered that from the tone of your voice last night," Asey said. "You see, just as I set out to drive Kay back to East Aspinnet, I spoke to the doc in the hall about that fifty-cent piece. Corner heard just enough so's he realized that I'd seen that coin-knife. He probably decided right away to get rid of it. But when he went to get into his truck, his tires had gone. He had to ride with me. I s'pose that knife was burnin' a hole in him, an' when he had Henry thrust under his nose, he took advantage of his opportunity. You see, he didn't know how long he might be ridin' around with me, an' he wanted to get rid of the thing, quick—pretty smart of him, too, because by the time Henry was filled to the burstin' point, findin' that knife in his innards wouldn't have mattered or meant a thing."

"How'd it come off his chain?" Jonah asked. "Carrying Phil to the buttery?"

"Most likely. I forgot to ask him."

"Look, why did he kill Phil, anyway?" Kay wanted to know. "What was his motive?"

"That part come hard," Asey said, "an' it's involved, because in a way, he had two motives. They was right there all the time, but they took a little puttin' together. Last night—or this mornin', dependin' on your point of view—Corner's clerk told me that Corner'd fired him. I gathered that his business wasn't so hot. On the other hand, the clerk said that last week, Corner'd promised him a raise. Get it?"

"No," Cummings said promptly.

"Wa-el, in other words, last week Corner must have

thought he had good prospects. This week, he didn't. I got to wonderin' if maybe he'd expected money, an' that led me to wonderin' if maybe he'd expected a loan, say."

"You mean, from Phil?" Kay asked.

"Uh-huh. Your brother come here an' sort of hurled himself into everythin', an' I wondered if a fellow like him mightn't maybe have dallied with the idea of gettin' into some local business. After all, hardware was sort of in his line, an' it seemed as if he'd decided to stay here, what with people suggestin' that he run for town office."

"*I* told him that," Tiny said with pride.

"But your brother had June trouble, an' will trouble, an' money trouble," Asey went on. "I wondered, s'pose Mundy's promised Corner a loan. S'pose he had it in mind to buy a partnership. N'en s'pose Mundy backed out, what with money trouble sort of pressin' down on him, an' everythin' bein' uncertain. Corner needed money pretty bad—one look at that truck of his proved that. I thought, s'pose that Mundy turned him down this afternoon—an' the almost more important part'd have been so much easier, Kay, if you'd only unbent an' told me more about him!"

"What d'you mean?" Kay asked.

"If you'd only told me that Corner'd asked you to marry him, an' you turned him down, an' he kept botherin' you till your brother told him to lay off! I had to pry that out of Corner, just now. But knowin' it beforehand," Asey said, "would've gone a long ways toward explainin' why the murderer wanted to involve you!"

"You mean that Bob put Phil in our house, and put my bike there at the head of the stairs to—to get back at me?" Kay said.

"Yup, an' I think he had some notion of helpin' to save you, kind of playin' the hero an' helpin' to get you off—after all, he could be reasonably *sure* you'd get off, because he knew you wasn't the murderer! But that tire business sort of handicapped him. He was apparently crazy to help you when I told him Hanson'd taken you off—only he sort of couldn't get started, without a car. An' besides, he had a very important chore to do."

"I still don't understand how this worked out," Jonah said. "Are you sure Phil promised him money, and then reneged?"

Asey nodded. "Corner admitted it. That skid an' the traction splint sort of unnerved him to the point where he was willin' to tell us anythin'. Yesterday, after nailin' up cases for Jennie at the workroom, Corner met Phil in the lane, an' they had a showdown. Mundy said he couldn't make the loan, because he was goin' to have to use most of his ready money to send June away. Said he'd reached the point where he had to do somethin' about June. Corner argued with him, an' when he found Mundy wasn't goin' to change his mind, he picked up the iron spider from the seat of his truck, an' let Mundy have it—remember, doc, you said he was hit from above? Corner was on the runnin' board of the truck, see?"

"But if he killed Phil," Jonah said, "he simply killed his chance of getting money, didn't he? I mean, he didn't gain by Phil's death!"

"No, but he thought he still had a good chance to get the money," Asey said. "You see, he knew about that new will. He was the notary that signed it. He knew Kay got the money, an' he thought quick— follow it?"

"No," Kay said. "I don't!"

"He thought to himself he'd involve you, be helpful gettin' you off, an' then you'd marry him out of gratitude, an' he'd get the money. Don't shake your head, Jonah. Corner admitted that, too."

"Why did Phil change that will in the first place?" Jonah wanted to know.

"That," Asey said, "took some fancywork, an' I finally got Mundy's lawyer in Dalton on the phone an' got to the root of it. Seems that June's mother's folks didn't care any more for Phil than June or her mother did, an' Phil'd learned long ago that there was some clause in this maternal trust fund that said if June was bequeathed anythin' by her father, or accepted any bequests from his estate, bang went the trust fund.

Originally that didn't matter, see, because Phil's capital was more'n the trust fund. But with his business shot, an' his income rapidly dwindlin' to nothin', an' the future uncertain, Phil decided to cut June off so's she'd always be sure of the trust fund, which was as safe as anythin' could be, an' more'n he could hope to leave her right now. See?"

"Why didn't he explain?" Kay said. "Oh, if he'd only explained!"

"To explain that to June," Jonah said, "wouldn't be anything you'd undertake lightly, and you know it! June would have wished everything—no, I can understand why Phil didn't go into the matter!"

"Now," Cummings said, "what about that infernal dummy I virtually spent the day guarding for you? What about that? I nearly broke the cellar door down, I was so anxious to find out what you'd spotted!"

"Oh," Asey said. "When I went down to fetch it for Corner, I noticed a deep scratch, just like Mundy's cut, on the back of the dummy's head. N'en all of a sudden it occurred to me that it wasn't so much that the dummy looked like Mundy, as you an' I first thought, doc. It was that Mundy'd been made to look like the dummy, with that hood an' the brown shoes. Now, Corner had the dummy in his truck when he killed Phil. An' after killin' him, as I said, he done some quick thinkin'. He had to be here for Jennie's class. He knew Jennie was goin' to be late—he admitted she'd

told him she was goin' to pick up a sandwich at the
drugstore, an' call it dinner, when he asked if he could
drive her home. An' he also knew, because Jennie'd
tipped him off, that there was goin' to be a problem,
an' that later, Jennie was goin' to take someone's place
as a spotter. So Corner figured he'd hide the body here
—it's hard to dispose of a body, you know," he added.
"Corner didn't want to leave it there in the lane, an'
he didn't want to leave it on his truck. So he decided
to leave it in here, an' then later, after the problem,
he'd sneak back an' take it to Mundy's. He knew for
sure that Jennie wouldn't be back till late."

"But look here," Cummings said, "he was at Hell
Hollow! He was hunting Mildred there when I found
him, when I was hunting for you?"

"Uh-huh. We assumed he'd been there all the time,"
Asey said, "but I learned different from the Thomas
girl. She was apologizin' for her mother for stoppin'
me. Said her mother was in a bad mood—an' among
the reasons for the bad mood, she said her mother'd cut
herself at Hell Hollow last night. I delved into the situation, an' found that her mother's group'd had a problem at the Hollow durin' the time Corner was s'posedly
there. In short, he wasn't there all the time."

"Hm," Cummings said. "So he came back here, not
knowing or guessing that we'd been here, and moved
Mundy, and then went back to the Hollow and hunted
until I came barging into his life, and blurted out the

whole story—to think I sent him back here with his keys!"

"Uh-huh. As he said, he had any number of keys that'd fit our front door," Asey said. "He was just as nice an' helpful, an' casual, about it all."

"But what about that cut?" Cummings asked. "Get to that!"

"After hittin' Mundy, he put him in the truck," Asey said. "An' in so doin', Mundy's head got cut on a little piece of glass that was stuck between the truck's floorboards—Corner never knew it, or noticed it. N'en he put on the hood—that accounts for the little blood-stain you noticed, see? An' the same piece of glass apparently made the same mark on the dummy when Corner stuck that into the truck. An' when I seen the dummy's cut, I sort of begun to put two an' two together, as you might say. Looked like both the dummy an' Mundy'd both been exposed to the same thing."

"What about those damned brown sneakers?" Cummings demanded.

"Oh, I found them," Asey said.

"You *found* them? Where? How?"

Asey grinned. "He had the sneakers in the truck. He admitted he'd swiped 'em from Tiny's hoard her family made her give to the Red Cross. An' he wanted to make Mundy look like the dummy, so he could carry the two of 'em into the house together, see?"

"But he didn't!" Hazard said. "I don't like to contradict you, but Grace and I were here, and we saw Corner come with the dummy!"

"Yup," Asey said, "but he'd been here before!"

"What?" Cummings sounded unbelieving.

"Uh-huh. He drove up the lane in the truck, with Mundy an' the dummy in it, an' carried 'em both into the house together—the door was unlocked, you remember. He put Mundy out in the buttery, an' then came out, bearin' the dummy. If anyone'd seen him, he could say with perfect truth that he had the dummy—"

"Is that why he took off Mundy's rubber boots, to carry out the illusion?" Cummings said.

"Mostly. An' also to keep the rubber boots from drippin' any incriminatin' trails of mud or wet. He told me he took off his own shoes on the doorstep," Asey said. "Then he went off, an' then he come back again, after the Hazards had arrived. Very clever of him, you see, 'cause if anyone'd asked the Hazards, they could only have told about his comin' with the dummy. It was those sneakers," he added, "that kind of made things hard for him later."

"Why?" Jonah asked.

"Wa-el, when he put Mundy in the cellar, he took off the sneakers an' put Mundy's own rubber boots back on him. An' then he tossed the brown sneakers into his truck. But, you see, when his truck tires give out, he had to come with me. He couldn't dare take 'em out then, before Kay an' me. He had to leave 'em there. An' furthermore, he didn't have much of a chance to come back an' get 'em, because I asked him if he'd be home, in case I wanted to phone him about anythin', an' so he sort of had to be there, just in case I did phone. But after I called an' asked about the spiders, an' said I'd go see his clerk, Corner felt free to come over here an' get the sneakers, see?"

"So that's what he was doing, prowling around here," Cummings said, "when he bumped into June?"

"Just so. He was bearin' the spider as a sort of alibi, like I'd guessed, an' as he groped around for the sneakers, June come runnin' down from the doorstep where she'd been waitin' for me. She acted just like we thought, doc, an' accused him of bein' the murderer—an' that was that."

"What'd he do with the sneakers afterwards?" Jonah asked. "How'd you find 'em? *Where'd* you find 'em?"

"That," Asey said, "was as clever a piece of work as he thought of. Bright an' early this mornin' he went to the Red Cross workroom, pried open a case, stuck 'em in, an' probably heaved a good big sigh of relief."

"But how'd you guess they were there, of all places?"

"Because he was so worried about gettin' them cases off," Asey said. " 'Member he mentioned it, Jonah, when I asked you two if you had a lot to do this mornin'? So, after I got him out of the way—"

"Why'd you send me off too?" Jonah interrupted. "Isolating me like that!"

"I figured you'd see that he stayed there," Asey said. "Anyway, I went an' investigated the cases before Hazard's man came to take 'em away, an' it wasn't too hard to find the right sneakers. In his haste, Corner'd pried open a case of sweaters, an' there was the brown sneakers, right on top!"

"What about the spider he had?" Cummings asked. "Was that one that Mundy had bought for himself?"

"Nope, I think the clerk only thought he sold that sixth one to Mundy, because Mundy talked so much about spiders, he stuck in the clerk's mind. I think Corner kept that sixth spider himself, intendin'—like everyone else—to give it to Mundy for a birthday present. Because," Asey said, "I hunted my head off at the store, an' I could only find records of five sales. Three charges, two cash."

"I think," Mrs. Tuesome said, "that you're *sim*ply marvelous! Of course, I *am* devastated about Henry, but then I suppose he died in a *cause*, really, didn't he?"

"I'll send you a substitute," Asey said, "with a proper contribution—an' now, I got to excuse myself, because I got a telegram a while ago orderin' me to rush back. That's really about all."

"You can't mean that there's anything more!" Cummings said.

"Oh, odds an' ends, that's all," Asey said. "Like about someone knowin' enough anatomy to know where to hit, an' how hard, an' where to place that jack in the cellar. An' about Fido."

"What about Fido, for God's sakes!"

"Some of the catnip from the bunch on the buttery door," Asey said, "somehow got into the cuff of Corner's pants. Fido wove around Mr. Hazard's legs, this mornin', but he was clawin' Corner like a tree—I thought you noticed that, doc. Think your car'll be ready to take me up to the airport in about an hour?"

"Sure," Cummings said. "It's only scratched a bit, Johnny said. I've got to go look at Winston and Franklin and Douglas, and I'll be back for you."

An hour and fifteen minutes later, Asey strode down the lane on foot, reproaching himself for turning down all the other offers of lifts that had been forthcoming. Now, no one was home. No one even answered at the Hazards'.

"Oh, well," he shifted his bag and avoided the puddle in which he'd tripped the previous evening, "I hitchhiked down, I guess I can hitchhike back—for Pete's sakes! Jennie!"

"Why, Asey Mayo!" Jennie got off her bike. "When'd you come home? Why didn't you let me know?"

"Did you," Asey said coldly, "get a telegram from me yesterday?"

"Why, goodness me, so I did—I mean, I got it," Jennie said, "but I never had a speck of time to open it! Dave brought it over to Red Cross, an' we was packin'—"

"Uh-huh. I know. Where'd you go, after your problem last night? Was you spottin'?"

"I substituted for Mary Snow," Jennie said, "an' then I had a nap at Maizie's, an' then I took John Shaw's place. He's got an awful cold. Then this morning, I went to Boston with Maizie to a demonstration—real incendiaries, think of it! I just got back, an' picked up my bike—I'm awful sorry I missed you, Asey. You must've found it pretty dull here, all alone."

"Er—don't you read the papers?" Asey asked. "Or listen to the radio?"

"I've been so busy since yesterday, I haven't even listened to Peter Paul Bray, an' you know I *never* miss him if I can help it—you got to go right now?"

"Uh-huh. I left you some candy," Asey said, "but I'm takin' back my laundry. I can see you've no time for it—"

"What time *is* it? Goodness, four-thirty? I've got to rush! I'll tell Syl I seen you when I write him," Jennie put one foot on a pedal, "an' if you can see any way of lettin' me have your sugar-ration stamps, let me know. I'm worried about preservin'—I got to rush. Good-by!"

"If it ain't saved," Asey said, "it won't be your fault. Good-by!"

"If what ain't saved?" Jennie called back as she pedaled off.

"The country. So long."

Cummings overtook him ten minutes later on the highway.

"Sorry to be late," he said. "Hop in—by George, Asey, my prescription certainly worked out! You look wonderful! You're a new man! There's a spring to your step, you're alert—I *knew* a good murder would take that tired look out of your eyes and make you glow!"

Asey chuckled.

"What's so funny?" Cummings demanded. "You had just the right kind of vacation you needed, and you know it!"

"Another hour of it," Asey said, "an' I'd have collapsed. No, doc, if I'm glowin', it ain't because of what you humorously call my vacation."

"No?"

"No," Asey said. "It's because I can't hardly wait to get back to the peace an' quiet of the Porter tank plant!"

THE END